MYSTICAL
UNION

Books by Don Robertson

THE THREE DAYS (1959)

BY ANTIETAM CREEK (1960)

THE RIVER AND THE WILDERNESS (1962)

A FLAG FULL OF STARS (1964)

THE GREATEST THING SINCE SLICED BREAD (1965)

THE SUM AND TOTAL OF NOW (1966)

PARADISE FALLS (1968)

THE GREATEST THING THAT ALMOST HAPPENED (1970)

PRAISE THE HUMAN SEASON (1974)

MISS MARGARET RIDPATH AND THE
   DISMANTLING OF THE UNIVERSE (1977)

MAKE A WISH (1978)

MYSTICAL UNION (1978)

MYSTICAL UNION

DON ROBERTSON

G. P. PUTNAM'S SONS
NEW YORK

COPYRIGHT ©1978 by Don Robertson

All rights reserved. This book, or parts thereof, may not be repro-
duced in any form without permission. Published simultaneously
in Canada by Longman Canada Limited, Toronto.

SBN: 399-12237-0

Library of Congress Cataloging in Publication Data

Robertson, Don, 1929–
  Mystical union.

  I. Title.
PZ4.R649My [PS3568.0248]   813′.5′4   78-2895

PRINTED IN THE UNITED STATES OF AMERICA

Contents

Portions of this novel appeared in the play *Mystical Union,* which was first performed September 8, 1977, in the River Street Playhouse, Chagrin Falls, Ohio.

I would like to thank Melody Sutherland and Mary Marshall for their advice and encouragement, and I am especially grateful to Melody Sutherland for providing what turned out to be the idea for the book's structure.

For Dolores Sutton (and . . . sequentially, by chapter . . . Donald A. Bianchi, Glenn W. Buerkel, Joni Buerkel, René G. Cremona, Helen Cullinan, Thomas Cullinan, Don Edelman, Jane Ernest, Ray Ernest, Dick Feagler, David O. Frazier, Joe Garry, Delene Guenther, Shirley Hanssen, Barbara Hark, Dotti-Jo Harvey, William F. Hickey, Maude Geraldine Izor, Dee-Ann Kah, Dr Ralph E. Kah, Herb Kamm, Lissa Keller, Julie Ketterer, Kay Krantz, Julian Krawcheck, Marie Krawcheck, W. S. Kuniczak, Karen Lambert, Ethel Laughlin, Mary Marshall, Tony Mastroianni, Diane Matthews, Wayne Merholz, Jeff Miller, Susan Miller, Lee J. Monroe, Richard B. Nelson, Mary Jane Nottage, Tom O'Connell, Barbara J. Quill, Mary Anne M. Sheboy, Phyllis Stoller, Mary Strassmeyer, Melody Sutherland, Barbara Tanner, Clyde C. Taylor, Martha Towns and Dick Wootten)

MYSTICAL
UNION

Christ preached it. Persons of the clergy perform the ritual. Men and women pledge themselves to it. Children come. Inlaws. Hatred. Betrayals. Times of gallantry and benevolence and generosity. It is a mystical union, all right, and here we rub against it as dozens of lives collide and interact. Voices are raised, but seldom in unison. So then is commotion, not union. So then is incoherence, not union. So then is a mix and clamor, not union. Marriage is at the center of all this, and it is of course accompanied by loneliness and unrequited passions, plus all that other good stuff, including children and inlaws and hatred and betrayals. Prayers are recited, and babies are born, and mourners cluster around coffins. If marriage is at the center of all this, then surely a certain America crowds at the periphery. If we study diligently enough, perhaps we shall glimpse an America of honeysuckle and barn roofs, galluses, sleeping cats, melting chocolate . . . all of it lovely, soft, a bit torpid . . . and yet at the same time it is an America of smiles where no smiles should exist, of a flatulent inertia, of fellowship as true as a torn paper sack, of tissued slogans and defunct sheetmetal optimism, rusted, perforated, despairing. It is, in any event, a complex and irritating America, certainly too complex and irritating to be apprehended as a complete vision by any single human being. But how else can any of this be approached? So we go ahead and place all these persons on exhibit anyway. It is true that they are and were incomplete, confused, vexed. We stipulate that. So do they. But whose responsibility is the incompleteness? How is the debris created? We wade in it, and our bellies are tight, and we walk on snakes, and what force has created the villainy? Why can we not simply be permitted to love? Why must we forever trip over snarled rope and old tires? Why all this goddamned mess?

DAISY PILGRIM

When Daisy Polk was eighteen and she married Lloyd Pilgrim, she knew the back of his neck just about as well as she knew her own face. The teacher at the LaBelle Grade School, a Miss McEwen, had believed in alphabetical seating. So there were eight years, not counting summers, that Daisy watched the skin toughen below Lloyd's hairline, that she watched soft blond babyish down change to spiky little hairs, that she watched a sort of weathering, an acknowledgment that he was a farm boy, that he worked outdoors, that the back of his neck almost always was naked to the strong hard sun that lay nearly every day across the low humps and ridges of northwest Ohio, of the village of LaBelle, of his father's farm. He was a solemn boy, and he chewed tobacco by the time he was twelve, and there were dozens of occasions when Miss McEwen smacked his knuckles with her ruler when she caught him chewing in class. But Lloyd neither howled, protested nor complained. If he was caught, he was caught. If he was not, he was not. Either way, he seemed to figure the world wasn't about to tip over and send all the people and all the animals and all the houses flying into the sky. Daisy never knew whether she loved him. She figured she was supposed to love him, and perhaps that was enough. She was the youngest of four daughters of a widower who was a maintenance of way foreman for the New York Central. Her birth had been a surprise to her parents, and it had killed her mother, who had been fortythree. [Daisy's three sisters all had been born

14

to her mother before the woman had been twentythree.] It all meant that Daisy's sisters were in effect her mothers. They were kind to her, though, and they did not remind her that she had killed their mother. But then of course they did not have to remind her. The statistics did all the reminding that was necessary; history did all the reminding that was necessary, and so there were nights when Daisy lay tautly in bed and drew her knees to her chin and perhaps listened to the wind, and perhaps listened to the sounds of the house, and perhaps tried to summon the pain her astonished mother must have felt, and perhaps even wept, or at least perhaps made fists and pressed them against her eyes, as though perhaps she were attempting to push her eyes into her skull and thus somehow do away with grief and guilt. Oh, there were times when her father permitted her to sit on his lap, and there even were times when he read to her from the newspaper, and he told her Teddy Roosevelt was the greatest American since Lincoln and perhaps even the greatest American ever. And not once did her father lift a hand against her. And seldom was he even short with her. Yet there was within him a dry and flabby despair; it streaked his eyes; it caused him to moisten his lips too often. He was a large man, but his belly was soft. He was astigmatic, and his breath too often smelled of cigars and whiskey. He had been a section hand for many years, and he had been very strong in those days, and he could pound spikes and carry rail twelve hours a day without hardly pausing to say ah, yes or no—but those many years had been many years before. The father Daisy knew was not the father her sisters had known or the man her late mother had known. His voice had been shredded, and it was as though he had breathed something sour and final and was unable to expel it from his craw. Daisy's sisters were all married and out of the house by the time Daisy was four. One moved with her husband to Terre Haute.

15

Another moved with her husband to Toledo. The third, Maud, moved with *her* husband, Toby O'Hara, an embalmer, into Poole's Mortuary, which was only two houses away. And so Maud visited Daisy and her father just about every day, and Maud brought food for her father, and Maud did her father's laundry and dusted her father's house and changed her father's bed linen. And Maud did Daisy's laundry and changed Daisy's bed linen until Daisy was ten, at which time Maud told Daisy it was about time she (Daisy) learned to do for herself. At the same time, though, Maud would not permit Daisy to do their father's laundry and change his bed linen. According to Maud, everything had to be just right for their father, and naturally Daisy—being only ten—could not be trusted with the responsibility. Daisy would have objected to all this, but she did not know how. Instead, she embraced her knees. When she married Lloyd Pilgrim, it probably was the best thing she could have done, and just about everyone agreed she had made a good match. But she never did know whether she loved him. The standards never had been explained to her. Toby O'Hara was the best man, and he kissed Daisy after the ceremony, and his mouth tasted peculiar . . . bitter, as though perhaps his lips had been basted with chemicals. He told Daisy she was beautiful, and it would have been nice if she'd been able to believe him. She heard Maud talking with her father at the reception, and Maud and her father were drinking bad whiskey, and Maud was telling her father not to worry about his house; everything would be as it always had been. Lloyd was gentle with Daisy that night. She was tall. When undone, her hair trailed to her waist. It was very blonde hair, and Lloyd told her it was enough to make him want to spin cobwebs to the moon. Then he smiled, and he told her a poet he never would be. And carefully he spread her across the bed. She was slender and highbreasted, but she was enormous where she had to be

16

enormous, and he took her more easily than either of them had expected. She tingled a little, and the sensation was not nearly as unpleasant as she had expected. They moved to his father's farm, which was just west of LaBelle. Both his father and mother were ailing (and both from heart trouble), and so Daisy immediately took control of the entire house. She was in charge of all the laundry, and she was in charge of all the bed linen, and she was in charge of all the cooking and dusting, and she even changed some of the furniture around and took down some old photographs from the walls. Lloyd's parents sat quietly and said nothing. Daisy was nineteen in 1920 when she gave birth to her first son, Jim. Two years later she gave birth to Lloyd Junior. Then, in 1924, the last son arrived. His name was Donald. By that time, both of her husband's parents had died. Or perhaps they'd not died. Perhaps they simply had vanished. At any rate, they no longer watched Daisy, and so she changed more furniture around, and she removed more of the old photographs. Most of them were portraits, and she didn't even know whom they were *of*. Nor did Lloyd. Or if he did, he never admitted it. Of her sons, Donald was her favorite. He seemed to have more spunk. He seemed to have more laughter. Sometimes he even would tweak Daisy's rump, and he would gleefully run and hide from her before she could do anything. Her oldest sister, Olive, died in Terre Haute in 1929. Her next sister, Sarah, died in Toledo in 1934. And Maud died in 1937. Which meant that Daisy's father then sold his home (he was retired) and came to live on the farm with Daisy and Lloyd and the boys. By that time Lloyd had converted the farm entirely to a dairy operation, and he was making a reasonably good yearly living, Depression or no Depression. Daisy was careful to keep her father's room immaculate, and she changed his bed linen twice a week. Lloyd gave her peculiar looks now and again, but he said nothing. She wished she had the courage to ask her father whether he believed she had murdered her mother. But instead she and her father discussed very little. Sometimes he talked about the new Roosevelt who was in the White House, the *crippled* Roosevelt. He didn't like this new Roosevelt for sour wax beans, and he told her the world was going to hell faster than a pig in a greased chute. And he and Lloyd sometimes would sit in the kitchen and muse on the state of the human race, and one word kept passing between them, and it was "bullshit." Daisy began inspecting herself in the bathroom mirror. Outside was a sound of cows and a stink of cows. She plucked at her flesh, and it fell away. She scrubbed at her flesh, and it flaked and reddened. Her hair had darkened. Her breasts had enlarged, but at the same time they had loosened. She held them up. She let them drop. She held them up. She let them drop. She smiled at her reflection. She was just like everyone else, and perhaps this was a comfort. She no longer was young. She no longer had three proxy mothers. Oh, there was no perhaps *about* the thing—it *was* a comfort. There were days, though, when she did play tag with Donald, and her father sat on the porch and watched them. Lloyd and Jim and Lloyd Junior thought they were crazy, but it wasn't as though the craziness were harming anyone, and so Daisy and Donald were permitted to continue with it. They ran and flapped. The son hollered, and the mother murmured. The mother's father sat on the porch and kept his thoughts to himself. Donald went off to war in 1943. Jim and Lloyd Junior were exempted because they were farm workers. Jim died in a truck accident in Wyoming in 1947. Daisy's husband, Lloyd, died in 1949. Her father died in 1951. Donald died in 1976. Daisy Polk Pilgrim herself died in 1977 of a stroke she suffered while buying a box of Rice Chex in the LaBelle IGA store. She was seventysix. She knew there were many conversations she never had understood. Perhaps she should have listened more carefully when her husband and her father had discussed their beloved "bullshit." And a person just never did know. Perhaps she even would have gained some sort of knowledge of murder.

BLAH

Mrs Soeder and Mrs Henshaw and Mrs Martin and Mrs Hamner, widows all, sat on Mrs Soeder's front porch one evening in June of 1961, and they all drank iced tea, and they all ate potato chips that they dipped in an onion spread.

And Mrs Soeder said: "I hear all the Kennedys are the same."

And Mrs Henshaw said: "About women, you mean?"

And Mrs Soeder said: "Yes. I understand they are terrible. I understand no woman is safe with either the president *or* the attorney general."

And Mrs Martin said: "Little *Bobby.* I wouldn't trust him any farther than I could throw an elm tree. If he came into a room, and I was alone in that room, I'd call for the police."

And Mrs Hamner said: "Before or after?"

And Mrs Martin said: "That's not funny, Bernice."

And Mrs Hamner said: "But I think they're sort of *attractive.*"

And Mrs Soeder said: "Oh, they're *attractive* all right. But so is the spider to the fly."

And Mrs Henshaw said: "Whatever happened to standards? Were they stolen while we weren't looking?"

And Mrs Martin said: "I expect so."

And Mrs Henshaw said: "I wouldn't even let Carl *touch* my *breasts* before we were married."

And Mrs Hamner said: "Myself, I was the same way with Fred."

And Mrs Soeder said: "I wonder what I'd do if I received an invitation from the White House . . ."

And Mrs Henshaw said: "An invitation to do what?"

And Mrs Soeder said: "Just an *invitation.* I didn't mean anything *dirty.* I only meant like an invitation to dinner . . . one of those big *state* dinners . . ."

And Mrs Hamner said: "But you're a Republican precinct committeewoman, for heaven's sake."

And Mrs Soeder said: "You don't have to be so *literal* about it, Bernice. I don't expect the Kennedys, and Peter Lawford and all the rest of them, to send a telegram to Paradise Falls, Ohio, and *summon* a little old Republican precinct committeewoman to sit at a place of honor at a banquet for *General de Gaulle* or somebody, but I'm simply talking from a standpoint of *curiosity.* I mean, even if *Nixon* had won, I wouldn't have been *invited* to the *White House,* and I *know* that, but can't an old woman be allowed to daydream?"

And Mrs Martin said: "Would you wear your new Eastern Star dress, Louise?"

And Mrs Soeder said: "No. Of course not. I've worn it *already.* At installations."

And Mrs Henshaw said: "But it's not likely that the Kennedys attend many Eastern Star installations."

And Mrs Soeder said: "Very funny."

And Mrs Henshaw said: "I thank you."

And Mrs Soeder said: "There are too many jimmies on my Eastern Star dress. Jackie Kennedy would not approve. I would have to buy something simpler."

And Mrs Hamner said: "I think we're all crazy."

And Mrs Martin said: "What?"

And Mrs Hamner said: "Here we are, talking about the

20

Kennedys, as though we think maybe a helicopter will land in the front yard, and *Himself* will step out."

And Mrs Soeder said: "Well, what's wrong with that?"

And Mrs Hamner said: "Nothing, I suppose."

And Mrs Henshaw said: "There are times when I wish I'd let Carl touch my breasts before we were married."

And Mrs Soeder said: "What?"

And Mrs Martin said: "How's that?"

And Mrs Hamner said: "Pardon?"

And Mrs Henshaw said: "What did I think they were? Gold? Some sort of delicate china that would break? The Holy Grail? They were just *breasts,* after all."

And Mrs Hamner said: "There, there, Eleanor. I'm sure Carl understood."

And Mrs Henshaw said: "But I'm not quite sure *I* do."

And Mrs Soeder said: "I saw Barbara Pilgrim down street today. I expect she's had *her* breasts touched a *lot.* A *whole* lot. A first husband, then a second husband, then the first husband again. And do you remember that Kenny Oliver who was before either of them? Surely you do. I don't know . . . that woman must have some sort of *secret.* She'll never see thirtyfive again, and that has to be a fact, but she looks about *twenty*five, and she just sort of *bounces* and *giggles* along, tra la, tra la, like she *knows some sort of secret.*"

And Mrs Henshaw said: "It could have something to do with her breasts."

And Mrs Martin said: "That's stupid."

And Mrs Hamner said: "I've visited her place, and she doesn't pick up after those boys of hers the way she should. I mean, she invited me, and we sat in the front room, and *there were marbles in a corner,* right down on the floor behind the TV. Marbles and an old wadded *comic book.* And she sat, and she smiled, and a person would have thought

21

she was Jackie Kennedy herself. Talk about your White House. My goodness, we sat there, and we talked about the fund drive for the library, and she gave me coffee, and she just smiled and smiled and smiled, buck teeth and all, and maybe the secret's like something that's broken in her head."

And Mrs Soeder said: "I don't even think she votes Republican."

And Mrs Martin said: "I wouldn't put it past her. Not to, I mean."

And Mrs Hamner said: "*Marbles.*"

And Mrs Soeder said: "And remember how she flaunted her . . . her . . . her *business* . . . with that Jack O'Connell fellow?"

And Mrs Hamner said: "I never have liked him."

And Mrs Soeder said: "If I live to be a hundred, I'll never understand why her first husband took her back. Oh, sure. I know Oscar Sellers, God rest him, needed help in the hardware store, and I know the man liked Oscar Sellers, but dear me, after the way she'd *humiliated* him with O'Connell . . ."

And Mrs Hamner said: "I wouldn't buy a *nickel stamp* from that O'Connell."

And Mrs Henshaw said: "The dip's almost gone."

And Mrs Martin said: "Sometimes, when the weather's warm, I can hear them."

And Mrs Soeder said: "Pardon?"

And Mrs Martin said: "When she and her husband go at it, and the window is open, especially on a hot night like this . . . well, you know my place is right catercornered across the street . . . and, well, I can hear every *sound* . . . every *grunt* . . . every even little teeny *giggle* . . ."

And Mrs Soeder said: "That's our Barbara Pilgrim, just giggling away to beat the band. Tra la, tra la."

And Mrs Henshaw said: "Carl was a good person. I probably should have let him."

And Mrs Soeder said: "Are you talking about your breasts again?"

And Mrs Henshaw said: "Yes. But I can change the subject if you like. The dip is *all* gone now."

And Mrs Martin said: "Is there a secret . . . *really* a secret?"

And Mrs Soeder said: "To what?"

And Mrs Martin said: "You said Barbara Pilgrim knows a secret."

And Mrs Soeder said: "I said it's *like* she knows a secret."

And Mrs Martin said: "And that's about as much information as we'll ever get, isn't it?"

Mrs Soeder did not reply. The four women breathed in unison for a moment. Then Mrs Soeder went inside and fetched more dip. A fly crawled across one of Mrs Martin's arms, and she slapped at it, and so began a discussion of *insects* and how *filthy* they were. The evening crept along, crept along, and the broken words rolled like death, and the voices were hoarse, and no secrets were revealed. No secrets of blood. No secrets of breath. No secrets of the belly. After a time the gathering was adjourned, and all four of the women were in their respective silent solitary beds by ten o'clock.

JACK O'CONNELL & BUCKLEY

John K. O'Connell—or Jack, as he was familiarly known to many—was sixtythree in 1969 when he declared voluntary bankruptcy. He had invested all his savings in a men's hair dye preparation, and he had borrowed nearly one hundred thousand dollars from a former employer. He had opened a small factory in Columbus, but the preparation had been too astringent, and all his money had vanished within six months. In addition, the former employer had sued him for the one hundred thousand dollars, and several disgruntled purchasers of the preparation had sued him for various lesser sums, charging that the preparation had either (a) not changed the color of their hair at all, (b) scorched their scalps, (c) caused their hair to fall out, (d) caused their hair to come loose in clumps, or (e) permanently whitened their hair. The story of O'Connell's misadventures was carried by the wire services, and the preparation . . . which was called New Youth . . . became the object of many jokes by television comedians. As a result of all this, O'Connell not only declared voluntary bankruptcy; he also very quickly began to lose his reason. He was a bachelor, and in early 1970 he was committed to the Columbus State Hospital by his only close relative, a brother, Patrick L., of New Lexington. O'Connell's former employer was of course infuriated, and the man's lawyer petitioned for a sanity hearing, but the petition was denied by the Franklin County Probate Court, and the fellow's one hundred thousand dollars vanished forever down the drain. He did not even share in the money received from the sale of the physical assets of O'Connell's small factory, since all *that* money went for back taxes—federal, state and local. As for the men whose hair and scalps had been damaged by the preparation . . . ah, it all surely was too bad . . .

O'Connell was harmless enough. He was a large man, and there was a trace of a sort of handsome arrogance about his mouth and at the corners of his eyes. He had lived much of his life in a place called Paradise Falls, and he told several of the other patients he had been enormously popular in Paradise Falls. "I had a wife there," he said. "A wife and three sons."

"Oh?" said a man named Buckley, a schizophrenic.

"Yes," said O'Connell. "And fine young fellows, too. The man you see now is not the man I've always been. My wife's name was Barbara, and we had such a glorous marriage as dreams are made of."

"Is that a fact?" said Buckley.

"Absolutely," said O'Connell. "You have no idea how we just couldn't *wait* to get at one another."

"Has she come to see you? I don't recall that anyone has come to see you."

"She died," said O'Connell.

"Oh," said Buckley. "I beg your pardon."

O'Connell was playing checkers with Buckley in a day room. A loud rain was falling outside, and some of the more timid patients were weeping. O'Connell's checkers were black, and he was losing. He hated being black. He always lost when he was black. He drew a shaky breath. He rubbed his scalp. It never had been touched by New Youth, and so he still had a great deal of hair. He said: "Yes. Poor Barbara. She and the boys were in an automobile accident. The car missed a curve on 33-A and it plunged into the Paradise River. They couldn't get out, and so they all drowned."

"Jesus Christ," said Buckley.

"Is it my move?" said O'Connell.

"It's my move," said Buckley.

"No it *isn't*," said O'Connell. "It's *my* move. I mean, isn't it bad enough that I'm black? Do I have to be *cheated* as well?" Then O'Connell drew his bathrobe more tightly around him. "Goddamned rain," he said. "It was a rainy day when Barbara and the boys went into the river. The car skidded. The police told me the skid marks were more than fifty feet. And then the water came in the windows, and that was the end of them."

"You've been here three months, maybe four," said Buckley. "How come I've never heard about this before?"

"You never asked," said O'Connell. He moved one of his black pieces into Buckley's back row. "King me," he said.

"Yes sir," said Buckley, and he kinged O'Connell's piece. Then he wiped out three of O'Connell's other pieces, jump, jump, jump. "It's a fair exchange as far as I'm concerned," he said, grinning.

"If you follow the instructions in the manual, nothing can possibly go wrong."

"What?"

"I could sell refrigerators like no one in Paradise Falls."

"What?"

"I am a graduate of Oberlin College, do you know that? And I have committed much Byron to memory. *Through life's road, so dim and dirty, I have druggd to three and thirty. What have these years left to me? Nothing—except thirtythree.* Or: *To be the father of the fatherless, to stretch the hand from the throne's height, and raise his offspring, who expired in other days—*"

"Your move," said Buckley, the schizophrenic.

"*—to make thy sire's sway by a kingdom less,*" said O'Connell, "*this is to be a monarch, and repress envy into unutterable praise. Dismiss thy guard, and trust thee to such traits, for who would lift a hand, except to bless?*"

"Ah, go piss in a milk bottle," said Buckley, rising, knocking the checkers and the board to the floor.

O'Connell's face was bland. "I met F. Scott Fitzgerald when I was very young. I also met Zelda. It was a tea dance, and he was pleased that I also was Irish. I danced three dances with Zelda, and she was drunker than he was, which was saying a mouthful and *then* some. Her face was chunkier than her photographs reveal. I thought she was pretty. I never thought she was beautiful."

Buckley walked away.

Mystical Union

O'Connell listened carefully to the rain. He touched his forehead. It hurt. He knew his poetry quotations were accurate. He knew they were the truth. He and Barbara had shared the poetry in a motel in Lancaster. He would sit up in bed and read to her, and she would rest her head against his chest, and now and then she would blow at the hairs there, and her cool breath created a thickness in his throat and behind his eyes. He told her he would be the best husband a woman could want, and he told her he would be a fine father to the boys. He glanced now at the windows, at the rain that smeared the windows, at the men who crouched in the corners of this day room. Did the library have a copy of *Childe Harold*? Oh, of course it did. It had to. He listened to the wind, and he summoned: "*Let winds be chill, let waves roll high, I fear not waves nor wind; yet marvel not, Sir Childe, that I am sorrowful in mind; for I have from my father gone, a mother whom I love, and have no friend, save thee alone, but thee—and One above.*" Nodding, O'Connell remembered the symphony Berlioz had written—*Harold in Italy*, a symphony with viola obbligato. Not as famous as the *Fantastique*, but surely quintessential Berlioz and surely worth more performances than it received. Nodding, O'Connell stood up. He stepped on the checkers and the checkerboard, and briefly he lost his balance. But he regained it, and he walked to the library without further incident. It did not have *Childe Harold*, and so O'Connell wept. Of course he wept. He went to his ward and he lay down and lost contol of himself, and the stink made the other men hoot and snigger and shriek, and an orderly had him clean it up. "If you don't clean it up," said the orderly, "I'll dip your fucking head in a bucket of that goddamned New Youth." Everyone laughed, even the men who had been shrieking. O'Connell stripped his bed, wrapping the sheets and the blanket around his own shit, which also clung to the seat of his pajamas and the seat of his bath-

27

robe. He made the bed with a clean blanket and clean sheets. Then he took a shower, and the orderly gave him clean pajamas and a clean robe. Both the pajamas and the robe were torn, but O'Connell said nothing. Barbara, who was dead, had loved him. Or perhaps Barbara was alive. Oh well, what difference did it make? O'Connell went to bed and fell asleep. He dreamed he was fighting for the freedom of Greece. And Barbara rewarded him with her golden body and her immense and benevolent smile. You are forever my Byron, she said. She stroked his instrument, and it was mighty. John K. O'Connell died of a pulmonary embolism in April of 1971.

Don Pilgrim & Lloyd Pilgrim

Looking back on him, sure, I'll admit that my father could be cranky, and he never did understand why Mama and I would go capering out into the front yard and play tag like a couple of kids who haven't got all their goddamned wits about them. But he was a good man, and I think he had a sort of wisdom. It's not often we encounter pure wisdom, which is the sort of wisdom I believe he had. By that I mean it never bent, and he never went back on it. Which is what I call pure wisdom. Which is something I don't believe people trip over every morning like it's a roller skate or a handful of marbles. Or at least *I* don't. Not old Don Pilgrim. I loved my father. He died in 1949, which is a piece back, but I'll always love him. He had a dairy farm (and it's still in the family) . . . three hundred acres, and his hands always smelled like milk . . . three hundred acres just outside a place called LaBelle, Ohio, which is in the northwestern part of the state, about halfway between Toledo and Elkhart on what we knew as the New York Central, the good old Water Level Route. The farm had a big barnyard, and my late wife, Barbara, used to kid me about the barnyard. I remember one time she said to me: "When you cross that barnyard, you don't walk. You tiptoe. Only it isn't through the tulips, if you follow my line of thought." And I said: "Well, what did you *expect* it to be? A dance floor?" And then Barbara laughed, and maybe she came to me and hugged me. I don't exactly recall, but I wouldn't have put such a thing past her, considering the sort of person she was. But anyway, my father—and wisdom. Yes sir, the wisdom of old Lloyd Pilgrim. It was 1941, and I was seventeen, and one morning right after breakfast he took me aside and told me there was something important I would have to learn. At first I thought hey, hot damn, he was going to take me to the whorehouse over by Maumeeville, but he right away disabused me of *that* notion. He marched me out to the car and told me to drive to the depot. The car was a '37 Hudson, and my brother Jim washed it maybe every other day or so. It was a dull gold, and Jim waxed it just about every Sunday afternoon. I was very proud that my father let me do the driving, and I took care with the clutch. I wanted the trip to be smooth. I didn't want to strip anything. So I drove to the depot (the famous LaBelle, Ohio, depot, which was about the size of your Aunt Gertrude's privy), and I parked the car, and we got out, and we walked to a bench, and I recall seeing a sign that was in the shape of a red diamond, and it said: RAILWAY EXPRESS AGENCY. And there in front of us were the four mainline tracks of the New York Central. *Four.* And *shiny.* I mean, in those days the railroad was *the railroad,* and it touched LaBelle, Ohio, which meant LaBelle, Ohio, touched the world, and that was what we saw as civilization, modern times, all that sort of thing. The *20th Century Limited* went through LaBelle. My God! Oh, not that it *stopped,* but at least we had a chance to *see* it. (I mean, there's really something inspiring about watching a club car full of drunks going past at eighty miles an hour. I mean, it's one thing to be drunk, but at *eighty miles an hour* . . . well, that has to be some sort of, um, ultimate.) I don't know exactly what I was thinking that morning, and I don't suppose it's all that important. At any rate, my father and I sat ourselves down on that bench. And we just sat there. It wasn't even nine o'clock in the morning, and there was a lot we had to do—cow flop to shovel or whatever—but all we did was sit there, the boy and his father, squinting at the sunlight reflected on all those great old blinding New York Central tracks. And flat country was all around us. We could see corn. Corn I don't know how tall. And the wind, what there was of it, was moving sideways through that corn in a sort of hiss. And there was a lot of sun and no clouds. Boxcars on a siding. A sound of somebody's rooster. And maybe a dog. I don't know. A smell of tar, creosote, coal oil, whatever. And I sat there with my father, and I waited for him to say something, and maybe for all I knew *he* was waiting for *me* to say something. Or for me to *do* something. Stand up and sing. Tapdance. Pass water into the wind. But I didn't know what it was all about, so I just sat there with him, and I listened to the rooster or the dog or whatever, and I supposed sooner or later something would happen, and maybe he would say something, and I supposed it would be very important, and maybe the sky would split open and rain frogs and lizards and saltwater taffy. And finally, glory be to God, he did speak. The sky did not split open, but the words did come, and I haven't forgotten them. He didn't look at me. I don't recall where he did look, but it wasn't at me. It was off like maybe toward the corn or the boxcars. And he said: "Donald, you can look in any direction, and that's the world. Beyond the horizon is the world. Those tracks go to the world. They take a person out of LaBelle. I mean, after all, what is there in LaBelle? Fourteen hundred people, right? The Future Farmers of America, right? Purina Feeds, right? Trees here and there. Girls with big tits. Girls with little tits. Flags. Brick sidewalks. Covered dish suppers. And—except for the tits—it's all a lot of dull bullshit, right? Of course it is, and you know that as well as I do. And so you look around, and you see the tracks and the horizon, and you see Hedy Lamarr at the picture show, and you read about the Duke of Windsor and Errol Flynn, and you say to yourself: *Hey, once I get shut of LaBelle, there'll be a whole lot waiting for me.* And the horizon is such a sweet thing you want to lick it like maybe it's an ice cream cone. And you say to yourself: *Any day now I'm getting out of here. La-Belle can kiss my ass, and the Future Farmers of America can shovel pig shit until they all fall down dead."* And my father stopped here for a breath. His hands were folded in his lap, but they were folded too tightly, if you know what I mean. He looked down at them, and maybe he smiled a little. I don't know. I didn't have all that good a view of his face. Anyway, I don't think it matters. His mouth finally was unlimbered, and so he started in again. He talked about LaBelle. He talked about the Future Farmers of America. And then he said to me: "Donald, one day I suppose the itch'll get to be too much for you. At which time . . . well, at which time you'll seek out the big world beyond this horizon and every other horizon. You'll trade in dull old LaBelle, the dogs and the roosters and the corn and the sidewalks. Maybe you'll go to a city, or maybe you'll sail away in a ship, or maybe you'll fly away in an airplane, but the thing is—you know what you'll find? You'll find that nothing's different. Nothing. Not a goddamned thing. When you escape the dullness of *this* place, you'll end up trying to escape the dullness of some *other* place. What do people say? The magazines and all? The movies? Don't they say it's a great big world out there? All right, I'll go

31

along with that, but there's nothing really all that different about it. The girls are put together, well, some with the big tits and some with the little tits, but they're more or less kind of all alike, you know? I mean, the *geography* is the same, you know? And everybody goes to the privy the same way, and the same lies are told, and the same goddamned *ambitions* exist, and if you believe anything else, you're just fooling yourself." And then my father did an unusual thing . . . an unusual thing for him. He reached toward me, and he hugged me, right out there in front of the corn and the boxcars and the rest of it, and he said: "Godalmighty, Donald, the bullshit of LaBelle is the bullshit of the world, and you can't slide a piece of paper under the difference. Not a scrap. Not a feather. Not a thing." And then my father pulled back from me. And he said: "But you'll have to leave. You'll have to learn for yourself. My words aren't worth a hill of beans, are they? You're going to be like most of the human race—trading one sort of bullshit for another sort of bullshit and calling it accomplishment . . . or progress . . . whatever." And then he decided there was nothing more he had to say. We walked back to the car, and this time he did the driving, and we went home, and we shoveled cow flop. I guess I believed him, and I guess I still do. That doesn't mean I avoided the mistakes. Jesus Christ, all the time I was married to Barbara I worked in a *hardware store*, and my life has been more or less like a sack of broken glass, you know? I am back on the farm now, and I operate an HO train display that I call Railroad City USA. I always have loved trains—maybe because they have something to do with horizons. But if this is so, then does it mean I think my father's words all were bullshit themselves? Does it mean I'm telling him I can't go along with the wisdom of ignorance and smallness? Oh, how he hated bullshit. Oh, how he would be angry with me if he knew what I keep suspecting from time to time. I mean, you take my mother and myself . . . our games of tag. What were we trying to escape? Weren't we like mice on a wheel? We would caper and leap and gasp, and my father would frown at us. I don't know. Maybe the sky doesn't even have the capacity to split open. Maybe it never was supposed to split open. Frogs and lizards and saltwater taffy? My God, I must be crazy. (My father was only forty-nine when his gall bladder gave way and he died. The year was 1949. There was nothing smooth about the way he died. He looked like his belly was being twisted with a pair of pliers. We all spoke to him, but I don't think he heard anything. Oh well. He probably would have called it all bullshit anyway.)

DOTTIE WASHBURN & TOM WASHBURN

Dottie Washburn pushed her husband onto the sofa and flopped down beside him and said: "All right now. Let's keep our voices down. I don't care how young the kids are. There's no reason they have to hear any of this." She embraced herself. She was twentynine, and she was blond, and her bosoms were substantial. She said: "I don't care *who* says *what*, and I don't care what whoever thought was seen. Nothing's happened between Harry McNiece and me, and if you think anything else, you might as well just pack up and get out of here."

Tom Washburn said nothing. He could not look at Dottie.

"Thirty seconds ago you were yelling at me," said Dottie. "Now you're a stone. How come?"

"An old fart like him . . ."

"You don't have to call him that kind of name."

"And you *feed him peanut butter and jelly sandwiches? Jesus Christ.*"

"With milk," said Dottie.

"Jesus Christ," said Tom Washburn.

"And we *talk.*"

"Oh. Sure. Terrific. And so that Unger biddy gets an eyeful."

"An eyeful?" said Dottie. "Because she saw Harry cross the backyard? Was he in the nude? Was he . . . was he . . . *masturbating?* Did he sort of, um, *wave himself* at her?"

"God damn you, Dottie, stop—!"

"Please don't shout. We have three children, remember? And they're supposed to be sleeping, remember? And the oldest is only five, remember? What do you want to do? tear them apart? give them a . . . a *trauma?*"

"A what? What's that mean? You been talking with McNiece too much." And now Tom Washburn was blinking, but at least he had brought his voice under control. He was squat. He was hairy. He often smelled of dust. Or bricks. Or both. He and Dottie had been married for seven years, and she supposed she loved him. Certainly he'd never gone out of his way to damage her. Of how many people could that be said?

"A trauma is like a bad experience that could affect them for the rest of their lives," said Dottie.

"But you could of told me," said Tom.

"Told you?"

"That he was coming over and eating his fucking peanut butter and jelly sandwiches. Christ Almighty, what does he do for you?"

"He *talks* to me," said Dottie. "And he *listens.* He's fifty years of age, and he's like all the rest of us—he's afraid.

But he's not afraid to admit it. So we talk. Books. Sometimes music. Sometimes the lives of famous people."

"The lives of famous people?" said Tom. "Shit, this isn't happening. This is off the goddamned wall. It's the goddamned *Gong Show*."

"No," said Dottie. "We talk about things I used to enjoy. And now and then he touches my hand."

"And he tries to do a job on your head, too, doesn't he? He wants to get into your knickers, doesn't he?"

"Well, what if he does? That doesn't mean I'm going to let him. And anyway, you ought to be flattered to know that your wife is wanted by another man."

"Another *man?* That old—"

"You don't have to call him names," said Dottie. "He is honest, and he hurts, and he is able to talk about more than *bricks* and *tile*, and—"

"Which means I'm a goddamned idiot, is that what you mean? All I do is work like a nigger so you and the kids will have a roof over your heads and won't starve to death, and it means I'm what? scum? a dummy?"

"I love you, Tom. But maybe I love him too."

"What?"

"I mean that."

"Oh, he's *already* done a job on your head, hasn't he?" said Tom. "I can just hear him telling you to lie down, honey, so he can fill you with the goddamned finer things of life. Like maybe his cock, huh? Can he get it up, huh? Can he?"

"How should I know?"

"Don't bullshit me. Don't do that, or God damn you, I'll kill you."

"I'm *not*. It's never been *that*. Never."

"Can I believe that?"

"Yes," said Dottie.

35

He took her by the shoulders. He pushed her from side to side. "There's going to be no more of this shit," he said. "No more Harry McNiece. No more finer things of life. No more peanut butter and jelly sandwiches. No more milk. No more talk. No more of any of it."

"I can't promise that," said Dottie.

"What?"

"I'm not going to make a promise I probably will break."

"I'm your husband."

"I know that. This has nothing to do with you, though."

"Nothing to do with *me*? Some old guy comes staggering in the back door every other day or so, and you give him peanut butter and jelly sandwiches, and you have your . . . your hoitytoity little conversations about the finer things of life . . . and you say it has nothing to do with *me*? Then what the hell *am* I? furniture? a tablecloth? a goddamned klutz who endorses a paycheck every two weeks?"

"Tom. God. Tom. Listen. There are times when I want to scream."

"What?"

"I mean, all the *days*. The *days* and the *days* and the *days*."

"What does that mean? Am I a flop? Am I boring?"

". . . no."

Tom Washburn's voice began to peel away. "You want me to take a book of . . . a book of . . . ah, *Shakespeare* . . . with me every day to the Paradise Falls Clay Products? I mean, then every time I go to the toilet I can stand over the urinal and read: *To pee or not to pee* . . ."

"What are you talking about?"

Tom Washburn embraced his wife. He howled into her neck and her hair.

"Sh," said Dottie.

Tom Washburn's head moved from side to side. He howled. He howled.

"All right," said Dottie.

Tom Washburn howled.

Dottie waited. She kissed the top of her husband's head. She stroked the back of his neck. "All right," she said. "Yes. Yes. All right."

Tom Washburn's howling eventually subsided. Finally he poked at his eyes and looked up. "You . . . think any of the kids heard me?"

"I don't believe so," said Dottie. "I don't hear anything, do you?"

"No . . ."

"We wouldn't want them to hear anything, would we?"

"No . . ."

"If nobody hears anything, and if nobody sees anything, then nothing happens, correct?"

"What?" said Tom.

"You're going to have to leave this to me to handle. I'm not about to stop plying him with the peanut butter and jelly sandwiches. If I did, then I might as well die."

"I don't believe that," said Tom.

"You'd better start learning to," said Dottie.

Tom opened his mouth. Perhaps he was about to howl again. But then he blinked, hesitated, closed his mouth.

Dottie patted one of his knees. "Yes," she said. "Yes. Very good."

Tom Washburn's eyes were clotted. They leaked.

HARRY McNIECE & BARBARA SELLERS

My father owned a little candystore and newsstand next door to the old Ritz Theater. Oh, the Ritz Theater still exists, don't get me wrong, but its dreadful hard varnished seats have been replaced, and its great proclamative lightbulbed marquee has been replaced, and it just isn't the same old moom pitcher show that I knew when I was a kid. I mean, do you remember lightbulbed marquees, when the bulbs flashed in sequence on the letters so that the word

R

I

T

Z

jumped at you, faded, jumped at you, faded, jumped at you and jumped at you and jumped at you as though it were pursuing your eyes and your mind, tearing apart the night in a sort of sweetly relentless defiance? In today's language, the Ritz's old marquee would be called, ah, "glitzy," and that is probably as good a word as any. The glitzy Ritz. Ah, indeed so. Well, I spent a good deal of my boyhood within the range of all that glitz, and I look back with fondness on it. And it comes in handy (the nostalgia, I mean) for the column I write that appears thrice weekly in the Paradise Falls *Journal-Democrat*, of which I am the editor. I am a Paradise Falls boy, plain and simple. Oh, I went away to college, and I have done some traveling, and my late wife and I even could have intelligently discussed the European Common Market had anyone ever asked us, but I really never have been much more than a product of my environment. If the proper study of man is man, then the proper study of this particular man, Harry McNiece, is the study of his environment, this town that lies almost at the exact place where the foothills of the Appalachians fall into the Midwest plains. Look to the east, foothills. Look to the south, foothills. Look to the north, foothills. Look to the west, though, and there lies the beginning of the plains, a more or less unbroken pattern of fences and fenceposts and farms and cities and grazing animals and low remorseless fields—and it extends to just this side of Denver, by God. *Denver.* Jesus, did you ever feel one of those topographical maps that sometimes can be found in libraries or classrooms? I have, and the plains are almost like the breastbone of a woman whose boobs have been placed a trifle too far apart. Oh, I suppose you think I am dirty, comparing topography with tits. Well, perhaps so, and there *are* certain events in my history that would seem to back up the contention. But this is not intended to be some enormous confession of lusts and betrayals and guilts. I simply want to spread out a small fragile incident, and it is a sweet incident, and there are many days when it comforts me . . . and perhaps even more than it should. It took place when I was twelve, which would have made the year 1939. I was a knobbed and adenoidal drink of water, and I was growing so fast my britches were forever hiking themselves above my ankles. For some reason, the source of which I cannot remember, that year I got into the habit of rising very early in the morning. (It is a habit, incidentally, I no longer possess, and thank God.) At any rate, I would go for walks, and sometimes I would walk all the way out to the Paradise County Fairgrounds and sit in the grandstand and look to the east and watch the sun poke through the mist and the hills. In the summer it nearly always was a great perfect steaming balloon, orange edged in gray and eventually blue. The grandstand always was cold with morning moisture, but I didn't care. I always seated myself, and if my britches were dampened, my britches were dampened. It was too important to me that I *sit* and *reflect*, that I try to place myself within some sort of context having to do with that hot and magisterial demonstration taking place in front of me. It had nothing to do with glitz. It had nothing to do with candy and magazines and Spencer Tracy. It made me to believe that I was rattling around within something that was awful, that was scary, but at the same time had some sort of tough and merciless rightness. Does all this seem too pretentious for a boy of twelve? Perhaps. But it fairly represents what I felt, and perhaps it kept my mind off the constant exposure of my ankles. And anyway, if we cannot storm the heavens when we are twelve, when can we? When do we again have that much foolish courage? So I sat there every morning, and then came a morning when I was joined by a girl named Barbara Sellers. She was fifteen, and she had braces on her teeth, and she was already too skinny, and she actually had *followed* me. She wore I believe a brown jumper and a white blouse, and her hair was pulled back, and she climbed the grandstand steps to me, and her smile was metallic and grand, and she said: "Well, Harry McNiece, as I live and breathe . . . what are you doing here at six o'clock in the morning?"

I could not speak. I looked away from her. I almost felt as though she had caught me masturbating . . . a practice, incidentally, I had begun about six months earlier. (Along with the sunrises, it had sustained me you have no idea how profoundly.)

"You don't have to be shy," said Barbara. She seated herself next to me. She had an odor of Lifebuoy. "If you're wondering why *I'm* here, well, yesterday morning I got up very

early because I had to go to the bathroom, and I happened
to look out the window, and I happened to see you walking
past, and I asked myself now what on earth could Harry
McNiece be doing trudging along at such an hour? So this
morning I set the alarm for five, and I washed my hands
and face, and I got dressed, and I drank a glass of milk, and
I sat at the front window, and I waited for you to come
along, and you did, and so I followed you, and now you're
here, and so am I, and what is it do you feel?"

My head moved from side to side. ". . . nothing," I said.

"Small?" said Barbara.

". . . what?"

"Do you come out here and look at the sun so you can feel
small?"

I shrugged.

"Or maybe proud?" said Barbara.

"Huh?"

"That maybe you're the only person in Paradise Falls
who's seeing what you're seeing? I mean, the sun and all.
The mist. It *is* beautiful, isn't it?"

". . . yes."

"Could I share it with you?"

"No," I said, speaking quickly.

"Oh," said Barbara.

"Yes," I said, speaking quickly.

"That's all right," said Barbara. "If it's real private, I can
understand that."

"I just sit here," I said. "I mean, if you want to sit here
too, it's okay."

Her smile again. She shook her head no. She stood up,
brushed at her skirt. "No," she said, "this is yours. I'm too
selfish. I'm too nosy. I'm sorry." She bent over me and
touched my face. "I'm not Greta Garbo, but I do know what
it's like to *vant* to be *alone*. I shouldn't be here. I like you,
Harry McNiece, you funny bag of bones you. And every-

thing's fine. I'm going home how. Maybe I'll go back to bed. But probably not. If I know my mother, she'll probably be having a cat fit, wondering where I am. And I'll probably be stuck with the breakfast dishes, even though it's Rosemary's turn. It's just that I had to *know* about this. I'm only going to live once, you see, and . . ." And here Barbara let her voice drain away. She turned from me and made her way down over the rows of grandstand benches, then ducked under the grandstand. And that was the end of her as far as my visits to the fairgrounds were concerned. She never returned. I had her many times when I masturbated, and she always was generous. She was married three times, twice to the same man, but I do not believe she ever told a soul about our meeting that morning. Even at fifteen, you see, she understood how damaged I would have been. She had touched me. She had touched my face. I believe she had known the terrible wonder I had been experiencing. She was not glitz, you see. She was bone and sinew. She was benevolence. She died in 1974 of a kidney disease, and I attended her funeral. A week later I picked a cluster of day lilies and took them to her grave. I still take day lilies to her grave. Day lilies are orange. You can find them everywhere, and there are times when they have a capacity to reflect that fine perfect early sun I discovered in 1939 when I was all knobs and pain and ardent imaginings.

EDITH SHIELDS & JIM PILGRIM

Jim Pilgrim's chin rested on the lip of the house trailer's tiny commode, and he was weeping, and Edith was trying to dab at his face with a damp washrag. Her name was Edith Shields, and she was enormous, and she loved him

42

like he was all the angels and all the devils and all the skies
and the end of the world. Now surely there was no more
vomit left in him, and so she figured it was time to pull him
to his feet. He wore only an undershirt, and it was frayed.
His rear end was speckled with moles. She wanted to pat
the moles, but she didn't suppose that would be a proper
thing to do. At least not right *now*. And so she said: "Yes.
Yes. It's all gone now, baby. Yes." And she reached past
him and flushed the commode.

The sound of the water made him draw back a little. He
gagged, shuddered, but nothing came from his mouth.

Edith's arms and hands were larger than Jim's. She
seized him and pulled him to his feet.

He leaned against her, and she could feel his limp cock
through her silk bathrobe. Until two months ago, she'd never owned a silk bathrobe in her whole entire life. But then
Jim had bought her one in Laramie. Its color was a brilliant
red, a red that deepened or faded depending on the available light, and he had several times told her it just about
drove him crazy. Now, though, he might as well have been
dead, and so she didn't bother to think too long on his talk
of craziness. It did no good to think too long on things that
were useless, and that was the truth. Grunting a little, she
helped him into the bedroom. He had put away several gal-
lons of beer . . . she had no idea how many . . . and it
had been inevitable that he would vomit. First the tears
had come, then the vomiting, then more tears. And now he
would mumble words having to do with how sorry he felt
for himself. He always did, and she supposed it was her
cross to bear. She had been born in Mississippi, and she had
been a genuine footwashing Baptist. There was no Baptist
church here in this Wyoming town, but she still *thought*
Baptist, and she still *felt* Baptist, and she supposed it all
would be with her until she died, or until the sky was
ripped open, or until whichever came first. She spread him

across the bed, and carefully she lay next to him, and she permitted him to weep into her chest. He stroked her robe, and he mumbled something to the effect that it felt good. He had a partial lower plate, and so his words sloshed.

"Yes, baby," said Edith, stroking his hair, stroking the places where he had no hair, kissing his forehead and his eyelids and his cheeks and his nose. Her husband, Wayne, had died three years ago, in France, just before Paris had been liberated, and Wayne also had been a hell of a drinker, and so it wasn't as though Edith didn't know anything about drinkers. She wondered how many times she had dabbed Wayne's face with a damp washrag. She wondered how many times she had dabbed Jim's face with a damp washrag. Oh, she wished she had a nickel for each time. She shook her head. She looked around. The trailer was altogether too cluttered, and she knew it. Tassels. Souvenir pillows. Empty Coors' bottles. Too many dirty dishes in the sink. And the bedclothes went all this way and that. Again Edith shook her head. For a woman who operated a successful diaper wash service, she kept a home that was like a damn *sty*, and she should have been ashamed of herself. But there was so much she always had to do with *Jim*. He and her business seemed to occupy all her hours, and she could not even remember the last time she had dusted this place. He was a sheep rancher, and he lived alone in a tiny gray clapboard house at the crest of a low rolling green hill, but he was maybe the worst sheep rancher in the entire state of Wyoming, and he was maybe a step ahead of the sheriff, maybe a step and a half. Which meant he drank. Which meant perhaps he had given up. But this couldn't be allowed to happen. She supposed he was very, very dumb, and she knew damn well he was feeling too sorry for himself, but what did those things have to do with her love? You loved the way you married—for better or for worse, correct?

". . . no," said Jim. He tried to roll away.

Edith hung on to him, and he was unable to move. "What's wrong?"

". . . it . . . no, none of it . . . it don't none of it make no sense no more . . ."

"Sense?"

". . . yeah."

"Are you talking about us?" said Edith.

"I'm . . . I'm talking about all of it," said Jim.

"Don't be silly," said Edith.

". . . you . . . you shouldn't ought to pick at me . . ."

"Hush."

"I ain't worth shit, and I never been worth shit. I can't read a goddamn billboard without moving my lips."

"What do I care about billboards?" said Edith.

Jim scrunched backward. He was trying to sit up. He propped himself with an elbow, but it gave way. He flopped back. He sighed. "Hell with it," he said. He breathed shallowly, then: "I came out here because I figured, well, it would be one last chance . . . but, shit, Edith, if it wasn't for you, I wouldn't even make out a goddamn *grocery list* every week. The way you nag at me . . . it's all loving, and I'm grateful for it, but don't you see? I mean, *don't you see?*"

"Don't I see what?"

"I'm stopping."

"Stopping? You mean giving up?"

Jim nodded.

". . . no," said Edith.

Jim made fists, and he tried to focus his eyes on them. "I'm supposed to be ranching sheep, right? But they keep disappearing on me. Or they die. Or maybe a wolf gets at them. I could stay awake all night and hold up a goddamn *lantern* and I'd see them vanish before my eyes. Pop's been good to me, loaning me the money for this place, telling me all right, get the hell out of Ohio, go west, you dumbbell,

45

and seek fame and fortune, but all that's ever happened to me is that my sheep keep going away from me—one way or the other. Look, you was a Baptist, right? And so maybe I'm being punished for my sins, right?"

"What sins?" said Edith.

"I don't know," said Jim. "Ah, you think maybe, um, fucking? or, um, maybe beer?"

"That's stupid," said Edith.

"I never made no claim to be nothing else," said Jim.

"I want to kiss you."

"Never mind."

"I want to kiss you real deep and easy, you know?" said Edith.

"Never mind," said Jim.

"Ah, but what's this I'm feeling?" said Edith, taking hold of Jim's cock, which was stiffening.

"Jesus Christ," said Jim.

Edith rolled on top of him, and she told him he did not have to move. But he did incline his head upward and gnaw softly on her nipples. She lowered herself on him, and his eyes remained open, and there was enough light so that she could see a sort of mournfulness in them, as though he had acknowledged a reluctant necessity. He held himself back, and she was more or less able to come with him. The mournfulness had been like a sort of gummy filter. After they were finished, she washed his cock with the damp washrag. He smiled. He told her he wished he were different. He told her it was no fun to move his lips while reading a billboard. He became drunk again the next night, but that time he became drunk alone, and he rammed his pickup into a telephone pole, and that was the end of him, and it all was as though a ceremony had been concluded, and she supposed now he was happy, but she wept anyway. She wept and she wept and she wept, and she embraced everyone in sight. And she didn't bother to clean the trailer for maybe six months more. Then, instead of cleaning it, she sold it, and she sold the diaper wash business, and she returned to Mississippi, where she married a man named Hammett, who had a cotton farm not far from Tupelo. It was a prosperous farm, and so she was buried stylishly after she died of a brain tumor in 1968. She wore a fine dress, and a Baptist clergyman prayed over her with immense zeal, the sort of zeal that caused sweat to trickle down into his eyes and make them sting.

BARBARA SELLERS & OSCAR SELLERS

Barbara Sellers, who was twelve, sat alone in the front room with her father. It was January of 1937, and her two younger sisters were out sledding, and her mother had gone to Circleville to visit an aunt who was ill with some sort of nerve affliction that made the poor woman's arms flap and her eyebrows curl and twitch. The day was Sunday, and a low blank sun had spread a mist over the snow that lay across the town of Paradise Falls. It was a perfect afternoon for the packing of snowballs, and Barbara would have loved being outdoors and waging a loud giggly snowball war with her friend Kenny Oliver. But this would have meant that her father would be left all alone, and Barbara did not want her father to be left all alone. So she sat in the front room and talked with him. She sat on the sofa. He sat in what the family acknowledged to be *his* chair. It was leather, and it had a broken spring, but he did not care about the broken spring, and he'd never bothered to have it repaired. According to him, the broken spring accommodated the contours of his body just fine, and he didn't want anyone fooling with the chair and perhaps taking away its comfort. Oscar Sellers was a successful hardware merchant, even now within this Depression, and it was not often that he lost an argument, especially over such a matter as a broken chair spring. And so now, as he sat and chatted with Barbara, he adjusted the cheeks of his buttocks, and he drank beer from a stein his wife had bought for him at the Lazarus store in Columbus, and his face was heavy and comfortable, and his eyes were perhaps a bit hazy. But he did manage to smile at Barbara (it almost was a timid smile, and it confined itself to the corners of his mouth; it was the smile of a man who never really had caught the hang of it), and he said: "Look, I know you probably want to go outside. It's all right if you do."

"No," said Barbara. "I am needed here."

"Needed?" said her father. "No. That's not so. What am I supposed to be? Sick? I've never felt better in my life."

Barbara smiled at her father. There were braces on her teeth, but she already knew more about smiling than Oscar Sellers ever would. Her smile came in a sort of *zip*, clownish and splendid, and it was wet, and she said: "I like being needed."

"What?"

"It's the best thing in the world. I like that better than anything."

"You're too young to be talking like this," said Oscar Sellers.

"Why? Has some sort of law been passed?"

"No. No. I'm not talking about *laws*. I'm talking about *you*. I'm saying all right, it's good for you to know that you're needed, but there's more."

"More?" said Barbara.

"You have to be needed by yourself."

"What?" said Barbara. Another smile. In those days, she nearly always smiled when she didn't know what else to do. Later, when she became a young woman, she would replace the smiles with frequent trips to the bathroom. They gave her time to think through a situation, to work out strategy. But here in 1937, when she was twelve, her principal delaying tactic was the smile. And so she permitted it to focus directly on her father, and finally again she said: "What?"

"I think we're talking about responsibility," said Oscar Sellers. "Your uncle Willie and I, though, well . . . when we were boys and we ran away from home because we didn't want to work in the mines and because your Grandpa Sellers beat us . . . well, our responsibility was to your Grandpa Sellers, wasn't it, God rest his soul? But we wouldn't have amounted to a sack of birdseed if we'd stayed. So we turned our backs on the responsibility."

"I'm talking about a different sort of responsibility," said Barbara.

"Oh?" said Oscar Sellers, sipping at this beer.

"I'm talking about a responsibility that comes out of love. I love you, Papa, and I don't want you just to sit here all afternoon like a *lump*."

"And maybe drink too much beer?" said Oscar Sellers, sipping at his beer.

"Yes," said Barbara. She glanced down at the carpeting. Perhaps she had said too much. It would not have been the first time.

Oscar Sellers said nothing.

"Tomorrow is time enough," said Barbara.

"Time enough for what?" said her father.

"For whatever I want to do. Throw snowballs or whatever."

"But you can't think that way forever."

"I know," said Barbara.

"If you do, the days'll all drain away."

"I *know*," said Barbara.

"There'll be too many stuffy rooms. Too much of a smell of beer."

"Yes," said Barbara.

"Duty isn't everything."

"I suppose not . . ."

"When Edward ran off with the Simpson woman, duty wasn't all that important."

"No. But *I'm* talking about duty that comes from *love*."

"All right," said Oscar Sellers, sipping at his beer.

"So everything is fine."

"But even people you love . . . well, sometimes you have to stand back a little from your duty toward them. Otherwise, they have no place they can call their own."

"I don't understand that," said Barbara.

"I hope you learn to," said her father.

"Why?"

"Because otherwise you could . . . you could love somebody until all the air went out of it . . ."

"Oh," said Barbara. "Does that mean you really want me to go? I mean, are you working at *thoughts* or whatever?"

Oscar Sellers grunted, and he even permitted a demonstration of whatever it was that passed as his smile. "Thoughts?" he said. "Thoughts on a Sunday afternoon with the beer so, um, tasty? God forbid. I mean, I may be crazy, but that doesn't mean I'm stupid."

Barbara laughed. She went to her father and plopped on his lap. She told him if he was crazy then the whole world was crazy. She spoke to him of snowmen. She spoke to him of her braces. She spoke to him of Kenny Oliver—leaving out, though, the fact that Kenny Oliver already had kissed her seventeen times since Christmas. She felt her father shift his weight, and she listened to the way the chair's leather squeaked. She said something to him about the broken spring, but he told her the broken spring was just fine. She carefully tried to work through her mind that even the people you loved had to be left alone from time to time. And then she said: "If I push in too close on you, please let me know."

"Push in too close?"

"Oh, I don't mean *now*. I don't mean your *lap*. I mean . . . well, you know what I mean . . ."

"I expect I do," said Oscar Sellers.

"But just don't get to thinking you're a *duty* . . ."

"All right," said Oscar Sellers.

"Thank you," said Barbara.

Barbara Sellers eventually married a man named Pilgrim. Then she divorced Pilgrim and married a man named O'Connell. Then she divorced O'Connell and married Pilgrim again. Then she divorced Pilgrim, and in 1974 she died. She was fifty. In that time she had come to know something of breath and love and laughter and even aloneness. But she never *quite* understood aloneness. She had a sister Phoebe, who never had married, and Phoebe had understood aloneness very well. But Barbara never *quite* grasped it. Oh, there were times when she did, times when she backed away and tucked herself within a sort of peace. Yet at the end she saw her life as being full of refrigerators and old tires, things scattered everywhere. And how could honest aloneness have existed within all that clutter? She did know how to share, and she did know how to love, and she did know right from wrong, and she did love God and all His works, and she always kept her hedges neatly trimmed, and the house had a new coat of paint every third year, and her smile was enough to splinter windowpanes, and there were many who truly loved her—but did she ever understand the *essence* of what her father had tried to say to her that Sunday afternoon in 1937? The answer sometimes was yes; the answer sometimes was no. But then the world sometimes is yes; the world sometimes is no. So then "always" is floundering. "Always" is bafflement. Still, one never should lose sight of smiles and benevolence. Oh, Barbara wept; she wept; Barbara did weep; she did indeed. But her mistakes came from unfocused goodness, never from malice or fear. So at least then the debris was not gathered out of inertia. She never stopped, and there were many smiles, and her arms forever curled out, enveloping and innocent.

Don Pilgrim

I stayed in Paradise Falls for about six weeks after my wife died. There was no real reason I should have, but I did. It wasn't as though Barbara was about to come clawing out of the grave, for Christ's sake. But I stuck around, and nearly every day I drove up to the cemetery, and I sifted through memories, picking at them and goddamn *picking* at them like maybe a baboon parting its flesh in search of gnats or lice or whatever the hell it is they carry.

I said wife. I mean former wife. I mean former wife two times. I mean former wife when she divorced me in 1956, and I mean former wife when she divorced me in 1972. Her maiden name was Barbara Sellers, and her father owned a hardware store. She was married to a phony dipshit named Jack O'Connell between the times she was married to me. She was fifty when she died, and that was 1974, and I understand it was like her kidneys had been stabbed and slivered, maybe with pins. At any rate, her death wasn't all that much fun. I was with her at the end, but I didn't say anything. Why should I have said anything? Why should things be different at the end from what they are any other time? What do you think happens? You think the Hand of God pries off the roof and drops a little package on us and the package is full of WISDOM all wrapped in cellophane and maybe smelling of fresh paint, courtesy of The Great Plastic Fucking WISDOM Factory in the Sky? Shit. I mean, honest to Christ . . .

My home now is on a farm just outside a place called La-Belle, Ohio. I own and operate an exhibit called Railroad City USA, and it's maybe one of the best HO layouts in the United States. It is something *I* have put together, on *my* time, in *my* way. The layout takes up most of an old barn that I restored. The barn and the farm are owned by my brother Lloyd, and I live there with him and his family. He lets me have the barn rentfree, and one of his younger sons, Ralph, helps me maintain the layout. The railroad is called the LaBelle & Pacific, and I officially have designated myself the president. Ralph is the vice president, and the title has made him happier than a rat in warm butter.

But anyway, Paradise Falls. Paradise Falls and Barbara. I loved her. I still do. She creates within me a flat ache that makes me feel like I've gulped down maybe a clam without taking it out of the shell, you know? We loved each other from maybe 1942 until the day she died, and I know goddamn good and well that is a fact, and I can bring back to mind a whole bunch of the good days we had, good days when we were alone and good days when we were with our three sons . . . you know, picnics, varnish, bed, her laughter (it sort of *gurgled* up, you know, like maybe it had been *goosed*) . . . you know, the outline of her ribs, the taste of her two tiny nipples, even her goddamned stretchmarks, even the times when she came out of the delivery room, her so small and all, and her face was drenched, and her eyes were tight, and she looked right through me . . . I mean, if there's love, even the pain makes at least a little sense. But Barbara and I never really made a final connection. I wonder how many people do. I expect some do. I mean, we read about them, don't we?

I don't know. Maybe it's because I was working all this stuff in my skull that I stayed in Paradise Falls the six weeks. There was no reason I shouldn't have gone back to LaBelle and the good old LaBelle & Pacific, but I just didn't seem to have the strength to pack my grip and crawl into my Mustang and drive away. Paradise Falls is in southeastern Ohio, and I lived there the times I was married to Barbara, and I worked in her father's hardware store, and I took over the place after he died in '59. But then in '73, about a year after I divorced her for the second time, she and her sisters sold the place to a fellow named Arthur Bloomer. Yeah, *Bloomer*. No shit. He's a *Bloomer*, all right. According to what I've heard, volume is down maybe twenty percent, and he's let the inventory go six ways to hell. About all he's got going for him is the fact that he hasn't changed the name from Sellers Bros Hardware. I mean, Christ's sake, if he used his own name, half the town would think the goddamned place had been converted to a fucking lingerie shop, la de da, here we go gathering nuts in May, nuts in May. Bloomer. Some name. Shit.

LaBelle is in northwestern Ohio, and the distance between it and Paradise Falls is forever, at least in my mind. Maybe that distance had something to do with why I kept putting off returning to my trains. Maybe I figured I never again would have the strength for the trip. It all beats me . . . but then so have a lot of other things. Still, I did manage to drive to the cemetery, and there were times when I brought flowers, and I cleared away old dead flowers . . . including bunches of day lilies that kept appearing from I didn't know where. The earth had been mounded over her grave, but then it began to sink, like maybe it had sighed, settled itself and given up. And this wasn't so bad. With each day and night, with each smear of rain, the goddamned *scabbed* aspect of the earth faded a little more. Ashes to ashes. Dust to dust. Scabs to earth. Okay. Fine. I

am all for the healing of wounds. The cemetery people had
spread grass seed, and I spread more grass seed. She had
enjoyed working in her garden. Have I mentioned that? I
don't think so. Well, there had been something about the
feel of it, she'd said to me. The feel of her muscles. The feel
of the earth. The feel of honest basic goddamned *sweat*. I
don't know (she'd never really gone into detail), but the de-
light surely had existed, and I can remember how she had
grinned, and her with teeth so big they could have been
rented as keys by the Steinway people. But hell, I loved her,
and so maybe I'm prejudiced, but it's not all that bad a prej-
udice, is it? I mean, it beats hating niggers, doesn't it?

But I finally did go home to LaBelle and my trains and
Ralph and all the rest of it. You see, there was an afternoon
when I drove into the cemetery and I saw someone kneeling
over the grave. It was a man, but I could not tell who it was
at that distance. I parked the car out of his range of vision. I
got out of the car and circled behind him. He was a big fellow, and he had a heavy belly. I recognized him. His name
was Harry McNiece, and he was editor of the Paradise Falls
Journal-Democrat. He wrote a column that I had read every now and again. His wife was sick, and he didn't have
any kids. Well, there he was, kneeling at Barbara's grave,
and he was placing a vase full of those day lilies next to a
basket of roses I'd left two days before. I leaned against a
tree, and I watched him, and I saw him shake his head. I
was only maybe twenty yards from him, but he didn't see
me. I watched him sort of *fluff* the day lilies, you know? And
then I watched him stand up. And then I watched him slap
his palms together, as though maybe a little dirt had stuck
to them. And then I watched him slap at his knees. I didn't
feel good about any of it. It almost was like I was watching
the man jack off. I mean, whatever it was he was doing, it
was *private*, and I had no goddamned right spying on him.
It didn't even matter that I'd been married to her twice. If

he once had loved her, or if he even loved her right then, it wasn't my business. So I walked back to my car, and I got inside, and I quietly closed the door, and I drove out of the cemetery, and I drove around Paradise Falls for maybe half an hour. I saw a little boy fall off a tricycle, and I heard him howl. I saw old Hugo G. Underwood, the lawyer, go sort of shuffling past the entrance to the Grace Episcopal Church, which was where Barbara and I had been married the first time. Underwood walked as though all his bones had been pulled out of him, like maybe with a suction pump. He once had been a member of the United States House of Representatives, and I even had voted for him. I might as well have voted for Mortimer Fucking Snerd. Oh, not that Underwood was such a bad sort of guy. Hell, I've known a whole lot worse people. But it's just that it was like being represented in Congress by a bowl of rice pudding. So I thought about him for a while. And I drove. And leaves were beginning to change. Just barely, but a *feeling* was there, you know? A feeling of dry pushing at damp, you know? So then I saw two little girls, and they were maybe eight years of age, and they were holding hands, and they both wore pink dresses and hornrimmed glasses, and they could have been twins except for the fact that one was fat and the other was thin, and the fat one was a nigger and the thin one was white. It was a few minutes later that I supposed Harry McNiece had left the cemetery, and so I returned, and sure enough—he was gone. I parked the car, walked to the grave and stared down at his lilies. Had he been an old boyfriend? No. She would have told me . . . and anyway, she had been older. So then why the day lilies? I frowned. I worked it in my mind maybe a minute, maybe two minutes; I don't know. Then I decided it really didn't matter that much, did it? I mean, she had *touched* him. Who cared how? What difference did it make? Hell, she had touched a lot of people. The boys, her parents, her sisters, myself, even that asshole she married after she divorced me the first time. So why then was I staying in Paradise Falls? Was I guarding her? From what? Love? Would she have wanted me to spend the rest of my life prowling around a cemetery? As long as Harry McNiece existed, as long as the affection she had created existed, what the hell could *I* add? I mean, there they were—lilies. What could I do? *Gild* the lilies? So then I felt warmth behind my eyes. And it became damp. So I bawled a little. And I snuffled. And I sneezed. And that night I packed my grip. And I said goodbye to Barbara's sisters. And I drove to LaBelle. And I told myself: She will be fine. And at dawn the next day I was back with my trains and Ralph and all the rest of it.

HUGO G. UNDERWOOD & BARBARA PILGRIM

She was pretty enough, if you like them perky and sort of, ah, chipmunked. By that I mean she had a rather noticeable overbite. But her legs were absolutely sensational, and she had a trim little body, remarkable in a woman who was a mother three times. Her name was Barbara Pilgrim, and her father was Oscar Sellers, who owned the hardware store nextdoor to Steinfelder's, and she came into my office one morning in October of 1955, and she tried to grin, but nothing much came of it, and so finally she simply flat out said: "Mr Underwood, I'm not going to beat around the bush. I want to . . . ah, I want to divorce my husband."

I was standing. So was she. She wore a plaid overcoat, and she was hugging a small beaded purse. I motioned her toward a chair, but then—just as she was seating herself—I said to her: "Oh, I beg your pardon. Would you like me to take your coat?" I came around from behind my desk.

"No," said Barbara Pilgrim. She had been poised over the chair. Now she finished seating herself, and she made another attempt at a grin. It was just as unsuccessful as the first attempt had been.

I went back behind my desk and sat down.

"I don't mean any offense," said Barbara Pilgrim. "It's just that I've been cold lately. It's not that I've been *ill* or anything. It's just that I've been *cold*." She gathered the coat's collar tightly around her neck. She crossed her legs, and I was able to see a great deal of her excellent thighs and knees.

I spread my hands. "Well, I suppose you're under an emotional strain."

"That is correct," said Barbara Pilgrim.

"I must say I am surprised. I've always liked Don Pilgrim. How long has he lived here? ten years? ever since the end of the war?"

"Yes," said Barbara Pilgrim. "He came here to live ten years and one month ago. Which was when we were married. Grace Episcopal Church. And then he went to work in my father's store. And we have the three boys."

"Yes. Three boys. I have four children myself. Or, that is to say, Mrs Underwood and I do. Anne is nineteen; Nancy is sixteen; Kenny is fifteen; Billy is twelve. I can hardly believe it. I just don't know where the time has gone."

"You and Mrs Underwood are fortunate that you have had such a good marriage."

I said nothing.

Barbara Pilgrim cleared her throat. Then: "I've talked it out with Don. He's agreed to let me have the boys. But I guess I'll have to be the one to do the suing, won't I?"

I held up a hand. It was time to ask the usual cautionary question. "Whoa now. Hold on. Are you sure you're doing the right thing?"

Barbara Pilgrim nodded. She did not look at me. She

said: "There's another man, you see, and I'll be marrying him as soon as the divorce is, ah, decreed. Isn't that the word—'decreed'? I got through Ohio U in three years, and a person would think I'd know the word, but I guess I'm maybe a little . . . um . . . um, nervous . . . "

"You got through Ohio U in three years? Well, good for you."

"It was during the war," said Barbara Pilgrim, "and I went summers. There wasn't all that much else to do. But do we have to talk about that? I mean, the divorce, Mr Underwood. I want to talk about the *divorce*."

I had been leaning forward with my elbows on the desk. I slumped back. I am not much of a lawyer. I am not much of anything. But I am rich, and that helps. I did not earn the money, and I have passed through most of my life in a sort of indifferent torpor. Still, a lot of people seem to think my money has given me some sort of grasp of wisdom, and they want me to dispense it to them . . . the Hugo G. Underwood Elixir of Success. And it was clear Barbara Pilgrim wanted some of it that day in 1955. I was *Hugo G. Underwood*, and I *had it made*, and for one term (1949–51) I even had been a member of the *United States House of Representatives*, and I owned the newspaper. And my wife's father was the one and only *Elmer Carmichael*, who was absolutely the *richest* man in town, what with his being president of the Paradise Falls Clay Products Co, chairman of the board of the Carmichael Construction Co and president of the Paradise County National Bank (formerly known as the Paradise Valley Farmers' & Merchants' Bank, before it was granted its national charter). So therefore, what with my own wealth plus the wealth I married, I never really have been permitted to be trivial, and most people are made uncomfortable when I try to wander into small talk. What they don't seem to realize is that I am at my best when I am taking part in small talk. I think small talk represents my finest moments. I really speak well when it comes to pies, the weather, begonias, Marilyn Monroe. It is a genuine shame most people don't realize the extent of this talent of mine. Perhaps, in some fragile way, I would be able to enrich them.

Barbara Pilgrim had been frowning at me. She again cleared her throat.

I blinked at her.

"I'm sorry," she said. "I didn't mean to be so *abrupt*. It's just that I've had so much on my *mind* . . . "

I smiled. "Of course," I said. "I am the one who is at fault." I hesitated. I deepened my voice, hoping to make it properly lawyerish. "Your husband is not contesting?"

"He wants to, but he won't ."

"And the other man . . . he is . . . ah, who is he?"

" . . . um, his name is Jack O'Connell, and he—"

"—sells appliances at Steinfelder's?"

"You know him?"

"Yes," I said. "He worked in my Congressional campaign back in 'fifty. Unfortunately, it was the one I lost." Another hesitation. Then: "He will marry you and assume all support of the children?"

"Yes."

"And this is agreeable to your husband?"

"Yes," said Barbara Pilgrim. "Don's people come from a place called LaBelle, which is up between Toledo and the Indiana line. He plans to go back there. Now, please, Mr. Underwood, about the suing . . . "

"Whether or not he leaves," I said, "you can sue him on grounds of gross neglect of duty. If you don't ask for alimony or child support, I expect the separation agreement can be drawn up quite easily, and the whole procedure'll go through the Common Pleas Court smooth as wax. Of course, ah, certain *implications* will be made . . . "

"Implications?"

"Word gets around. And the talk'll be that you perhaps had some sort of . . . ah, adulterous relationship with O'Connell."

Barbara Pilgrim looked directly at me.

"Oh," I said.

Later, after I had taken notes for the separation agreement and had ushered Barbara Pilgrim out of my office, I seated myself, swiveled my chair around and looked out toward the Paradise County Court House. It stood in a square across the street, and an immense and filthy statue was atop its cupola. The statue was of a chastely draped woman, and the word BEAUTY was engraved on its base. The statue was peering, supplicating. I reached for the telephone, and I had the longdistance operator place a call to a Miss Shirley Edwards, in Washington, D.C. She worked in the offices of the Democratic National Committee, and she had been my mistress for a number of years. I'd not seen her in about six weeks. She had superb legs, and Barbara Pilgrim's legs had put me in mind of them. Shirley came on the line, and she told me she loved me. She also told me her cat was sick. Its name was Robert A. Taft. She said yes, she would be pleased to meet me the following evening in our usual motel in Columbus. I went home that night and told my wife I would be attending a meeting of the state central committee the next evening. I don't know whether Jane believed me, and I don't really care. I drove to Columbus the next day, and I could not erase from my mind that look Barbara Pilgrim had given me when I had spoken of her relationship with O'Connell. I was not much good with Shirley Edwards, and I'm afraid the lady was more than a little vexed. We had been lovers since 1948. Our arrangement came to an end in May of 1956 when she married a man who owned a seafood restaurant in Chevy Chase. I was fortynine by then, and I sent the newlyweds a matched set of carving knives and forks and skewers. It even included a little thermometer. You stuck the thermometer in the meat, and juices popped out, and you discovered how warm the meat was.

DON PILGRIM & FRIENDS

Don Pilgrim, whose former wife had died eight days earlier, sat with several of his friends in a rear booth of the Sportsman's Bar & Grill. It was the afternoon of Friday, August 9, 1974, and everyone was drinking beer, and Gerald R. Ford was the new President of the United States, but Gerald R. Ford was not the principal topic of conversation. Nor was his predecessor, Richard M. Nixon. Instead, everyone was talking about a woman named Miss Margaret Ridpath, who at noon today . . . at just about the time Ford had taken the oath of office . . . had shot and killed three young and as yet unidentified bank robbers. In so doing, Miss Ridpath had herself been shot and killed, and the bank robbers had shot and killed a bank guard named Otto York. She had used Otto York's gun on the bank robbers (one of them had been a girl), killing two of them inside the Paradise Falls State Bank and pursuing the third outside onto Main Street. Mortally wounded, the young fellow had collapsed. Also mortally wounded, Miss Ridpath had knelt next to him. She now had two guns, having appropriated the second one from one of the robbers she had killed in the bank. She pressed both the guns against the third bank robber's head, and he asked her not to kill him, but she refused. Then, after blowing away most of his head, she also collapsed, and she died within an hour. Don Pilgrim had been standing about thirty feet from this final scene, and now he shook his head, sipped at a Rolling Rock and said to

his friends: "And to think of all the years I called her Miss
Margaret Birdbath. I mean, she always seemed so prissy
and all. A goodlooking woman, though. I'll give her that.
How old do you suppose she was? sixty? Well, she was a hell
of a wellpreserved sixty. Good tits and whatever."

"She was past sixty . . . closer to sixtyfive," said Ferd
Burmeister, a druggist.

"In her day, she could of married just about anyone," said
Wes Izor, who worked in the Sellers Bros Hardware Store.

"Smart," said Dave Pullen, a farmer. "Her and her
bridge."

Don Pilgrim nodded. Miss Ridpath had been a bridge
player of national reputation. She'd had a crazy old mother,
though, and she'd had to live with the crazy old mother and
a housekeeper. Don's late former wife, Barbara, had been
one of the few people in town capable of holding a conversation with loony old Mrs Ridpath.

"Well, Margaret Birdbath sure did go out like John
Wayne," said Lou Smith, who operated the Isaly's. "And
you should of seen the inside of the bank. Me, I ran in, and
people were screaming, and them two punks was laying on
the floor, and poor old Otto York was laying on the floor,
and blood was everywhere, and it was *slick*, you know?"

"Jesus," said Wes Izor.

"John Wayne," said Don Pilgrim, looking at Lou Smith.
"Right. John Wayne. We'll think back on her, and she'll be
John Fucking Wayne, won't she?"

"Huh?" said Lou Smith.

"So?" said Dave Pullen.

"You trying to make some sort of point?" said Ferd
Burmeister to Don Pilgrim.

Don Pilgrim was not a tall man. His body was square and
rigid. He made fists. He now lived near a town called La-
Belle, where he operated a model railroad display. He had
lived in Paradise Falls for many years, though (he had been

married twice to Barbara), and he was no stranger to any of the men in this booth. So he said: "Shit. It'll come to be like a goddamned *legend*, and we'll set our memories by it, won't we?"

"Do what?" said Wes Izor.

"Set our what?" said Lou Smith.

Don Pilgrim sighed. Both his hands loosened, then curled around his can of Rolling Rock. He said : "Set our memories. The way we set our memories on where we were and what we were doing when Pearl Harbor was bombed. Or when Kennedy was killed. Five years from now a man and his wife will be talking, and she'll say to him: 'Henry, this is the best summer for corn we've had since, ah, 'seventyfour; which I remember on account of it also was the year good old Miss Margaret Birdbath got into the gun battle.' Or an old man will say: 'Shit, I ain't been laid since the year the blood came all, ah, *slick* on the floor of the Paradise Falls State Bank.'"

"So?" said Dave Pullen. "What's so terrible about that? It's the way people's minds operate."

"A sort of shorthand?" said Don Pilgrim.

"Right," said Dave Pullen.

"So it'll all then come down to shorthand," said Don Pilgrim

"Maybe so," said Ferd Burmeister.

"Shit," said Don Pilgrim.

"What's wrong, buddy?" said Wes Izor.

Don Pilgrim looked at Wes Izor. "Maybe we ought to remember more of it," said Don Pilgrim.

Wes Izor was tall and pink, and the veins in his nose had blown apart, and there were some who called him Izor the Eyesore. He and Don Pilgrim had worked together in the hardware store for many years . . . back in the days when Don Pilgrim had been married to Barbara, whose late father and an uncle had founded the place during World War

64

Mystical Union

I. Wes Izor was not all that bad a fellow, though, despite his crapulous appearance, and so he said: "Look, Don, we don't want to make you mad. I mean, with Barbara gone and all, and we all know you still had a whole lot of feeling for her, and—"

"Never mind Barbara," said Don Pilgrim, leaning forward. "I'm not talking about *Barbara*. I'm talking about that goddamned *shit* in the bank and out there on Main Street." Don Pilgrim hesitated. He finished off the can of Rolling Rock. Then he crushed the empty can in his cupped hands. "I'm talking about . . . ah, everything . . . I mean, how we can just shrug away every fucking thing on account of we keep telling ourselves the craziness maybe only is temporary, and if we said something about how *really* bad it was, the thing that happened today, then we wouldn't be . . . ah, *cool* or whatever . . . and we wouldn't be . . . *men*. But I mean, Miss Margaret Birdbath—what was it *happened* to her? I mean, *her*, of all people, what with the sort of person she was. Quiet, right? Wouldn't say shit if she had a mouthful, right? But all we *really* want to do is *forget*, don't we? Turn her into a legend. A goddamned John Wayne. Like that fucker Nixon . . . all we want to do is forget *him*, too, don't we?" Another hesitation. Don Pilgrim glared at the other men, and none of them spoke. Lou Smith and Dave Pullen actually looked away. Finally Don Pilgrim resumed. He said: "A story's been working in my mind. A memory. It takes place in Germany, and the year is good old glorious 1945, and our company comes to this . . . this *place* . . . this *camp*. The SS people, who were about the only ones left still fighting, had hauled ass out of there, and so we walked through the open gates, and what did we see? We saw fucking *skeletons*—that's what we saw. Skeletons in dirty striped suits, and some of the skeletons were breathing, and they sort of clustered around us like *dogs*, you know?

And they smelled like *shit*, you know? And I threw up all my fucking *cookies*, you know? And we tried to feed them, only they ate too fast, so *they* threw up. Jesus Christ, it was 1945, and it could of been this morning. The place was called Camp Schwartzenscheiss or some goddamned thing. And you know something? About a mile and a half away was a *village* called Schwartzenscheiss, and a platoon of us went in there, and we found the fucking burgomeister, and he told us oh no, no, vee knew nothingk aboudt the gamp ant vhat vas goingk on. And if you believed *that*, you believed shit tasted like cottage cheese. So what we did was, we rounded up every fucking man, woman and child in that village . . . maybe there were three hundred of them . . . and we marched those fuckers *to* the camp, and we marched them *through* the camp, and some of them bawled, and some of them threw up *their* fucking cookies . . . and the goddamned burgomeister even tore at his shirt and beat at his chest. And God *damn* but what it all felt good . . . to have those German assholes *see* and not be able to *hide from* what they'd done. And the way the skeletons looked up at them. It was like those Germans were being kissed on the lips by the devil and their fucking *mouths* were falling off, you know? And then we marched them back to their village, and they were moaning and groaning and carrying on, and they kept saying they didn't *know*, they didn't *know*. And we told them to save that sort of bullshit for the barnyard. And it all was fine. And we were righteous as hell. The only thing is—the next day we were laying all around that village, and some of us were fucking the girls in that village, and others of us were drinking beer sold to us by the same fucking people we'd marched through the camp, and it was like well, okay, let's forget it. Done is done, and past is past. And I was no better than anybody else. I got drunk, and I got fucked . . . by the burgomeister's daughter, no less, and she even copped my joint. So I forgot real fast, didn't I? When it comes to a choice between skeletons and getting your joint copped, what the hell, you can only do the natural thing, right? So all right . . . all right . . . so we forget on account of maybe we *have* to. But shit, doesn't that mean we'll never stop with all this blood? That goddamned Nixon, why don't we take him to Vietnam and show him what happened? Jesus Christ. God damn . . ."

They all looked away from Don Pilgrim. No one spoke.

Don Pilgrim wept.

Ferd Burmeister cleared his throat.

Don Pilgrim covered his face, and after a time everyone went away.

BARBARA PILGRIM

I could talk to Phoebe about as well as I could talk to the walls, but Rosemary always was there to listen . . . or at least weep, which I suppose was better than nothing. I was the oldest. Then came Phoebe, then Rosemary. We were the daughters of Mr and Mrs Oscar W. Sellers, and our father was the sole owner and proprietor of the Sellers Bros Hardware Store. The other Sellers brother had been my Uncle Willie, but he had died in a canoeing accident before I was born. There were times my father spoke of Uncle Willie at some length. It never really was set in my father's mind why Uncle Willie had been called to glory so quickly and so abruptly. "In this life," my father would say, "a person doesn't even have to give offense. All he has to do is be in the wrong place at the wrong time. Or make a tiny mistake, give way to some sort of silly carelessness. Willie was a good fellow, not a fellow to cut corners, not a fellow to go

back on his word. I knew him better than anybody on this
earth knew him. His wife. Anybody. Which is why I visit
his grave so often. Which is why I drag you along. You and
your sisters and your mother." And then perhaps my father
would embrace me, and it was as though he were asking me
to forgive him for boring us. But I didn't forgive him. Oh,
not because I was cruel, but only because I didn't understand the question. I loved him. I loved them all. My girlhood was a decent and good girlhood (and I mean "decent"
and "good" as defined both above and below the
waist . . . I was, you see, a virgin on my wedding night),
and I have more good memories than bad ones. Many more.
Shadows, for instance. Have you ever watched the way they
progress across a lawn on a bright summer day when only
trees and roofs lie between the lawn and the sky? It ought
to remind you that there is some sort of glorious mech-
anism that keeps functioning no matter how much *we* holler, no matter how cruel *we* are, no matter how badly *we* die,
no matter the silliness of the questions *we* ask. In the time
it takes to say this, oh my goodness how the shadows do
change, blend, scatter, vanish. I would watch those shadows, and I would wait for a sudden cloud, some whim of
God, and the pattern would be smeared and split, and a new
pattern would evolve, and it was this sort of thing that
passed as a summer afternoon in Paradise Falls in the '20s
and the '30s and even into the '40s. So then I stipulate shadows. So then I also stipulate the way my boyfriend Kenny
Oliver would take me dancing, the way he always insisted
on placing a flower in my hair, arranging a gardenia just so
and then stepping back and telling me what? I had stepped
from the pages of a book? I was the answer to all dreams?
Oh, how can memorys of a girlhood exist without a Kenny
Oliver standing jauntily within its fragile circumference?
He always wore bow ties, and he was a gorgeous dancer,
and he enjoyed kissing me . . . even though I

was . . . well, the word is "bucktoothed," and there's no sense denying it . . . and I wore enough orthodonture to set half the compass blades in the world all awhirl like dead leaves in a high wind. Time pushed him away—history— the war—but those things have done nothing to damage the *memory* of him. Could it be that some people exist only as ornaments to our recollection of the past? Kenny Oliver left Paradise Falls years ago, and no one really knows where he is or what he is doing (and he may even be dead), and I know I should mourn the fact that he no longer is with us, but I cannot. Here, now, in 1972, everyone would laugh at his bow ties and his gardeniaed kindnesses and his arcane and anachronistic talent for the fox trot and jitterbugging, and so therefore isn't it better that he has vanished? And isn't it better that I see him as the coiled and genially bouncing boy from the days when I was that green and toothy and enthusiastic Barbara Sellers many people said could outgrin the sun if she was of a mind. But that was only my *image*. Perhaps it had at least a glint of accuracy, but there was too little within it that had to do with pain. I studied shadows, and there were other times when I reached for something larger than the biscuited and glidered and lemonaded dimensions of my girlhood, but mostly I settled for those dimensions. There was so much, you see, I never was *told*, so much I never was *shown*. I eventually married a man named Don Pilgrim, and then I divorced him and married a man named Jack O'Connell, and then I divorced Jack O'Connell and married Don Pilgrim again, and now—believe it or not—I am in the process of divorcing Don Pilgrim for the second time. I have no idea where I'm headed. I'm not even all that certain where I've been. There was a Mr Amberson, and he taught English and coached the track team at Paradise Falls High School, and I loved that Mr Amberson, and perhaps he supplies the only real, accurate and coherent definition of what I was. And maybe from *that* I can determine where I am now. He was a small man, precise and I suppose rather delicate (he and his wife both died last year), but he always took the time to listen to me. We would sit in his empty classroom after school was out for the day, and he would brush chalkdust off the sleeves of his jacket, and he would press down his shirtcuffs so that they would not bunch or wrinkle, and he would say to me: "There is no way, Barbara, I can force you to be something your nature and your inclinations prevent you from being. I can say one thing, however—namely, you have a gift for words. But I cannot make you exercise it. All I can do is acknowledge it. I am only a smalltown teacher, but that does not mean I am entirely a nincompoop, and so when I say you have talent, I hope you treat my opinion with respect. Your essay on Nathan Hale. Your essay on your cat. When *National Scholastic* published them, a further acknowledgment was made, correct? Do you have any idea how many essays are submitted for publication to *National Scholastic*? Thousands, I expect. *Thousands.* And *you've* been published *twice.* What was that phrase you used to describe your cat, that she moved *'wispy and quick and was gone like the vanished dreams of dead lovers whose tombstones have been overturned and whose names have melted into the earth as though blotted by some immense uncaring thumb'*? Florid, yes. But at least a mind was functioning. At least images were being created. And the people at *National Scholastic* agreed with me, didn't they? They also felt the summoning of the words, didn't they? To compare the movement of a cat with vanished dreams is unquestionably excessive, but you were not ashamed, were you? It was what you felt at the time, wasn't it? It was an honest statement, correct?" And Mr Amberson smiled at me, and I of course was seeing him through a mist (there is no other word for it; oh, I know how schoolgirlish it is, but what can I do when faced with its rightness?), and I wanted to touch his hand, to weep, to tell him he was my inspiration, to plead with him to take me someplace away from this *town* and his *wife* and *children* and all these *shadows* and *wispy cats* and explain to me how I could find the courage to be the sort of person he wanted me to be. I wanted to brush at his sleeves and his cuffs, to wrap him within whatever benevolence I possessed. But I did nothing. I simply sort of shrugged. The year was 1942, and I knew I would do what was expected of me. I was eighteen that year, and I knew my girlhood was over. I would be leaving for Ohio University in the fall . . . if, as the saying went, God was willing and the creeks didn't rise . . . and I would indeed do all the proper things and say all the proper words. And Kenny Oliver surely would vanish, and I would not have the time for shadows and cats. Instead I would seek to take exercises that would expand my chest. And I would seek a man—wartime shortage or no wartime shortage. And marriage would come. And babies. For where is it written that intelligence and sensitivity (if indeed I ever have owned either) automatically include courage? So then I no longer was a girl. Ah ha ha ha, where are the jacks of yesteryear? where is the rubber ball? where are the boys who pull your hair? where are the gold stars for perfect spelling papers? Oh, I loved him. I loved Mr Amberson. But so what? I never moved toward him, nor he toward me. Still, I did love him. It was not a lot of silly and hapless mooning over someone I knew was unattainable. I loved him because, plainly and simply, he bothered to penetrate that thing within me that was shattered later . . . either by timidity or inertia. Jack O'Connell, my second husband, tried to rediscover the thing, but the effort was made only for his own purposes, and so he failed, and he revealed himself to be little more than a mad impotent windbag. My other husband, Don Pilgrim, was (and is) a good man, but he knew (and knows) as much about this as he knew (and knows) about needlepoint.

So then let it all go, Barbara. Forget it, Barbara. The girl is gone, Barbara. Your sister Phoebe never would talk with you about any of it, and your sister Rosemary never even would have understood it, let alone talked about it. So mourn then alone, Barbara. The days of promise, of latticed shadows, of roofs and dollbabies and erasers and paint sets and silly hairy dogs. Phoebe lives alone now in a house that is full of caged birds. Rosemary watches soap operas and loves her children and her husband, even if he doesn't have much of a chin. They are what they are, and they accept. So then do the same, Barbara. So then mourn whatever you like, but accept the walls that crowd you, nudging your shoulders. If it all is debris, then it all is debris. At least you see it. At least you understand the choice you made. At least now and then you spy an edge of what you missed. That just may be an accomplishment.

Barbara Pilgrim & Rosemary Cross

All through the summer of 1974, as Barbara Pilgrim lay in the Paradise Valley Memorial Hospital and felt the kidney disease tear at her interior landscape as though that landscape were nothing more substantial than sticks and excelsior and bits of dry gobbed useless glue, as though her belly were a ripped sack leaking damply anonymous shreds and fragments, as she lay in that hospital and was hooked to the machine and was unhooked from the machine, as she was hooked and unhooked, hooked, hooked, hooked, unhooked, unhooked, unhooked, unhooked, as pain came boiling into her throat, as she was sedated, as her eyes rolled, as she made fists and beat them against the bedclothes, as the ritual of the hooking and the unhooking was performed by a stout nurse who had three moles on her throat, and those three moles put Barbara in mind of the Belt of Orion, as all this awful crunching and smearing laid back Barbara's flesh, humiliating her, making her last days vile and incontinent, she was visited every afternoon by Rosemary Cross, who was the younger of her two sisters and perhaps was the most tearful and melancholy woman in the Western world. And so it evolved to *Barbara* to attempt to lighten *Rosemary's* burden, and finally one afternoon Barbara said to a weeping Rosemary: "Hey now, just who's supposed to be sick anyway?"

Rosemary, who had been poking at her eyes with her thumbs, blinked at Barbara. "I'm . . . I'm sorry . . ."

"Well, it's your nature, isn't it? I mean, you cry when a petal falls off a daisy, don't you?"

". . . yes," said Rosemary, blowing her nose.

Something small and insistent ripped across Barbara's belly for a moment. She tightened her eyes, but in no other way did she reveal her pain. She did not want to set Rosemary off again. Instead she breathed shakily for a moment, then said: "I had another letter from Don today." She nodded. "Another very nice letter. He writes well, do you know that? Anyway, he wrote of this and that, and I was moved, and he even asked me whether I just didn't want to lie down and never get up . . ."

Rosemary said nothing. She did not like Don Pilgrim. She never had liked Don Pilgrim. Apparently Don Pilgrim did not often enough make her weep. He was Barbara's former husband. Actually, he had been Barbara's former husband twice. Between her marriages to him, she briefly had been married to a man named Jack O'Connell, but *that* marriage had been a farce. The marriages to Don Pilgrim had not been farces, though, and even Rosemary knew that. And so she spoke carefully (and Barbara noted the care) when she said: "Why hasn't he offered to come here?"

73

"He thinks maybe it's better this way," said Barbara.
"And maybe so do I." Here Barbara moved her head affirmatively. Don Pilgrim owned and operated a model railroad exhibit near the village of LaBelle, which was in the northwestern part of the state, not far from the Indiana line. He had opened the exhibit last fall, a little more than a year after leaving Barbara for the second time. "I resent it . . . at least a little," she said. "But . . . well, maybe I can understand . . ."

"How?" said Rosemary.

"He thinks all the words have been said. What if he would come here? What if we would touch? Would that make this damned pain any easier?"

". . . I don't know . . . I . . . oh dear God, Barbara, why *you*?"

Barbara sighed. "Well, why *not* me?" she said. "What am I—something special? You ever see any sign that God reached down and touched me?" A smile. "I'm *touched*, all right, but not by God. And anyway, the word really is 'teched.' Who says 'teched'? Mammy Yokum in the funnypapers?"

"I don't know . . . I don't read the funnypapers . . ."

Barbara chuckled, and the force of it made her wince a little. "No," she said, "I don't suppose you do. Not *you*."

Rosemary glanced away from her dying sister.

"Indulging me?" said Barbara.

Rosemary said nothing.

Barbara spoke slowly, easily. She knew precisely what she had to say, and so she moved the words from her throat with great calm. She said: "Do you think you can understand the difference between grief and fear? I mean, I am sorry, but I am not afraid. Don and I shared many good things, and he is a good person, and Mama and Papa were good persons, and our oldmaid sister Phoebe is a good person, and even *you* are a good person, and not even Jack

74

O'Connell was all *that* bad . . . and remember Kenny
Oliver, what a good dancer he was? And remember Mr Amberson, God rest him, how I loved him back in high school,
however many years ago *that* was? And the boys . . . Don
and I had three good sons, and they have been our pride and
joy. So, sure, Rosemary, I expect I have a *right* to be *sorry*.
But I'll be *damned* if I'll *cave in*."

"That's . . . that's fine . . ." said Rosemary.

"Now don't cry," said Barbara. "I order it."

Rosemary nodded.

"A Polack came into a doctor's office," said Barbara, "and
a frog was on the Polack's head, and the frog said: 'Doctor,
please take this wart off my ass.'"

Rosemary looked at Barbara.

"It was the *frog* that spoke," said Barbara.

"Oh," said Rosemary.

"Well, don't fall off your chair."

"All right," said Rosemary.

"Sheesh," said Barbara, sighing.

"I don't follow things like that too well," said Rosemary.

"So I've noticed," said Barbara.

"I . . . um, I had my hair trimmed this morning. Phoebe
thinned it out a little. It was a slow morning, and she was
able to take me right away."

"I thought I noticed something different."

"How does it look?"

"Fine," said Barbara. "You always were the family beauty, and you know it."

"That's not so."

"Well, if you didn't *bawl* so much, it *would* be so."

"I can't help it . . ." said Rosemary, leaning forward and
beginning to weep.

Barbara reached out and patted Rosemary's hair. "Ah,"
she said, "it does feel lighter. And it certainly looks better.
Now. Now. Hold on with that. You want to flood this room?"

"Don . . . shouldn't Don *really* be here? Never mind your *words* . . . tell me what you *feel.* And I mean *really* feel."

"What I really feel is whatever he wants me to feel," said Barbara. "I love him, and that's the least I can do."

"That's the . . . that's the noblest . . ."

"Baloney," said Barbara.

"What?" said Rosemary.

"I love him, so whatever he wants, I want. Period."

"Even if he wants to be cruel?"

"Cruel?"

"Staying away . . ."

"Maybe cruel is the best. Did you ever think of that? If he comes here, it'd be a reminder, don't you see?"

"A reminder of what?"

"Wreckage," said Barbara.

"What?"

"*Wreckage,*" said Barbara. "Old sheds with their roofs caved in. Teddybears with no eyes. Photographs of people whose names we've forgotten. A reminder of things that can't be restored. Not ever."

Rosemary wept.

"No," said Barbara. "Please." She had an overbite. She gnawed on her lower lip.

Rosemary curled forward, and her hands were pressed against her face, and the sound of her weeping was cavernous.

Barbara expelled her breath. "All right," she said. "All *right.*" She patted her sister's head, and then she drew her sister atop her on the bed, and she embraced her sister, and she kissed her sister's cheeks, and she licked away a great many of her sister's tears. The Orion nurse eventually came along and led Rosemary away. Barbara closed her eyes and summoned images of grapes and old cars and mouths and the distant hills.

76

JACK O'CONNELL & BARBARA PILGRIM

At fortysix, Jack O'Connell was past his prime, and he knew it. Still, there *were* traces, however battered, of what he always had considered his handsomeness, and he *did* have a way of talking that gave a certain grandly magisterial authority to his words. He pushed at them; he chiseled them; he attempted to create the impression that he was speaking in tones that had a quality of bronzed tablets. He was an appliance salesman at Steinfelder's Department Store in Paradise Falls, Ohio, and it was no easy thing for a man of such, um, humble station to speak in tones that had a quality of bronzed tablets, but he worked at it, and he was reasonably successful. There were women who were impressed with him. He was a graduate of Oberlin College, and he could recite Byron and Whitman, and he was able to define sonata form, and he thought of himself as having a way with syllables. They served him well, the syllables . . . at least as far as women were concerned. He was no *rapist*, no *brute*. Either he talked his way into their adorable little panties or he stayed out. He'd never married. At one time he had been enormously ambitious, and he had insisted on viewing his life from the capitalized pinnacle of what he liked to think of as THE BRIGHT SIDE. But there had been no particular focus to his ambition (he could define it only in adjectives, never in specific nouns and verbs), and at thirtyfive or so he had felt it slide away like runny icing on an overbaked cake. So then what remained was the rhetoric, the procession of adjectives, the vacant poetry . . . plus of course an intelligence that from time to time was able to use them as a key that unlocked adorable little panties.

Such as the panties that at this moment were being worn by a young housewife named Barbara Pilgrim, who was tiny, whose teeth were prominent, who nonetheless had quick and chipper good looks, who was the mother of three little boys, whose husband apparently had neglected her beyond her power to endure. She sat next to O'Connell in his '49 Plymouth, and it was March of 1952, and they were on their way to a motel in Lancaster. It was a comfortable little place, and O'Connell had used it several times. Today would be his first time with this Barbara Pilgrim. She had walked into Steinfelder's two months ago, and she had bought a refrigerator that had been featured in an after-Christmas sale. O'Connell had taken his time in ringing up the sale, and he had made special note of the fact that she had splendid legs. He also had made special note of the fact that she was drawn, that she was a little snappish, that she unquestionably was not the happiest woman in the world. He knew her husband slightly. The man's name was Don Pilgrim, and he worked nextdoor in the Sellers Bros Hardware Store. He and O'Connell had occasionally bought drinks for each other in the Sportsman's Bar & Grill. Pilgrim was a chunky man, compact, and he had a tough and farmerish way of talking. To O'Connell, it was no particular surprise that Pilgrim's wife was drawn and snappish; he didn't suppose she received much gentleness or compassion at home. And so, well, O'Connell began a campaign aimed at the investiture of Mrs Pilgrim's panties. If there were two qualities he possessed in abundance (or at least gave the impression of possessing in abundance), they were gentleness and compassion. And so he arranged to drive past the Pilgrim home on South High Street at least three or four times a day, and it was not long before he learned that Mrs Pilgrim packed her three little boys into a large wagon and went promenading with them just about every day at noon, weather permitting. She appeared to be swallowing immense mouthfuls of air, and he was able to see her mouth open and close, and he said to himself: My God, she looks as though she's drowning. From this discovery he was able to move reasonably quickly. First he would *accidentally* meet her on a sidewalk, and they would briefly chat of the weather, or General MacArthur, or President Truman, or John L. Lewis, and within a week she was inviting him into her house, and they would sit at the kitchen table and drink tea while the three little boys hollered and gurgled, and within a month he was kissing her and stroking her nipples and telling her he loved her. And he was quoting poetry to her. Byron or whatever. And her babies were plucking at her ankles and her legs. And he told her she needed to be brave. And he told her she only lived once. And he spoke of Yeats and Maud Gonne. Of Berlioz and Henrietta Smithson—neglecting to mention, though, the historical fact that Henrietta Smithson, who had been Berlioz's ideal, had been a damned poor wife after Berlioz finally had won her. But the fine bronzed voice of Jack O'Connell succeeded; it did its job of work on this Barbara Pilgrim, and now she was on her way to Lancaster with him (she was supposed to be on a shopping trip to Columbus, and her sons had been left with a sister, a woman named Cross), and she sat in a sort of crouch, her buttocks and her back jammed against the door on the passenger's side, and she said: "Jack, I have more to lose than you do. I don't know. I *still* don't know."

"Yes you do," said Jack O'Connell. "What do you propose to do with the rest of your life? *Cope* with it as though it were a bucket leaking muddy water? I love you, Barbara. I honestly do. I mean you no harm. If I didn't love you, do you think I would endanger your life this way? What sort of monster would that make me?" A curve. A snowbank. O'Connell's hands were easy and strong on the wheel, and the car smoothly negotiated the curve. This was Ohio US

33-A, and it was narrow, and a great deal of traffic whisked past in the other direction. There had been a thaw, and the snowbanks were gray.

"He *is* good, you know," said Barbara Pilgrim.

"Good?"

"In bed. I mean, this isn't as though I'm *frustrated* . . . or at least not all *that* much . . ."

"There are many ways of being frustrated," said O'Connell, clearing his throat. "The frustration of minds that cannot meet. Of words that remain unspoken. Of hands that reach out but never touch."

Barbara Pilgrim looked sharply at O'Connell. Then, grinning, clucking, she said: "Jack, for God's sake, *all right.* You don't have to go all platitudinous on me."

"Do you love me?"

"Yes."

"Are you certain?"

"*Yes.*"

"Then tell me. Say to me: 'Barbara Pilgrim loves Jack O'Connell.'"

"Barbara Pilgrim loves Jack O'Connell," said Barbara Pilgrim, speaking quietly.

"Do you love Don?"

". . . no."

"Are you sure?"

". . . yes."

"Am I gentle with you? Am I considerate? Do I seek your views? Do I listen to you?"

"Yes," said Barbara Pilgrim.

"Do you enjoy my mouth on your breast?"

"*Yes.*"

"I never bite you, do I?"

"*No.*"

"So then who really is good?"

"Good?" said Barbara Pilgrim.

"When it comes to loving you," said O'Connell.

"I don't know yet. Ask me in an hour or so."

"That's better," said O'Connell.

"Better?"

"A little bit ago you said you didn't know."

"And you think maybe I *do* know?"

"Yes," said O'Connell.

"I don't understand this," said Barbara Pilgrim.

"A little while ago, you said you didn't know. I took it that you meant you didn't know whether you should go through with all this. *Now*, though, when you say you don't know, the context is different, isn't it? You're saying to me you *won't* know until the *effort* is made, correct?"

"Oh," said Barbara Pilgrim. "All right."

O'Connell smiled. He said to himself: I am the Sugar Ray Robinson of cheap romantic rhetoric. Feet, do your stuff. He and Barbara Pilgrim were silent the rest of the way to the motel. They went to their room, and they were cautious with each other, and it turned out better than most first times were (at least in O'Connell's experience), and afterward he kissed her belly and murmured bits of Byron. Her panties had been tossed on a chair, and from time to time he glanced at them, and he had a vision of Tennyson, and he said to himself: Victory. Empire. And in the meantime his murmured musical words came all warm and bronzed, smooth as shit in fresh cornbread.

BARBARA PILGRIM & MRS RIDPATH

Mrs Ridpath had been fat and crazy for many years. By 1970, however, she was not so fat, although she was just as crazy. Warm days she sat in her front yard in an old canvas chair that had the word STAR printed on its back. She waved at passersby, and now and then one would stop and chat with her. Her husband had committed suicide back sometime in the '20s. The suicide had had to do with the death of another woman, and it had been the reason Mrs Ridpath's brain and reason had flown apart. Still, she meant no harm, and there were times when she was lucid, when she even was able to grasp and control a sort of lovely rhetoric. Barbara Pilgrim, a housewife who lived around the corner in a house on High Street, appreciated the rhetoric. There were others who appreciated the rhetoric, but Barbara Pilgrim perhaps appreciated it most of all, and so she always made a point to visit with Mrs Ridpath when Mrs Ridpath was enthroned in the STAR chair in the Ridpath front yard. And so Barbara Pilgrim smiled widely one August afternoon when she saw Mrs Ridpath taking the sun. And she crossed the yard and touched one of Mrs Ridpath's cheeks and said: "Hello, Mrs Ridpath. Have you ever seen a day that is more of a blessing?"

Mrs Ridpath rubbed her mouth. She bared her dentures. Finally she said: "I'll have to think on that one. There have been so many, but the thing is . . . maybe I've forgotten what a blessing is . . . I mean, when you have to suffer the way *I* have to suffer, your mind doesn't give you much time for *days* . . ."

"Now, *now*," said Barbara. "If you can't take the . . . the, ah, the separate *little* things that make up a life . . . and sort of list them . . . or at least file them away . . . you're depriving yourself of too much . . ."

"Ah, but you forget," said Mrs Ridpath. "I'm a loony. Everyone says so. If I wasn't a loony, why would my daughter hire Pauline Jones to care for me? Wouldn't I be able to care for myself?"

"You're about as loony as a fox," said Barbara. "You

make more sense than the President makes. You make more sense than my husband makes. You make more sense than anyone I know."

"But there are times when I just sort of get off on the wrong track . . ."

"Pardon?"

"I start talking about hummingbirds."

"What?"

"They sort of flick into my mind. Hummingbirds and the memory of my husband, and how he loved Dorothy Hall so much he killed himself after she died. How come, huh? Would he have killed himself if *I'd* died? I mean, all right, yes, hummingbirds flick into my mind. And the taste of a fountain Coke. And do you remember Wanda Ripple, who used to care for me? She made me a lime pie every Christmas. I can taste those lime pies. The 1943 one was the best, and that is the absolute truth."

Barbara Pilgrim was tiny and slender. She squatted next to Mrs Ridpath's chair. She was wearing a sunsuit and Adidas. She was able to balance herself easily. She said: "Tell me all about whatever you want to tell me." She squeezed one of Mrs Ridpath's knees. "I'll listen very carefully," said Barbara. "Dreams. Truth. Little bits, flying things. Whatever you want to say, say it . . ."

"Do you love me?" said Mrs Ridpath.

"Of course," said Barbara.

"Why?"

Barbara smiled. "Why not?" she said. "When did you give me any reason not to? And besides, I like the way your words sound . . ."

"Suppose I was to talk about ants."

"Go ahead," said Barbara.

"You don't *mind*?"

"Not a bit."

"I mean, the word I *said* was *ants.*"

"I don't care if you said 'cockroaches.' Whatever you want to talk about, talk about."

"Really?"

"*Yes.*"

"My goodness," said Mrs Ridpath. "Thank you." She swallowed. Then: "When I was seven years of age, and my name was Inez McClory, and I lived with my mama and my papa in St Louis, I was playing in the back yard, playing in the dirt, doing I don't know what, sort of *scooping* at it, I expect . . . well, anyhow, that was more years ago than you'll ever understand . . . anyhow, somehow I sat on an anthill . . . and at first I didn't realize it . . . but then I had a sort of peculiar *feeling*, you know?"

"I believe so."

"Squirms."

"Yes," said Barbara.

"Dear little Inez McClory, so prim and proper, and she had ants in her pants, and that is the absolute truth. And I moved this way, and I moved that way, but the ants moved right along with me . . ."

"So why didn't you stand up?"

"I did. I *did*. But the ants came right along up with me. So I ran around the yard, and I slapped at my rump, and I rubbed my rump against a tree, and I was bawling, and so finally Mama came out, and I told her what the matter was, and you know what she did?"

"Laugh?" said Barbara.

"Yes," said Mrs Ridpath. "She laughed, and I recollect she even cried a little, and then she took me into the house, and she washed my bottom with maybe it was lye . . . on account of the sting I felt, I mean."

"I expect *so*," said Barbara.

"How come I do this?" said Mrs Ridpath, blinking.

"Do what?" said Barbara.

"Bring up something like that. Something from so many years back."

Barbara's knees had begun to ache. She stood up. She bent over Mrs Ridpath and kissed her on the forehead. "Why shouldn't you?" she said. "Myself, I'm only fortysix, but I have a lot of things stored up, too. And I drag them out all the time. Why shouldn't I? Why shouldn't anybody? We're told that in order to be brave we have to face the future. All right. Fine. I'll accept that. But what's wrong with treasuring the past? And anyway, it's not just anyone who has ants in her pants. Myself, I once went on a hayride, and the horse kept, ah, *farting*. I don't know *why* I remember *that*, but I *do*, and somehow it even *comforts* me. Because, you see, the memory maybe isn't all that important, but the *place* the memory takes us *is*. Because what do we have to show for ourselves except the things we've done, the things we've seen, the people we've met—and the love, my God yes, the *love*."

"So it's all right then to talk about hummingbirds?" said Mrs Ridpath.

"Or ants," said Barbara.

"Suicide?"

"If you want to."

"Dance programs? Willow trees? Music no one else can hear?"

"Of course."

"The taste of a fountain Coke is like heaven to me. I told all my children about what their father did. I was clear as a bell with them. It wasn't until later that I became a loony. And don't say I'm not a loony. I know a loony when I see one. I know myself when I see myself. I understand mirrors. I used to walk naked a great deal. Every day there she was, Inez Ridpath, prowling the house, and she was naked as a jaybird. But, you see, she was naked because that way she was ready to die. She came into the world naked, and she would go out of it naked. But now I don't bother with being naked. I've decided I'm going to outlive the world, and in the meantime I don't want to catch a chill. Ha. Ha. Ha. Just because I'm a loony, that doesn't mean I don't have a sense of humor."

"I love you," said Barbara.

"Pardon?" said Mrs Ridpath.

Barbara plucked at the collar of her sunsuit. "I love you," she said.

"Which means always then we can talk of humming-birds?"

"You bet," said Barbara.

Mrs Ridpath's hands were spread across her lap. They were spotted and ropy, and she blinked at them. She said: "There were hummingbirds outside the window the day after my son Paul was born." She looked at Barbara. "Are you sure now I can talk about them?"

"Yes," said Barbara, and her eyes were warm.

"Thank you," said Mrs Ridpath.

Barbara nodded, and her throat was full of what perhaps was hot grease.

REGINA INGERSOLL & MRS WATTERSON

In 1937, which was the year Regina Ingersoll died of tuberculosis, she weighed barely ninety pounds. She once had been beautiful . . . or so she had told the other patients in the TB ward of the public hospital in Cincinnati . . . but in 1937 no traces of that beauty remained. Still, she insisted on wearing bright wet lipstick, plus rouge, plus some sort of eye paint. And she said: "As long as I am flirting with death, I might as well be at my most attractive."

She spent most of her last few months talking with a Mrs Watterson, an elderly widow who also was dying of TB, and Mrs Watterson said: "But don't you think you are being excessive?"

"I always have been excessive," said Regina Ingersoll. "It is my nature."

"But perhaps you could change your nature," said Mrs Watterson.

"Too late," said Regina Ingersoll. "Too late."

"I suppose . . ." said Mrs Watterson.

"I have lived in Paris," said Regina Ingersoll, "and I met my husband there, and I loved him very much. That was long, long ago, and you should have seen me. But he *hurt* me. He was *too large* for me. How can a woman live with a man who is too large for her? I mean can you possibly understand the pain?"

"Yes," said Mrs Watterson.

"Other women feel that sort of pain, don't they?"

"Yes."

"Did you?"

"No," said Mrs Watterson. "I was . . . ah, *commodious* . . . and, well, Frank never complained . . . and the children were no trouble at all . . ."

"They're a comfort to you, aren't they?"

"Of course."

"Like last week when your daughter brought you the toffee and the back issues of *Liberty*."

Mrs Watterson nodded. Briefly she closed her eyes. Then she opened them, and again she nodded. She and Regina Ingersoll were sitting in the solarium, and perhaps the day was too bright.

"Nobody brings *me* a thing," said Regina Ingersoll.

Mrs Watterson said nothing.

"But that's all right," said Regina Ingersoll.

Mrs Watterson blinked, cleared her throat.

"When one is alone *before,* then it isn't so dreadful to be alone *after,*" said Regina Ingersoll. She smiled a little, and some of her heavy lipstick had smeared her upper front teeth. Her mouth made it appear that she had just spat up blood.

Mrs Watterson nodded.

"Do you understand what I mean?" said Regina Ingersoll.

"Not quite," said Mrs Watterson.

"Then why did you nod?"

"I expect I was just trying to be polite."

"Politeness is not necessary," said Regina Ingersoll. "Not *now.* Not between *us.* Not when *we* know what *we* know."

"All right," said Mrs Watterson, sighing. She wanted to be somewhere else, but there was nowhere to go. She had eaten all the toffee. She had read all the back issues of *Liberty.* She had sorted all her memories, all the recollected laughter, the pain, the babies, agates, photographs, scraps of music, dear wet green grass, her husband's final tight rouged coffined face. "All right, Regina," said Mrs Watterson, "if you want to be naked, be naked."

"Thank you," said Regina Ingersoll. "I'm simply saying—I have no children, no brothers, no sisters, no lover, no husband, no friend. I am a vanished human being, do you understand?"

"Of course I do," said Mrs Watterson.

"But I refuse to feel sorry for myself."

"Good for you."

"If I have vanished, then how can I be afraid of death? I mean, I'm *already* dead, wouldn't you say?"

Mrs Watterson nodded.

"So I try to restore my beauty, and I suppose you think I'm grotesque, but in my day I was enough to make the walls shake, and that is the *truth.* I was Regina Walker from Harrisburg, and it's a wonder the traction company didn't run a special branch line to my front door for all the boys who came calling on me. Skimmers. Hard bow ties. Teeth. Do you remember how beautiful teeth were when we all were young? So it's not as though I've *always* been dead. And then I was married, and it was a grand ceremony indeed, and people came from as far away as *Minneapolis, Minnesota.* His name was Carl Ingersoll, and I met him in Paris in June of 1920. He was from Chicago, and he was a painter, and we sat on the same ottoman at a party, and we talked, and two weeks later he asked me to marry him, and I said yes, yes, *yes*, and I persuaded him to come home to Harrisburg with me so the ceremony could be performed in my church. I am an Episcopalian, you see, and in those days I held my church to be very precious. And Carl, the dear, was most gracious. And so I took him to Harrisburg, and my family welcomed him . . . he had *connections* in Chicago, you see . . . and the ceremony was just as grand as grand can be . . . the cake was four feet high, and more than five hundred persons were invited to the reception, and there was an orchestra, and I wore white, and I was indeed a virgin . . . indeed . . . indeed . . ." And here Regina Ingersoll hesitated. She was seated in a wheelchair. She clawed at its arms. "Then . . . then . . . that night . . . well, no matter what we tried . . . it was . . . it was as though he was tearing me open with a . . . with a . . . *bayonet.*"

"There," said Mrs Watterson.

"I want to *finish*," said Regina Ingersoll. "The thing needs one last time to be what? flung into the wind? I suppose so. Well, ah, the upshot was that there was nothing anyone could do. He gave me all that *pain*, you see. And so, well, it all collapsed . . ."

Mrs Watterson rubbed her palms together.

"I don't even know where he is," said Regina Ingersoll. "I don't even know whether he's alive or dead or what. I've deliberately avoided trying to find out. Oh, the rest of my life was uneventful enough, and for years I was pursued by men, and once, when I was teaching school in a place called Paradise Falls, there was a man who interested me and whose . . . um, *dimensions* . . . I dearly wanted to know . . . but nothing came of it, and Regina Walker Ingersoll has dropped out of sight, and her family lost all its money in the Crash . . . 'twentynine and 'thirty and all that . . . and her father died . . . and her mother died . . . and she had no brothers or sisters . . . and so here she is . . . and you have *no idea* what she once was . . . and so she primps for her last day as though it were a Junior League cotillion . . . and ah dear God, it's as though all my life I've been on my hands and knees and I've been licking dust . . . do you know what I mean?"

Mrs Watterson nodded.

"And you have no wisdom for me, do you?" said Regina Ingersoll.

"Of course not," said Mrs Watterson.

"The sun is nice and warm," said Regina Ingersoll.

"That is the truth," said Mrs Watterson.

"There ought to be more than licking dust," said Regina Ingersoll.

"Or toffee," said Mrs Watterson.

"What?" said Regina Ingersoll.

"Nothing," said Mrs Watterson.

Regina Ingersoll died in September of 1937. Only Mrs Watterson attended her funeral. Mrs Watterson died in November of 1937. There was a large turnout for Mrs Watterson's funeral, and all six of her children were on hand, and they spoke of waste, and they spoke of tragedy, and one of them . . . a daughter . . . even spoke of toffee.

OSCAR PILGRIM

I'd just turned twentysix in October of '76, and it was my first year as head football coach at Tarkington High School in Fort Wayne, Indiana. We had won two of our first four games . . . which wasn't bad, especially when you took into account the fact that the 1975 team had gone one, eight and one and had scored only six touchdowns for the whole damn season. The first thing I'd done was install a modified wishbone, and in one game we'd scored forty points. Which was exactly the number of points we'd scored in all of '75 under old Roy Brinkerhoff. He'd never really liked me a whole lot, and he'd fought to have his job passed down to Frank Ripley, the other assistant. But I am a better football man than Frank Ripley ever will be, and the people in charge knew it. So I got the job, and Roy Brinkerhoff and his wife retired to a trailer park in Sarasota. I guess they play cards and go through scrapbooks. I don't really know. The thing of it is, though . . . I never *did* anything to the man. There was no reason for him to have behaved the way he did. Beverly and I had him and his Wilma over to supper I don't know how many times, and I honest to God even kind of tried to be the son the old guy never had. But the thing is . . . no matter what I did, no matter how much Beverly and myself went out of our way, he just seemed to resent us. Why, in '74 Beverly even baked him a chocolate mint birthday cake, and we got half a dozen of the guys from the team to sing him happy birthday to you, happy birthday to you, blah blah, but he acted as though he couldn't of cared less. So, like I said, I guess he never really liked me a whole lot. Beverly tells me maybe we were too pushy. I don't like to think that. I don't like to think I would be that sort of, um, *tricky* person. Puts me in mind of a certain political figure of not so long a while back, you know? And I'd never been brought up to be tricky. Oh, my father and my mother had their troubles (they were married twice, and they were divorced twice), but they did teach straight behavior to me and my two brothers. Which was why Bobby finally did confess that he'd knocked up Karen Fletcher. And it was why Donald Junior went to Canada to get away from the war. (The Karen Fletcher thing, though, was nip and tuck all the way. Bobby married her just four hours before the baby was born, and Pop practically had to hold him by an ear while the ceremony was being performed. As for Karen, why, she was so worked up she almost had the baby right there on the floor. She'd only been seven months gone, but the shock of actually standing there with Bobby as her husband was too much for her, and I guess her plumbing got to churning. There she was, sixteen, and there Bobby was, also sixteen, and they held hands in the ambulance all the way to the hospital. That was 1967, and I'll tell you something—it's all really been a surprise to us. The baby was a boy, and they've had two more boys since then, and now Bobby is studying at Bexley Hall to be a priest in the Episcopal church, and he and Karen appear to be happy as two warm bugs. Which just goes to show you—although just what, I don't know.) But, anyway, getting back to straight behavior, I am *Oscar Pilgrim*, by Jesus, and that name has come to *mean* something, and there's no reason in the world for anyone to believe I undercut Frank Ripley. *Sure* I wanted the job, but I got it on *merit*; I got it because I had *worked hard*; I got it because I *know football*. I was a halfback at Paradise Falls High School, and I was a defensive back at Bowling Green, and the New Orleans Saints even gave me a tryout as a free agent, and so it's not as though I'm somebody who's just walked in off the street. Yes, I did send in a résumé. Yes, I did send in letters from my old coaches. So? I didn't ask them to lie for me. I only asked them to state the truth as they knew it—and the truth is: *I have a keen football mind.* So, honest to God, I don't want to hear anything more about Frank Ripley. I had a talk with my father about the situation. It was the summer of '76, and I'd just received the appointment, and I called him longdistance from Fort Wayne to LaBelle, Ohio, where he operated a model train exhibit in an old barn on my uncle Lloyd's farm, and I told him the news, and he said: "It all was square?" And I said: "Of course it was." And my father said: "Then I congratulate you. Only there's one word I want to give you. Don't blow the thing up away out of all proportion. Do the best you can, but then be able to walk away from it. Otherwise, you'll get all caught up in *ambition* and *envy* and a whole lot of bullshit you don't really need. Do you understand what I'm saying to you?" And I said: "Sure, Pop. And don't worry. I won't let it get out of hand." And I was telling him the truth, and it is a truth I still believe. Oh, sure, when I made my application I did jot down a little note stating that Frank Ripley had won no games and had lost six when he had filled in for Roy Brinkerhoff in '69 while Roy had been laid up by an attack of the appendicitis, but was that so terrible? What happened? Did Roy find out about it? I mean, I don't think *Frank* knows, on account of he is *my* assistant *now*, and I don't hear a peep from him one week to the next. Oh, shit. The hell with it. What I'm really talking about here is October of '76, which was when my father died. It came too quickly for anybody to understand. He had stopped at a restaurant on the Indiana Toll Road, and he had been buying a comb from a machine in the men's room, and he bent down to take the comb from the machine, and a heart attack got him, and he probably was dead before he hit the floor. The funeral was on a Friday morning, which meant I would have plenty of time to drive from LaBelle back to Fort Wayne and coach my boys that night against Central Tech. I took Beverly with me to the funeral, but we left our little daughter, Valerie, with Beverly's mother. Valerie was only two, and she wouldn't have understood any of it, and what the hell, she might have wet her pants, right? Oh, don't get me wrong—Beverly and myself love our little girl (she has blond hair and a precious pug nose, honest to Christ), but why should we have shoved a funeral down her throat? Why, Pop would have yelled at me for fair, and I wouldn't have blamed him. So Beverly and I sat with Bobby and Karen and their three little boys in the front row of the La-Belle United Church of Christ. Donald Junior wasn't there. Ford still hadn't cleared up the amnesty question, and so Donald Junior had had to stay in Canada. But a great many people *were* on hand, including Uncle Lloyd and old Grandma Pilgrim and a truckload of other Pilgrims . . . kids, cousins and whatnot, all of them LaBelle Pilgrims, and we didn't know them all that well. And two or three dozen model train freaks showed up. They were from all over the state. Plus Pop's *ladyfriend*, a woman named Hannah Bellamy. And even Aunt Phoebe, from Paradise Falls. She would not sit with us. She told us she was sorry; she meant no offense, but she just wanted to be alone. I never have understood Aunt Phoebe, and I don't suppose I ever will. Maybe I'm a little afraid of her. Sometimes I think she's found something that just may be truth, and the knowledge is so large that it's just about ripped out her tongue. Large? Yes, and maybe not only large but scarifying. So Aunt Phoebe sat alone, and her eyes were like flat agates, toneless and without moisture, and Pop's coffin was gray, and the minister said something to the effect that Pop was as naked now, as pure now, as happy and as favored, as he had been the day of his birth. I wasn't able to follow that line of talk, and so I let my mind wander. My father had worked in

94

a hardware store in Paradise Falls. He'd not given much of a damn about the hardware store. A long time later, after he'd divorced Mom the second time, he said to me: "Oscar, each of us has a personal and maybe even silly thing inside himself . . . a *dream,* a *notion* . . . and it has nothing to do with anyone else, nothing to do with *love* or *sharing* or all those *words* that are supposed to mean, um, *ultimate,* um, *joy.* With me, the dream or notion or whatever is my trains. I am God with my trains, and oh yes, I know my attitude has hurt your mother. But don't you see? If I hadn't done something about it, maybe I'd have killed her. Does that frighten you? Well, by God, there's at least a *little* truth to what I'm saying. Oh, I loved your mother, and I still do love your mother, and we had good times, and you boys have been good boys, but there always was something in maybe, oh I don't know, maybe my *belly* that all my life has been *pounded at,* as though there's a whole different Don Pilgrim who's never been let out into the sunlight. Please, Oscar. For Christ's sake please try to understand." And then Pop looked away from me, and I didn't know what to say, and so finally I got to talking about Ohio State and Michigan. And now, at Pop's funeral, I remembered that particular conversation. I looked at Bobby, and maybe *he* understood. Maybe I would talk with him about the thing. He and Karen sat erectly, and their three little boys sat erectly, and they all appeared to be listening. I wondered whether we should have brought Valerie. So what if she *had* wet her pants. It was her grandfather, wasn't it? I glanced at Beverly. She smelled like gardenias. Whenever there was some important occasion, she always smelled like gardenias. (Our quarterback, Timmy Franz, had sprained the thumb of his throwing hand. I hoped he had worked it out.) We rode to the cemetery in limousines, and Aunt Phoebe for some reason hugged the Bellamy woman after the graveside prayers were said. Some of us were served coffee in the Bellamy woman's front room, and Uncle Lloyd spoke of cows, and I took my brother Bobby aside and I said to him: "Was Pop selfish?" And Bobby said: "Pop was human." And I said: "That's no answer." And Bobby said: "It's the best I can do." I walked away from him. Our mother had been dead two years. She had missed Pop. She had wanted him to return to Paradise Falls, to the hardware store, to the house where Donald Junior and Bobby and I had been raised. But he'd refused. His trains had been more important. But near the end Mom had said to me: "There were good things. Your father reminds me of them in his letters. We correspond a great deal, and I enjoy the labor of putting down the words. Maybe we're ruined, but at least there was excitement now and then, and at least we have no real bitterness. Not *now*. Not with all this wreckage we have to contend with." I don't know altogether what Mom meant, but she was sort of smiling as she said the words, and so I suppose it was all right. (Bobby's three little boys were polite, and they listened to everything that was said to them. Should we have brought Valerie? Jesus Christ. And never mind about Frank Ripley. I don't want to hear about Frank Ripley, Pop. Please, Pop? Please?)

Amberson & Barbara Sellers

It was a Saturday afternoon in April of 1945. Anne and I had been notified earlier that week of the death of our son Henry, who had been killed while serving as a first Lieutenant of infantry with Patton's Third Army in Germany. Our other son, Lewis, had come home on emergency leave, and he and our daughter, Florence, were comforting Anne as well as they could. But she was not accepting much comfort. Henry, the oldest, had been her favorite, and she had called him her Always Boy. His arrival had been difficult, and he had cost her dearly in pain. She knew it was unfair to Lewis and Florence to call Henry her Always Boy, and she'd insisted to them that she didn't *love* them any the less, but her reasoning was a trifle shaky. If she didn't love Henry more than she loved Lewis and Florence, why was it necessary that she bestow on him such a grandiloquent title as Always Boy? It was clear to me that Lewis was bothered by the contradiction; he was an ambitious fellow, and his entire life was spent in a clenched pursuit of enough *accomplishment* so that Anne and I somehow would *recognize* him (he actually even eventually went and got himself elected mayor of Paradise Falls) and perhaps then bestow on him the full and unimpeded gift of our love. Florence, though, wasn't so disturbed by her mother's special love for Henry. That was the thing about Florence, and it still is the thing about Florence . . . she may never cause the planet to spew flame and explode, but she does have balance, and she does try to understand, and I honestly believe she is congenitally incapable of holding a grudge. So she for one was able to face up to her mother's relentless elevation of Henry into something that perhaps prowled at the right hand of Almighty God. He was intelligent, this Henry, and he smiled much of the time, and his mind and benevolence set him apart from the rest of the world to the extent that there were those who actually disliked him, or at least were afraid of him, which meant the Always Boy almost always was alone. Which meant there perhaps even were those who believed him to be demented. He was large and handsome, and he could have been a fine athlete, and he could have been enormously popular with girls—but he was neither. No. I amend that. I admit he could have been a fine athlete, but I am not so certain he could have been enormously popular with girls. You see, there was something

97

about him that was so gently *intimidating*, and it *confound-ed*, and it made him appear peculiar, and it kept both sexes at arm's length. Oh, I know I am speaking here in generali-ties, and he lacks specific dimension, doesn't he? The saint-ly outcast and all that. But how can one accurately and tell-ingly define a boy who mourned . . . and deeply . . . when the interurban line to Columbus was abandoned back in '31? And he mourned dead kittens, broken flowers, burst balloons. I know, I *know* how misty he is, and I wish I had more skill at invoking the language so that he could ade-quately be described. But I do not, and so I have no choice but to *state* that he was so intelligent he was frightening, to *state* that he was so good he was peculiar. When he enlisted, in early '42, when he abruptly dropped out of Kenyon and came home, he told Anne and me we had to have faith he was doing the right thing. He *stated* it. He was, in that sense, just as didactic as I am. He had a strange notion he was an awkward clodhopping oaf (or perhaps it was his idea of some sort of didactic joke), but at any rate he patted one of Anne's hands and said to her: "If I stayed home, it would be like *hiding*. And all my life I've been hiding. Either that, or I've been standing off to one side. You've fussed over me, and most of my teachers have fussed over me, but the rest of the world has said go peddle your fish, Henry Amberson, you're a crackpot. You and your clodhopping . . ." Anne tried to argue with him, but she did understand the truth of his words, and she accepted it. It was a truth that had to do with his own sort of acceptance, and he sought to penetrate it. In short, he wanted to be more like other people. He wanted fellowship. And perhaps he found it in the army. But not for long. And so we mourned. And Anne mourned most of all. She howled, and Florence embraced her. She sat on the floor, and Florence embraced her. And Florence was only fifteen that year. And Florence said: "Yes. Yes. Fine. Yes." And she stroked her mother. And she smoothed her mother's hair. And our younger son, Lewis, a captain of ordnance stationed in Ravenna, Ohio, tried to say words having to do with heroism, but he choked on them; it was as though shells and pebbles had been forced through a funnel and down his throat. And so finally then, on that Saturday afternoon, I had to get out of the house, away from all howlings, all words, all shells and pebbles. So I walked to the Elysian Park, and I listened to new leaves. There had been rain, but sunlight had burned it away, and so I seated myself on a bench in the picnic shelter, and I very *carefully* listened to the new leaves, and I almost *resented* them. After all, why weren't they mourning Henry? Why hadn't the universe paused in its mighty wheelings and designs? But then I shook my head, and I hoped God would not punish me too severely for my presumption. (As might by now be suspected, I do occasionally let pompousness seize me. For instance, now and then I have a notion that I want to run so fast I will run off the face of the planet. Ah, but then I was a track coach, and perhaps my dream was an occupational hazard.) But, at any rate, I was soaking myself in all that prolix internal windbaggery when I abruptly was aware of a girl walking toward me. Her name was Barbara Sellers, and she had been a pupil of mine, ah, two or three years earlier. She was small and dark, and her teeth were prominent, but she nonetheless was quite pretty, and she had been one of the finest pupils I ever had taught (I was, you see, an English teacher at Paradise Falls High School from September of 1920 through June of 1962). She had written several fine essays, and two of them had been published by *National Scholastic.* And she was doing splendidly at Ohio University, and she would earn a diploma in three years under an accelerated program. I had kept in touch with her, and from time to time I had gently hectored her on not letting her writing potential shrivel through neglect. I had the feeling, you see, that she would settle for less than what she was capable of achieving. Many people do . . . and especially girls . . . or at least in those days. But now, when she came to me, neither of us was thinking of her writing potential. Instead she simply sat next to me, and she was pale, and she said: "I won't say the dumb words, Mr Amberson. I *can't.*"

I looked at her.

She was wearing a white blouse, dark green jumper and skirt, white socks and penny loafers. (I can give no coherent reason why I remember these details, but they are vivid, and I know they are precise.) A loose white ribbon held back her dark hair. She fussed at the ribbon for a moment, and then she said: "He was too special for the dumb words."

I nodded.

"He was kind to everything."

I nodded.

"I'm surprised he ever became a soldier."

"Well, you see, he wanted to—"

"Be, um, be like everyone else?" said Barbara Sellers.

"Yes . . . in a sense . . . or at least to be accepted . . ."

"*I* liked him," said Barbara Sellers. "He played jacks with me once—do you know that?"

"Jacks?"

"Yes *sir*," said Barbara Sellers. "I was playing with I think it was my baby sister Rosemary, and she had to go to the bathroom or something, and then along came this *great big grinning Henry Amberson*, and he sat down with me, and he and I bounced the ball and scooped up the jacks and did the whole thing. And he even kept playing after Rosemary had come back. The three of us just really had the nicest time . . ."

I nodded.

"I came home this morning for the weekend," said Barbara Sellers, "and I heard about it soon as I walked in the door. So I started over for your place, but I saw you walking along, so I followed you. You don't mind, do you? I mean, I thought maybe you'd go someplace quiet, and sure enough, you did."

I nodded.

"If I'm too nosy or pushy, let me know, but is Mrs Amberson all right?"

"Not really," I said.

Barbara Sellers nodded. "She really liked him a lot. I mean, a person didn't have to be very smart to know *that.*"

I looked at Barbara Sellers. "The people from Graves Registration have been in touch with me," I said, "and they tell me Henry's body can be shipped home as soon as the war is over. They want to know if we want the body. I suppose we do, don't we?"

Barbara Sellers exhaled. She said nothing.

"A short time with him was better than no time at all," I said.

"*Yes,*" said Barbara Sellers.

"An afternoon. A breath. That . . . that . . . *smile . . .*"

"*Yes,*" said Barbara Sellers.

"It doesn't matter where he's buried, does it?"

"I don't believe so," said Barbara Sellers.

"Are these your dumb words?"

She patted one of my knees.

My eyes were too warm, and so I closed them.

"I want to say everything will be all right," she said, "but I think that would be a lie."

I nodded. I did not open my eyes. I supposed we would bring him back. I supposed Anne would insist on it. But it didn't matter—as long as we tried to refrain from saying the dumb words. And so I opened my warm eyes and said to Barbara Sellers: "Thank you."

DOTTIE WASHBURN & KIDS

Munching, wiping at Kevin's plastic bib, shushing Martha, holding little Tommy to her bosom and spooning up Gerber's peaches, Dottie Washburn sat in the coffee shop of the Holiday Inn in Independence, Ohio, and tried not to think of her absent husband and her absent lover. After all, it was *she* who had left *them* behind, taking all three of her children plus the more than two thousand dollars she and Tom had had in a joint savings account at the Paradise Falls State Bank. She was an intelligent young woman, pretty in a vaguely heavybosomed blond way—but now she was not quite so sure about her intelligence. Oh, she always had *believed* she was intelligent. But how intelligent was she to have put herself in this fix? How intelligent was it to have three children the oldest of whom (Martha) was five? And children were so *precocious* these days, so *into* everything. Why, Martha even was able to balance herself on a skateboard. Her father had taught her. Dottie wondered whether the children missed their father. So far Martha and Kevin had said nothing about him. Little Tommy wasn't speaking all that clearly yet, and so he didn't really count.

A waitress came to Dottie's table and asked her if there would be anything else. The woman was tall, and she was perhaps forty, and she smiled at the children. "I must say . . . they certainly are well behaved," the woman said.

Dottie returned the smile. "Well, you're catching them on an unusual morning." A hesitation. Dottie knew there was no more that really needed to be said, but she could not help it. She said: "We are on our own, you see. We have cut our ties, you see."

"Pardon?" said the waitress.

Dottie blinked at the waitress, and a slackness had come into the woman's face. "Oh, never mind," said Dottie, "it was just a figure of speech. We're on a little vacation, is all. And it's like the whole world's been shoved at us, you know? It's a little frightening, you know?"

"Oh yes," said the waitress. "Would you, ah, care for your check?"

"Why?" said Dottie. "Is it ill?"

"What?"

"Never mind. I tried to make a joke, but it was a very bad one, and it doesn't deserve being repeated."

"Oh," said the waitress.

Later, after paying the restaurant check and the room bill, Dottie drove north into Cleveland on Interstate 77 and then northeast toward Buffalo on Interstate 90. Her car was a '73 Nova, and it clanked and knocked, but the sounds of the children erased most of the clanking and knocking. Kids climbed over her. They rubbed at her with their hands and their buttocks and their thighs. It was an October morning, bright, cloudless, uncommitted, and now and then she was able to see sunlight spread in quick speckles off the fragments of Lake Erie she glimpsed every so often. She did not have the slightest idea where she was headed. Her parents were dead, but she did have a sister in Grand Rapids and a brother in Detroit; it certainly wasn't as though she were *alone*. Grace was a good sister, too, and Frank always had been a good brother, and Dottie knew either of them would welcome her and the kids without asking too many questions. But she could not be with them. She could only be with people who would ask no questions at all. She could only be with people like that waitress back in the Holiday Inn—people who never would understand or try to understand. A runaway housewife who made a feeble joke about caring for a *check* was probably your average everyday runofthemill wacko, and she was better off communicating with no one. Still, it was nearly impossible for her not to want to communicate with her own mind, and so . . . as she drove, as the kids hollered and crawled, as now and then she absently shushed them or pushed away their hands . . . she reluctantly called herself to testify. Q: *Mrs Washburn, it is men who retreat from unpleasant situations, and it is women who remain at home. Why then have you flown in the face of conventional behavior?* A: Because I have too complicated a situation. Q: *How so?* A: I have . . . or had . . . both a husband and a lover, but neither really did all that much for me. Yet they were hanging in there, so to speak. Even though I was weary, they were not. And so I reached a point of exasperation. And so here I am, and perhaps the wheels will fall off this poor car, and perhaps the kids will drive me up the wall with their *noise* and their *mess* and all, but at least it will be *my* wall, and I won't forever be hassled by propaganda. Q: *Propaganda?* A: Absolutely. On the one hand, Tom is my own age, and he is strong, and he works hard. On the other hand, Harry McNiece is fifty years old, and he is too fat, and I suppose he talks too much, but he does understand me better than any man ever has, and he does understand what is missing from my life. And he tries to supply those things—but he hasn't been able. And I'm sorry, but he is a poor lover; he is a widower, and maybe there is too much he has forgotten. But at least he *listens*; Tom seldom even seems able to try. Why is this? Would he somehow lose macho? Oh, there have been times when he has wept, but his tears have been the tears of a spoiled child, if you know what I mean. My lover . . . my sorry excuse for a lover . . . also now and then weeps. Perhaps out of nostalgia. I don't know. He says he loves me. Damn it, they *both* say they love me, and I get so much propaganda I could throw up. Harry speaks to me of literature and music and famous persons. Tom speaks to me of home and the kids. And both Harry and Tom insist they want to know who I am, and Harry carries it one step farther and speaks of mutuality, but what am I to believe? Remember that commercial: "What'§ a mother to *do*"? Well, what am I to do? And why do I think of Harry and Tom in the present tense? Q: *Could it be that the matter still is unresolved?* A: No! A plague on both their houses! I am free now, and hooray! Q: *With three very small children?* A: Never mind! Q: *What will you do? The two thousand dollars won't last very long, and then what will happen? Will you become a waitress like that woman back there in Independence? What will happen to the kids? Who will care for them? Be practical, Dottie! Face the truth! Why, suppose you find a man who fills your needs, whatever they are. Will he want to marry four people? And how will you be able to marry when you're already married? Don't you see? The reasons wives (and/or mothers) don't disappear is because they can't. If you are in an unpleasant situation, if you feel unfulfilled or whatever, these things are a terrible shame, but flight will solve nothing.* A: I never have heard such sanctimonious . . . SHIT . . . in my life! I am twenty-nine years old, don't you understand, and if I don't get out now, I never will! Q: *But it's not enough just to get out. You have to go someplace.* A: I have a husband who is a nice turkey, and I have a lover who is a nice windbag, and you're telling me they're better than what I'll probably have to face? Q: *Yes. And the possibility exists that you're not as exasperated as you think you are. The possibility even exists that you're not exasperated at all.* A: What? Q: *Maybe you love them both . . . in different ways. Maybe what you perceive as exasperation is really only . . . indecision. Have you ever thought of the situation in that light?* A: I don't want to talk about it anymore! And Dottie pushed angrily at Kevin, who was trying to lick one of her knees. He slid to the floor, and he began to wail. Groaning, Dottie pulled to the side of the road, stopped the car, shut off the engine, lifted Kevin to her lap, stroked him, crooned over him, kissed his cheeks and forehead. Her husband worked in a brickyard. Her lover was editor of the Paradise Falls *Journal-Democrat* and wrote a safely amusing thrice weekly column. She sighed. Cars and trucks roared past, and the sound of them made little Tommy, the baby, weep and choke. So Dottie hugged him along with Kevin. Martha was quietly humming in the back seat, and she was plucking at her Big Bird doll. Dottie drove to an exit ramp south of Conneaut. She found a pay booth and telephoned Paradise Falls, reversing the charges. There was no answer at home, and so she called the *Journal-Democrat,* and she was told Harry McNiece . . . editor, columnist, incompetent lover . . . had committed suicide the night before. Pills and alcohol. Dottie abruptly hung up. The children were hollering inside the car. Martha had rolled down a window, and she was leaning out, and Dottie called to her to be careful. Dottie walked back to the car. She cupped her hands and placed them against her blouse. Her nipples were erect. She could not believe this. She thought of Harry and his paunch. She thought of the way he had kissed her nipples. He had not been so incompetent at *that* particular activity. She drove all the way back to Paradise Falls, stopping only to buy gasoline, feed the children and let them make bad. She did not weep. She probably was as dead as Harry McNiece (he had spoken of *mutuality,* and he had tried so terribly hard), and she felt as though she were being squeezed by ropes and heavy belts. She told herself she was ridiculous. She told herself it all was a soap opera. She told herself the world would little note nor long remember her pain. She asked herself more questions, but grief kept getting in the way of the answers. (There had been times when she had fed peanut butter and jelly sandwiches and milk to Harry McNiece. She and Harry had been to bed exactly twice. It had not been good. And now he was dead, and had he surrendered or had he been trying to say something? Dottie wanted to flop and gasp. She wanted to tear at her chest. She drove too fast, and the car rattled, and the children sang and whimpered, and she was being sucked back into a dark hole, and she knew this, and she also knew the hole would be closed behind her. She grimaced. Tomorrow she would vacuum and dust. She and the kids had been gone four days, and surely there was a great deal that would have to be done. If a dark hole is to be a dark hole, it might as well be habitable.)

LLOYD PILGRIM

When a boy is whipped by his father, and the father speaks words, the boy is wise to heed those words . . . at least while they're being spoken. Little Lloyd Pilgrim was not all that often whipped by his father, but the whippings always were accompanied by oratory, and little Lloyd's father would say: "I don't never want to see you strike an animal unless you're punishing it or killing it. When you hit a dumb sheep just because it's a dumb sheep, that makes you cruel, and I won't abide no cruelty around this here place. If you really fix to be cruel, then you'd better fix to be cruel some other place, on account of I'll God damn see to it that all the gates'll be closed to you and all the doors'll be slammed in your face . . . on this farm, I mean, this farm where your mama and me feed you, and your bed is warm. Nothing like a warm bed, right, boy?" And: "The Methodist

God ain't the worst God, on account of I expect the Papist God is the worst God, what with the funny language and all them priests who got peckers but can't do nothing with them. And there's the stink of the incense, too, if you get what I mean. That's your Papist God for you, and it must be a hell of a thing to be a Papist and to die and not even *understand* what they're *saying* over you. So be grateful for your Methodist God, boy. And don't you no more pick your nose in church like you done this morning. On account of if you want hell, I can give you hell. Hell on earth. Hell on that there skinny rump of yours. Feel the fires, boy? Eh? Eh?" And: "The next time I see you carrying a goddamned William Jennings Bryan sign in a parade, I'm going to nail your flesh to the barn door and boil the rest of you down for rendered fat and throw your bones in the goddamned kitchen stove. I mean, I can stand just about anything. I expect I even could stand it if I found you buggering a goddamned chicken—*but I will not tolerate you carrying no goddamned sign for no goddamned Democrat. And especially that fat rascal who wants to tear down the country, that goddamned Bryan, him and first his goddamned free and unlimited coinage of silver, and that passes, and he loses, but he runs again, and he loses again, and now he's running again, and he's hardly even stopped for breath, and what has the country done to deserve such a goddamned bag of gas flung in its face almost every four years? Tell me, boy! Eh? Eh?"* But the beatings really were not that frequent, and the oratory did at least divert some of Lloyd's attention from his pain. And anyway, none of this should come down as the history of a life begun in meanness and abuse. The Pilgrim farm, in northwestern Ohio near a place called LaBelle, was really rather tranquil, and Lloyd's life was not governed by the beatings; rather it was *punctuated* by them . . . the way the lives of other children perhaps are punctuated by picnics and laughter and blue flowers and first love. Lloyd and

108

his two younger sisters, Rebecca and Helen, passed through their green days easily, and sometimes they even giggled over their father's oratory, and they allowed as how perhaps their father should have run for public office. "He's got the wind for it," said Rebecca. "Surely," said Helen. "And the tongue," said Lloyd. And then he and his sisters sniggered behind their hands, and the girls scampered off to play run sheepy run or whatever, but Lloyd would sit in the shade of a barn roof and now and then muse on his father's tongue. And Lloyd would read newspapers and listen to public officials, and the newspapers and the public officials were no different from his father's tongue, and the word that kept nudging into Lloyd's mind was "bullshit." And in 1917 (spring . . . a good spring . . . it soaked the earth but did not drown it), when the good old US of A became involved in the Great War, Lloyd could not get it shut of his mind that the whole shooting match was bullshit. What did *he* care about the Kaiser? What did *he* care about Belgian nuns and Nurse Edith Cavell and the *Lusitania* and the fields of Flanders and the goddamned Zimmerman Telegram and the exploits of Captain Fonck? He was seventeen in that year of 1917, and he was glad he was too young for the draft. His father often spoke to him of how important it was that the war be won, and maybe it all *was* important, but Lloyd wasn't too sure. Suppose the worst thing of all happened—suppose the good old US of A lost the war. What would then take place? Would a company of jackbooted Prussians march into LaBelle and pull down Old Glory from the post office flagpole? But wasn't the US of A too large? To occupy every village and town and city and outhouse and cowshed in the good old US of A, how many companies of jackbooted Prussians would be needed? a million? two million? In other words then, would anything really change if the US of A decided the hell with the war; it all was a lot of that wellknown substance known as bullshit?

So why then were so many people dying? over what? for
what? in whose name? There were times when Lloyd simply sat crosslegged on the earth, and he ripped away clumps
of earth and grass, and he sighed, and he couldn't understand why anyone would want to die in the name of *words*.
He supposed there was a key to all of it, and he supposed everyone else in the world understood the key—but he was
damned if *he* did. Which meant either he was very stupid or
he had found a key of his own, a special key, a key to bullshit. He would sit solemnly, this Lloyd Pilgrim, and he
would bite off a hunk of tobacco and work it easily between
his jaws (he had been chewing the stuff since shortly after
his twelfth birthday), and he would look around, and perhaps he would watch a redwinged blackbird, or perhaps he
would watch a *dozen* redwinged blackbirds as they lined
themselves on a fence as though they were troops mustered
for inspection, and every so often he would give a great
whoop, and he would wave his arms, and the redwinged
blackbirds would fly in every which direction, and he would
holler at them: "You're *redwinged blackbirds*, for Christ's
sake! You're not *sheep!*" And it almost was as though he
was accusing the world's entire population of redwinged
blackbirds of practicing a sort of ordered and obedient bullshit of their own, and so he would glare at the great white
chunk of sky that lay over the fields and the house and the
barns and the outbuildings, and could his Methodist God be
responsible? Sometimes Lloyd would spit a brown gob, and
sometimes a chicken would come along and peck at the
brown gob, and Lloyd would shoo away the chicken, and
now and then he almost would grin. Almost. But never entirely. Never. This was because of bullshit—and the question of bullshit, which pursued him until the day he died.
His sisters married when they were quite young, and they
moved away . . . Rebecca to Ishpeming, Michigan, and
Helen to East Chicago, Indiana. Both their husbands were,

of all things, motorcar salesmen, and talk about your *bull-shit*. Lloyd himself was married in 1919, and the girl's name was Daisy Polk. She was quiet, and she never gave Lloyd as much as a stitch of trouble, but she did take over the house, and no mistake. She had sat behind him in school for eight years, and he supposed he loved her. Surely she was pretty enough, if prettiness was what was required. As a matter of fact, on their wedding night he allowed as how her hair was enough to make him want to spin cobwebs to the moon. Then he smiled, and he told her a poet he never would be, and at the same time he told *himself*: Hey, listen to the bullshit. He moved well through the marriage, and he was a good father to his three sons . . . Jim, Lloyd Junior and Donald. He watched his parents die, and he watched the boys grow, and he watched Daisy move the furniture and take down photographs from the walls, and she permitted him to take her whenever he liked, and she never complained. She was his first woman, and she was his last woman. He never spoke all that much, but he did take each of his sons aside privately and did try to explain a little of what he believed was bullshit. He read magazines, you see. He looked at newsreels, you see. Daisy's father came to live with them, and there were some good sour disgruntled times when Lloyd was able to discuss bullshit with that old man. The farm was converted to a total dairy operation, and it thrived. Daisy's favorite boy was Donald, the youngest. There were times when she and Donald would play tag in the front yard. It all put Lloyd in mind of cages. He did not like to think of cages, and so he would look up at the raw chunked sky. The magazines and the newsreels slapped at his mind, and he figured old Hitler and the rest of them would get to slaughtering people like human beings were pigs leaking on a concrete floor. And sure enough, hell yes, along came 1939, and Lloyd said to his fatherinlaw: "It wouldn't be so bad if it was the same people come up out of their graves so they can do it all over again. But it's *new* people." And Lloyd's fatherinlaw, a large and gelatinous man who once had been a maintenance of way foreman for the New York Central, said: "And more's the pity. I mean, the bullshit just never stops, does it?" And Lloyd said: "How come I've only had one woman?" And his fatherinlaw said: "What?" And Lloyd said: "This here place, I like it good enough, and I surely ain't never wanted to go away. On account of . . . well . . ." And Lloyd's fatherinlaw said: "On account of what?" And Lloyd said: "On account of wouldn't none of it be no different." And Lloyd's fatherinlaw grinned loosely and said: "I think maybe you got the secret of the universe." And Lloyd Pilgrim shrugged. Maybe he didn't have the secret of the universe, but maybe he did have the secret of bullshit. The world could keep its kings and its dictators and its banks and its wars. Here was enough. So Lloyd Pilgrim chewed and mused. He milked cows. Sometimes they would kick at him, but he never beat them. They were only dumb brutes, and he knew they really had meant him no harm. (He would kill the old cows, but he never was able to look at their eyes when he slit their throats. It was best when he cut all the way through their vocal cords. That way, they made little noise. God damn, a dry cow was a sorry creature, and so why were there times when Lloyd Pilgrim had to press his face against a wall and choke back hot fluids?) He read. He saw. Pictures came and went. Words. Proclamations. Oaths. Lamentations. And all of it was bullshit. So he chewed. And he began to think of himself as *old* Lloyd Pilgrim before he was fortyfive. (And he choked back more hot fluids. And he thought of tongues.) And he was fortynine when he died. His gall bladder had been shredded, and so he was an *old* fortynine. Words were said over him, and they were properly comfortable and sanctimonious, and he

unquestionably would have classified all of them as bullshit.

BLAH & BLAH

Mrs Emma Lucille Thackeray Wootten, widow of Herman Leo Wootten, who for years had been acknowledged to
be the best plumber in Paradise Falls, died of intestinal
cancer on Monday, April 1, 1968. She then was laid out in
the Zimmerman Funeral Home for three days and nights,
and her funeral and burial took place the afternoon of Friday, April 5, 1968, the day after Martin Luther King had
been assassinated in Memphis, Tennessee. Late that afternoon, after the burial of Mrs Wootten, four elderly widows
gathered in the front room of the home of a woman named
Soeder, who was the oldest of them and whose bones trem-
bled. She somehow managed to serve tea, however, and she
broke out several packages of Pecan Sandies, which all four
of the women acknowledged to be their favorite cookies in
the whole wide world. The other three were named Henshaw, Martin and Hamner, and they and Mrs Soeder had
been friends since the beginning of time. They sipped at
their tea, and they munched on their Pecan Sandies, and
Mrs Soeder said: "I don't believe I've ever seen so many
Eastern Star people this side of a state convention."

And Mrs Martin said: "And who was that woman with
the dyed hair and the curl pasted right smack in the middle
of her forehead?"

And Mrs Hamner said: "Oh, she was one of the people
from Bissoula."

And Mrs Martin said: "I beg your pardon?"

113

And Mrs Hamner said: "Bissoula. I believe it's in Montana. Or maybe Wyoming. Well, anyway, remember back in 'fiftyseven or so, when Emma was installed as Worthy High Priestess?"

And Mrs Martin said: "Not really."

And Mrs Hamner said: "It was the woman with the curl who installed her."

And Mrs Henshaw said: "A woman from Montana or Wyoming or wherever?"

And Mrs Hamner said: "No. She lived in Columbus then. But she had the curl and all, and I told myself I wouldn't forget her if I lived to be a hundred."

And Mrs Soeder said: "Which is when, Bernice? the day after tomorrow?"

And Mrs Hamner said: "Very *funny*, I'm *sure*. Especially coming from a woman, a socalled *friend* of mine, who's forever saying the same thing. If I live to be a hundred. If I live to be a hundred. Nya. Nya. Blah. Blah."

And Mrs Martin said: "Now, now, Bernice."

And Mrs Hamner said: "Well, if I *have* picked up such a phrase, I've picked it up from *her*."

And Mrs Soeder said: "You ought to *hear* yourself, Bernice."

And Mrs Hamner said: "Do *you* ever hear *your*self, Louise? I mean, *really*? I mean, every other *sentence* is . . . um . . . um . . . *decorated* with 'if I live to be a hundred,' 'if I live to be a hundred,' nya, nya, blah, blah."

And Mrs Martin said: "Bernice, I do believe you've made your point."

And Mrs Henshaw said: "Louise didn't mean anything by it."

And Mrs Soeder said: "If I hurt your feelings, Bernice, I apologize."

And Mrs Hamner said: ". . . all right."

And Mrs Martin said: "Here, Bernice. Have a cookie."

And Mrs Henshaw said: "Yes. A nice cookie for Bernice."

And Mrs Hamner said: ". . . all right."

And Mrs Martin said: "Yes. That's better. And anyway, we don't want to fuss like this and take anything away from the memory of Emma."

And Mrs Hamner said: "Can you *imagine* . . . *dying* a curl *black* and *pasting* it in the *middle* of your *forehead*? The woman looked like *ZaSu Pitts*, I *swear*."

And Mrs Martin said: "But we shouldn't be talking about *her*. We should be talking about *Emma*. Who was a good woman, even if she was too pushy, wouldn't you say?"

And Mrs Soeder said: "Pushy? She *invented* pushy. A person would have thought the Eastern Star was the United States Marine Corps. She was a Worthy High Priestess to make all the other Worthy High Priestesses in the world fall down dead."

And Mrs Henshaw said: "You have a point."

And Mrs Soeder said: "When that Mr Carleton spoke this afternoon of her *humility* and her *selflessness*, it was all I could do to keep from falling on the floor and laughing myself into a coma. He's a nice young man, that Mr Carleton, but he never knew the Emma Wootten *we* knew, did he? Listen, I don't know what *you* think, but it seems to *me* that all four of us have been more than a little active in Eastern Star for a great many years, correct? But compared with *her*, it's as though we sat with our rear ends in cement. The way she always insisted that the minutes be read. And the way she dressed for each meeting as though she were being presented to the Queen of England."

And Mrs Martin said: "Well, that always was her way. I don't think Herman really cared all that much about the Masons, but he *was* a thirtythird degree when he passed on, and I expect he was afraid *not* to be. If Emma *wanted* a thing, she *went after* it, and no mistake. Herman was allergic to dogs, do you know that? Something about their fur.

115

But Emma had Dandy how long? fifteen years? oh, a *good* fifteen years. And Dandy was as furry as anything. Hairy as the devil. And he slept at the foot of their bed, can you imagine such a thing?"

And Mrs Henshaw said: "Yes."

And Mrs Soeder said: "That was our Emma."

And Mrs Hamner said: "And that was the *ugliest* dog I ever *saw.*"

And Mrs Martin said: "Maybe Emma was the way she was because she had only the one child. I mean, what with poor Mary ending up in that *special school* and dying so young. One child, and the child turns out to be feebleminded. A shame."

And Mrs Hamner said: "I don't believe I *ever* heard Emma admit Mary was not right in the head. Only I *do* know Emma carried toilet paper in her purse whenever she went anyplace with Mary. Just in case, you know."

And Mrs Soeder said: "That is a fact, all right. I saw the toilet paper myself once. She and Mary came visiting here, and they sat right in this room, and I must say Mary was on her best behavior, didn't utter a word, didn't break wind, didn't even belch, sat quiet as a mouse and looked at me with those big awful loose eyes of hers, and Emma rattled on about one thing and another, and all in all it was a very nice little visit, very proper, but then for some reason Emma's purse slid off her lap, and the catch snapped open, and a roll of toilet paper sort of bounced out, if you know what I mean."

And Mrs Henshaw said: "Do you suppose she was so pushy because she wanted to keep her mind off other things? Do you suppose that was why her voice was so loud? On account of maybe there were thoughts and feelings she wanted to drown out?"

And Mrs Soeder said: "Wouldn't surprise me a bit."

And Mrs Martin said: "It's funny that the colored man should be killed right now. Funny I mean because *he* was pushy *too.*"

And Mrs Soeder said: "But *Emma's* pushiness didn't *hurt* anyone. It didn't . . . um . . . *disrupt* things. Did any of you watch the *Today* show this morning? Did you see the way those people were rioting? Memphis. Washington. Baltimore. I don't know where all. And if you ask me, it doesn't have a whole lot to do with King. It's just an excuse for them to *vent* their *natures.* To *loot* or whatever. But he *was* pushy, no doubt about it. And the thing that happened to him was bound to have happened to him. Sooner or later."

And Mrs Henshaw said: "My father called them niggers. He called them niggers until the day he died. He was from Virginia originally, and he *liked* them just fine. But he always called them niggers."

And Mrs Hamner said: "Thank God *our* colored people are all right."

And Mrs Martin said: "Amen."

And Mrs Hamner said: "What with the world blowing up and all, it's nice to know our colored people respect us and keep to themselves. I remember 1916 very well, don't you? When Elmer Carmichael brought them up from Mississippi to break the strike at the Paradise Falls Clay Products. They were good people. They *are* good people."

And Mrs Martin said: "Amen."

And Mrs Soeder said: "I wonder if they'll ever catch the fellow who did it."

And Mrs Hamner said: "They'll catch *somebody.* Bobby Kennedy and them, they have to. They need the colored vote."

And Mrs Martin said: "Amen."

And Mrs Henshaw said: "I wonder if they're standing in line together."

117

And Mrs Soeder said: "What?"

And Mrs Henshaw said: "Emma and that King fellow. At the Pearly Gates."

And Mrs Soeder said: "Oh. Well, if they are, I expect I know what they're doing."

And Mrs Henshaw said: "And what would that be?"

And Mrs Soeder said: "Pushing."

The women laughed. The sound of their laughter was like torn matchsticks. Then the conversation drifted back to the late Emma Lucille Thackeray Wootten, and everyone agreed that her death must have been terribly painful. Heads were shaken. The Pecan Sandies were carefully chewed, so dentures would not slip. The women breathed as carefully as they chewed, and they were properly grateful to be alive. Poor Emma, they said, poor Emma, poor Emma, and of course at the same time they rejoiced. Their victory jigged and clapped in their eyes.

HARRY MCNIECE & TRICIA

Harry McNiece, editor of the Paradise Falls *Journal-Democrat*, was in Columbus in July of 1976 to attend a Sigma Delta Chi conference on journalistic ethics. All expenses were being paid by the paper's owner, a man named Underwood, and so McNiece had decided to drink a great deal. One night he sat alone in the bar of his motel, and he worked on putting away as many martinis as his constitution could accommodate. His wife had died a year earlier of liver cancer, and he actually had not been to bed with a woman for nearly three years all told. That woman had been a prostitute, and she had solicited him here in this bar. Later, after an encounter that really hadn't amounted

118

to much, the woman had given him her telephone number, and she had told him to stop *trying* so goddamned hard, for Christ's sake. He had dialed the number an hour or so ago, but a recorded voice had informed him it had been disconnected. There almost had been a note of jubilation in the recorded voice, as though it were taunting him, telling him: Up yours, Honeybunch; there's no way you'll get laid tonight. So now McNiece poked at his third martini, and he watched the bartender, and the fellow was wearing a cheap reddish toupee that kept sliding a trifle off to one side. He did not smile, and he put McNiece a little in mind of a cretinous and surly Howard Cosell. It was a Thursday night, and a number of the Sigma Delta Chi men were drinking at two tables that had been drawn together in a corner of the room. McNiece knew most of those men. They were from such places as Middletown, Logan, Marion, Canton, Wauseon, Youngstown, East Liverpool, Xenia, Painesville, Washington Court House. He had known several of them for a number of years, and they talked mostly of (a) automation, (b) pussy, (c) unions and (d) linage rates. Most of them had tight rimless faces, and some of them gave off a curious odor of sour underwear. McNiece didn't want to have anything to do with them. McNiece wanted to get laid, God damn it. McNiece's mother had not brought him up to be a Trappist monk, and *enough* was God damn good and well *enough*. He was sipping at his fourth martini when a young woman named Tricia sat down next to him. He knew her name was Tricia because the word was knitted in script on her tote bag. She was slender, and her hair was long and straight, and he took her to be perhaps nineteen. But the bartender did not question her when she ordered a Kahlua and cream. She smiled at McNiece after the bartender brought her the drink. And McNiece smiled. And he swallowed. And then he said to the bartender: "Please put that on my tab."

"I thank you very much," said Tricia.

"It is my pleasure," said McNiece.

"That's nice to hear," said Tricia.

"I beg your pardon?" said McNiece.

"A reference to pleasure. Especially coming from a person your age."

"A person *my* age?" said McNiece.

Tricia's smile was uneven, and her teeth were of various sizes, and she probably was older than McNiece at first had thought. "Well," she said, "there are some people from your, um, *generation* who seem to believe pleasure is somehow a source of, um, *guilt.* Myself, I am a great believer in permissiveness . . . consenting adults . . . whatever . . ."

"Oh," said McNiece, "well, yes . . . so am I . . ."

"Even when one of the adults is a prostitute, right?"

"Pardon?"

"Whore. Hooker. I am a whore, sir. W-H-O-R-E. And to think I once attended Capital University. Oh, is the world ever going to hell in a handcart . . ."

McNiece cleared his throat and sipped at his martini.

"I *enjoy* it," said Tricia. "I'm not a *nympho* or anything like *that,* but I *do* enjoy it. Each man is different. Each man is special."

McNiece exhaled.

Tricia nodded. She wore jeans, a white blouse, no brassiere. She turned toward McNiece. "Look at my boobs," she said. "See the little buttons sticking out? *You're* doing that, my friend. I swear to God you are. How old are you? fifty?"

"Close," said McNiece. he set down his glass and rubbed both his palms against his knees. "I am fortynine."

"And lonely and horny, correct?"

". . . correct."

"A hundred dollars gets you *this* consenting adult for the entire night—provided you also buy her breakfast. You like

120

shortie nighties? I have one in my tote bag here. And don't let my name throw you. I'm not related to Nixon."

"I didn't think so," said McNiece.

"He should be so lucky," said Tricia.

"There's . . . there's something I have to ask you . . ."

"If it's something kinky," said Tricia, "never mind. I don't want to hear about it. If you'd care for head, fine, but I'm not into *whips* or any of *that* crap."

"No. No. I don't mean whips. I mean love."

"You mean what?"

"I mean I'll have to tell you I love you. And I'll have to kiss you."

"Oh," said Tricia.

"Well?" said McNiece.

"I don't know . . ."

McNiece pressed the palm of his left hand against the knuckles of his right hand. "I . . . the thing is, I have to have more than pleasure. About three years ago I met a girl here. *Young woman*, rather. And the pleasure was all right. But I . . . well . . ."

"You're not into the zipless fuck then, are you?"

"The . . . the what?"

"Read *Fear of Flying*. Read what Isadora Wing has to say about the perfect fuck. The uncommitted fuck. The zipless fuck. Anonymous. Final."

"You mean the book by the Jong woman?"

"Yes."

"I didn't read it," said McNiece.

"I know," said Tricia.

McNiece was silent.

"The kissing doesn't bother me," said Tricia.

McNiece looked at her.

"A lot of people think hookers don't kiss. That's a lot of crap. If a john wants to kiss a hooker, if he wants to run the risk or whatever . . . fine, that's up to *him*. It doesn't matter to *me* one way or the other. But this love thing is different. Is that where you're *really* at—into *love*? I mean, what do you want to do? play music on FM?"

"Maybe."

"This is really bizarre."

"Why?"

"I can act at a long list of things. Devotion. Courage. Whatever. And I mean, I'll confess . . . I even can act at making my nipples pop. I mean, *look* at them. But *love* is, um, *different* . . ."

"Jean Harlow would rub her nipples with ice."

"Who?"

"Never mind. I'm only talking about something *I* read in a book."

"Which is supposed to mean?"

"Which is supposed to mean that maybe things don't change," said McNiece.

"Oh."

". . . ah, perhaps I could let you have twentyfive dollars more," said McNiece.

"Because of the love thing?"

"Yes."

Tricia nodded. She smiled. "All right," she said. "Love it is. And maybe you'll even be able to *talk* me into *lubricating*. A boy did that a long time ago. I suppose I was in love with him. His name was Paul, and the pigs hit him on the head in Chicago in 'sixtyeight, and I'm older than you thought, aren't I?" She finished her drink. McNiece paid the tab. He took her up to his room, and he switched on the FM, and he undressed her, and they listened to Enoch Light, and he kissed her, and his words were ardent, and she did in fact lubricate, and she did in fact not laugh.

122

RIP

It starts out sort of funny, doesn't it? I mean, two kids meet in a hay wagon, and I just about need a road map and a compass and a magnifying glass before I can find her chest. Then, the next thing I know, I'm working in her precious daddy's hardware store and I'm about to be crushed to death by a goddamned avalanche of snowshovels and sawblades. So, for want of anything better to do, I knock her up three times, and all of sudden the funny isn't even *sort* of funny. I mean, it's like I'm wrapped in straps, and maybe my legs'll be shaved, and Pat O'Brien will come along and pray over me and Barton MacLane will pull the switch. Ah, but that's not fair. I shouldn't bitch so much. Barbara and I have had our troubles, and we'll probably have more, but there have been humorous times, too. Or at least *we* think they've been humorous. For instance, take Bobby, our youngest son. When he was sixteen, Barbara and I became grandparents. The girl's name was Karen Fletcher, and he married her four hours before the baby was born. I just about had to *hold* him by an *ear*, and poor Karen was so surprised she had the kid I think it was two months prematurely. But do you want to know something? Bobby and Karen are happy, and he has every intention of studying to be an Episcopal priest. God save the Holy Episcopal Church. Hell, God save us all. Still, I can look back on that time and see it as being funny. Bobby the lover, the look on his face when I found out he had Karen in the family situation. It was like all his teeth had fallen in, you know? And so I finally had to laugh. Barbara was with me, and she also had to laugh. Oh, we are real parents. There our boy is, and he is tormented right up the goddamned wall by thoughts of bastardy, and all Barbara and I can do is laugh. Oh, well, what were we *supposed* to do? Claim it was a virgin birth? Look for a star in the east? Old fellows with beards and staffs? The angel of the Lord? No, there are times when Barbara and I become sort of silly. Even in the bad days, something every so often will come along to make us laugh. Like the time back in 1964 or so when the mayor of Paradise Falls, whose name was Amberson and who was a son of a highschool teacher Barbara had liked a whole lot, made a Fourth of July speech on a platform at the Elysian Park and stood there and said: "*If this sation is to nurvive, we must all pace up to our fart!*" A thousand people were there, but I'll tell you the truth—the mayor said the words with such conviction that Barbara and I were the only ones who laughed. I expect maybe no one else was paying attention, but Jesus Christ, you should have seen the dirty looks we got. Ah, so what. I mean, a good laugh is a good laugh, and dirty looks are a cheap price, right? At least that's the way I feel, and it's the way Barbara feels, and I think it's the way my brother Jim would feel. I bring him into this because there's a story I want to tell, a true story every word of it, and it has to do with my brother Jim. I think it's funny. And Barbara thinks it's funny. And God damn it, I think Jim would, too. Anyway, it took place soon after the war. I had two brothers—Lloyd Junior and Jim. I served in the ETO during the war, but Lloyd Junior and Jim stayed home on the family's dairy farm near LaBelle, Ohio, and shoveled cow pies for the war effort. Jim became restless, though, not too long after the Japs gave up, and so in early '46 Pop loaned him enough money to buy a small ranch out in Wyoming. Sheep, that sort of thing. Well, Jim was in Wyoming not even two years when his pickup skidded into a telephone pole and that was the end of him. His sheep ranch hadn't exactly been coining money, and I guess he'd come to the conclusion that he wasn't John Wayne, and so he'd gotten pretty down in the mouth. Anyway, even though I was living down in Paradise Falls and working my ass off in Barbara's dear Papapoo's hardware store, I was the one my LaBelle relatives elected to go out to Wyoming and take care of everything, the funeral arrangements and all the rest of it. I flew there in a little DC3 puddlejumper, and the sheriff of that Wyoming county told me old Jim had put away about a goddamned *keg* of Coors' beer. Maybe that's an exaggeration, but who gives a shit? After you get to a certain point, it really doesn't matter all that much. And okay, the possibility does exist that he eightysixed himself against that pole *deliberately*. But what *difference* does it make? Dead is dead, and anyway, it was *his* business. The town nearest his ranch was a sad little place, crowded by high grass, with all the buildings rubbed gray by the wind and the winters. Jim was a bachelor, and there wasn't anyone there to mourn him except some woman who ran a diaper wash service. Her name was Edith . . . ah, Edith Shields. Big bazooms, you know? Believe me, I remember them well. And she surely did bawl and carry on, and I recall that she clasped me very warmly to her massive breastworks. And, ah, finally she got around to giving me an envelope, and there was a note inside that envelope, a note written by my brother Jim. It said, close as I can remember:

To Whom It May Concern:
    When I die, I do not want to be buried in the ground. I do not want to have nothing to do with the ground. All my life I been a prisoner of the ground, and of animules, and of cow flop and sheep dip and pig shit. I got no more goddamned use for the ground. And so, when I die, I respectfully request I be cremated and my ashes scattered over the Atlantic Ocean off of Cape Cod, Connecticut. I never seen Cape Cod, Connecti-

cut, and I never seen the Atlantic Ocean neither, but I don't care. Anything's better than being buried in the ground.

Okay. Just a second. Sure, I know Cape Cod is in Massachusetts. But Jim didn't. We think he flunked geography— same as he flunked sheep ranching and telephone poles. Oh, look, nobody's perfect. Take myself, for instance. Until Barbara straightened me out, I thought Cape Cod was in Rhode Island. But Jim was . . . well, what can I say except maybe to point out that the good Lord probably broke the mold *before* He made Jim. Well, anyhow, the note finished off with:

This here is all the way I see it clear and sober, and I respectfully request that my wishes in this matter be paid attention to. Very sincerely, James G. Pilgrim, written here on this 23rd day of March in the year 1947 in the presence of God Almighty and my good friend and true companion, Edith Shields.

So it was all very clear, right? The nearest crematory . . . or crematorium . . . or cremorium . . . or creamery . . . or whatever the hell they're called . . . was in Laramie, and I had to hire a hearse to take old Jim there, and this Edith Shields went along, and she sat in the front seat between me and the driver, and when she wasn't hugging me she was hugging the driver, and *that* old boy looked happier than a pig in whale shit. And then we were in Laramie, and they shoved old Jim's coffin into a fire, and after a while some undertaker came up to me and gave me an urn. It was like maybe a sugar bowl, with a top screwed on, and the undertaker said: "There's nothing in there except some ashes and maybe a piece of bone and maybe a tooth or two." And then the undertaker smiled, and it was like he'd just given me a Chinese dinner to take home. I mean, your average undertaker is a prince of a fellow, no question about it. Well, anyhow, Jim . . . and his ashes and the bone and the tooth or whatever. I very carefully packed the urn in my suitcase, and I flew to Boston, hopping from DC3 to DC3, and then for something like I think it was fifty dollars I hired a Piper Club or some such thing to take me out over Cape Cod. The urn still was in my suitcase, and I hadn't even bothered to open the suitcase so I could change my clothes . . . all I wanted was to get the thing over with and go home. So I climb in the Piper Cub with some guy, the pilot, and we take off, and before you know it we're over the ocean at Cape Cod. So I start to open the suitcase. The guy hollers back at me: *"Any special place you want to throw out the ashes?"* I tell him no; one place is as good as another. *Any special place?* Jesus. What did he think he were talking about? A table in a restaurant? Ah, but then maybe he was just trying to be polite or something. I'll give him the benefit of the doubt. So I fumble with the latches and the straps on the suitcase. And I open the thing. And somehow the top has come unscrewed from the urn. And there's old Jim, spread across my clothes and my shaving stuff like . . . oh, I don't know . . . talcum powder. Well, the pilot takes one look at *that* and we goddamn near go into a crash dive, and I don't know whether to shit or call for rosary beads, and there's poor old Jim, blowing all around the cabin, along with my shirts and who knows what all. So just what am I supposed to do? comb him out of my clothes? suck him up with a vacuum cleaner? So I do the only thing I can think of to do. I toss the whole shooting match out the window—suitcase, clothes, ashes and all. And the wind sort of carries him away, you know? It is quite a sight. There Jim is—riding to glory by way of American Tourister, right along with four shirts, six ties, six pairs of shorts, six undershirts, my razor and all the rest of my shaving stuff, a bottle of Bromo-Seltzer, a paperback copy of *The Grapes of Wrath,* by John Steinbeck, plus what is maybe the best suit I've ever owned. Well, I suppose there's a moral to this. If you want to cremate somebody, stay out of Laramie, Wyoming, where the people who screw urns aren't really very good at it.

PHOEBE SELLERS

Harry McNiece, who was editor of the Paradise Falls *Journal-Democrat,* killed himself a few months ago. He apparently got drunk and took too many pills . . . Valium, I believe. I'm told he left behind a note concerning a woman, something having to do with unrequited love. My facts may be all out of whack, but I did know Harry McNiece, and I can believe he had the capacity to kill himself because of unrequited love. He and I had a few dates when we were in high school, and his eyes became all wet and warm whenever he saw me, and one night he said to me: "Phoebe, please don't make fun of me when I tell you I love you." And I said: "Okay, I won't make fun, but I don't believe it. I got two sisters, and maybe you could be in love with *them,* but you aren't in love with *me.* You'd be better off being in love with a brick wall, and you know it." But Harry kept at me; he insisted he was in love with me, and so I let him kiss me, and I even let him put one of his hands on my chest. It was 1944, and we both were seventeen, and I didn't suppose any of it mattered all that much. Barbara, my older sister, was full of laughter and kindness. Rosemary, my younger sister, was the beauty of the family, even if she did pule and whimper too much for my taste. So where did that leave me, Phoebe, the *middle* Sellers girl? I really had no territory, *did* I? Even now, and I'm pushing fiftyone, my face is not something you'd photograph for use on the labels of poison bottles. In other words, my features all are arranged in the places where custom and human geography dictate they be. My hair is dark, and I always keep it carefully groomed, and I always pay close attention to my makeup . . . as well I should, seeing as how I own and operate the Astor Beauty Shop, which is far and away the town's finest, she said modestly. But my features *are* heavy; my mouth *is* too pouty, and my eyes *are* too large. And my body is . . . ah, I think the word "solid" does the job. My breasts are good, and I have quite a narrow waist, but there's never been all that much in my body that's given promise of yielding. And men like bodies that yield, don't they? They like women who *flutter* all over them, don't they? Who *flutter* and *flatter*, correct? Myself, I've never been able to do those things. I've always lived alone—even when I was a child and at least *officially* was living with my father and my mother and Barbara and Rosemary. *Statistically,* I was a member of a family. *Within myself,* though, I was an orphan, and the people who reared me were nothing more than goodhearted strangers. Any my sisters really were *actresses* paid to make certain I wouldn't be *altogether* lonely. I don't know why I felt that way. Perhaps because Barbara and Rosemary had preempted so much, leaving me with no area I could call my own, no perfect and private place where I could spread out my *own* intelligence or beauty or talent or wit. And so I developed my only real skill, which I call "thereness." I always was *there.* Good old Phoebe always could be *counted on.* If you needed help, you went to *Phoebe.* If you needed a skirt hemmed, *Phoebe* would kneel at your feet and do the work with the pins. *Phoebe* comforted you when you had a fight with a boyfriend; *Phoebe* told you not to let him know he had flattened you; *Phoebe* could be counted on to lash back at people who picked on you; *Phoebe* had a good strong tongue; *Phoebe* was tough; *Phoebe* was

129

not afraid. Oh, I was that Phoebe Sellers all right, and I still am that Phoebe Sellers. In Paradise Falls, where insects peep and the great oily odor of roses is so strong it makes the roof of your mouth pop spit, where the sound of freeways and automobiles still has not quite been able to overcome the murmuring of the river, where old women rub their knuckles and briskly snap beans and talk of Hoover and the Depression and the old C&O car shops and the days when you could see a movie at the Ritz or the Cameo for a nickel, where elderly lawyers prop their feet on their windowsills and squint and blink out at the sky and God and think perhaps of virility and warm words, in this reasonably quiet and reasonably gentle town I have a reputation for the most jarring sort of honesty, and I suppose it is why most people think I never married. But they are wrong. The reason I never married is my fear of pain. I have had many chances to be married, and I probably still could be married, but I really do not see the sense of it. My sister Barbara was married three times (twice to the same man), and the experience was so glorious she died of kidney trouble at the age of fifty. And do you know what the last word she said was? It was "debris." Don Pilgrim (the man she'd married twice, and divorced twice) was in the hospital room with us, and she looked directly at *him* when she said the word. Oh my God, poor Barbara. I believe there were things she could have been, but the marriage wrung those things out of her. As for poor puling Rosemary, what can I say? She's been married only once, and the thing apparently has been a success (as far as marriages go), but she is the most boring woman between here and the Panama Canal. Her big thing is to watch the Ohio Lottery on television each week, and she tells me she loves Amy Carter so much she could just about hug the poor child to *death*. Now, I ask you, what sort of woman is it who has such a passion for *Amy Carter*? If Rosalyn Carter is the First Lady, and Billy

Carter is the First Brother, then Amy surely must be the First Brat. So much then for Rosemary's taste. So much for her life. And so much for marriage. It killed one of my sisters, and it has turned the other into a lobotomized repository for enough sentimentality to put half the world into insulin shock. So I stay alone. It is now the spring of 1978, and I play a little bridge, and every now and again I am visited by men who find my body interesting (my favorite lover is a fellow named Norman Starr, and he likes to call himself my star lover, which I suppose he is), and we do all the good and easy and relaxed things, and we are courteous, and afterward I always put on a robe and serve coffee and brandy and cheese and crackers. My house is full of caged birds, and sometimes they set up a terrible commotion, but most of my men do not seem to be annoyed. Norman even has gone so far as to tell me that sometimes the racket excites him. According to him, it's almost as though we're being applauded. Oh, I know the symbolism you can attach to the caged birds, to my canaries and parakeets and parrots, and you can say they represent all the *wives* and *husbands* and *units* and *relationships* I've never been able to understand, and I suppose you're right. But I don't give a damn. Because, you see, I have at least walked around the edges of *wives* and *husbands* and *units* and *relationships*, and I know something of the lies and evasions that are necessary in order that the machinery continue to function, and I just won't have any of it. I would rather confront truth. I don't know the origin of my preference, but there it is. It exists tough and heavy as an imbedded boulder that has been pounded into the side of a mountain by centuries and winds and the Hand of God. When you are a girl and you are preempted, when you must be *grateful* to Barbara for handing you down something and at the same time must be *careful* so that you do not damage it before you hand it down to Rosemary, when each day is drawn in shadow, when your only characteristic is your *thereness,* your good old *depend-ability,* your good old skill with *pins,* when you are hugged and loved not because of what you *are* but because of what you *did,* then your only comfort comes from yourself, from your view of truth. Does all this mean then that I never have loved? Absolutely not. Do you think I would be feeling so sorry for myself if that were the case? But I never was able to take the risk, to face the inevitability of attrition, of words curdling, of flesh falling away. And there was one time when I didn't even have the choice. The man was Don Pilgrim . . . *the* Don Pilgrim. He was rough, jaunty, a grinner, and there were times his language was so foul it was a wonder the floors didn't curl, but I saw within him the sort of humanness I can understand. You see, he seemed to want to make do with what he *had* rather than waste his time with *dreams* and *pretense.* I loved him I don't know how many years, and I would imagine his humor be-ing directed at *me* instead of dear sweet perky adorable crinklenosed *Barbara* with her cunning *buck teeth* and her *college degree* and all the rest of it. But I never did a thing about the situation; I never touched him; I never even hint-ed. He probably would have laughed at me, correct? He probably would have told me I was crazy, correct? So I did nothing. I simply was *there.* I borrowed enough money from my father to set myself up in business (the money long since has been paid back), and I am as honest with people as they want me to be. And I become angry when they ask me for truth and I give them truth and it makes them uncom-fortable. If they don't want to run the risk of being made uncomfortable, why do they ask for truth? What do they *re-ally* want? *Lies?* Oh, don't you understand how much better it is to live alone in a house full of caged birds? When they set up a commotion, we all know it is a witless commotion; we don't attach *words* to it and try to give it *significance.* There are days when my breasts swell, do you know that? I have gone through The Change, but nonetheless there are days when my old boobs balloon up, and my bra straps cut into my shoulders. What does this mean—that something within me keeps resisting time and decay and wanting to look back over a shoulder? Oh, dear God. (Don Pilgrim was buried in a place called LaBelle, which is west of Toledo and not far from the Indiana line. He had died of a heart attack, and he had been only fiftytwo. That was a year and a half ago. I still hurt. I recall how he grinned. I recall his warm hard language. I try not to think back too often on my sister's final word. Whatever debris existed, it was *their* debris; it had nothing to do with *me*. I embraced a stranger the day Don was buried. It was a woman, and I believe she had been his mistress. I stood next to his grave, and the smell of the earth was so raw it made me want to throw up, and I had to embrace *someone*, you know? Even if I was endangering myself, for once in my life I had to take the chance. You still don't understand me, correct? You see me on the floor, and my mouth bristles with pins, and you look right through me, correct? I am *there*. I am *there*. I am *always* there. But at the same time I say to you I am *invisible*. I can be tough, and I can be an independent old number, but quick, close your eyes! Tell me what I am wearing! Tell me the color of my earrings! You can't, can you? I *am* invisible, correct? Admit it! WOULD YOU LIKE ME TO SPEAK MORE LOUDLY? WOULD YOU LIKE THE CAGED BIRDS TO JOIN IN?)

LETTERS

Don Pilgrim and his wife, Barbara, were divorced for the first time in February of 1956. She then married a man named John K. (Jack) O'Connell, with whom she had been having an affair for several years. Pilgrim returned to his family's dairy farm near LaBelle, Ohio. The new Mrs O'Connell remained in Paradise Falls, Ohio, where her father operated a hardware store and her husband worked as an appliance salesman. She and her former husband did correspond, though, and here are excerpts from some of their letters:

Dear Don — Jack and I have separated, and I am suing him for divorce. I often think of you and wonder what you are doing. Do you like living on the farm again? As I recall, you never liked cows very much. Are they any more pleasant than they used to be? Do you think of me at all?

Dear Barbara — That surely is too bad about you and Jack. Sincerely, Don.

Dear Don — It was a genuine pleasure to receive your chatty letter. I think I'll have it mounted with my Ohio U diploma.

Dear Barbara — I wouldn't have them mounted if I were you. Maybe holding hands would be enough.

Dear Don — The boys keep asking about their daddy. They never did like Jack, and they never were able to call him their daddy. Oscar even thought Jack was a sissy.

Dear Barbara — I guess Oscar's not as dumb as we thought.

Dear Don — I wish you'd stop trying to joke about all this. It's not easy. Now and then Jack sends me little notes. They are full of poetry quotations, and I don't know whether he regrets what happened or *what* he feels. If he *regrets* it, then he shouldn't have let it happen, right? The grape arbor is having a good year, and do you remember Emma Wootten? She is the pushiest woman I've ever known, and now she's the new Worthy High Priestess at Eastern Star.

Mystical Union

Dear Barbara — Thank you very much for the latest Eastern Star news bulletin. I've been wondering myself to distraction about Emma Wootten and her legendary pushiness. Well, she may be too pushy, but at the same time, God knows, it's good to see that from time to time ambition can be fulfilled. By the way, I'm getting so I don't mind the cows. And the solitude is wonderful. There's only myself here, and of course Lloyd Junior, and his wife, and their seven kids, and one hundred sixtythree cows, and the silent brooding majesty of the great Midwest plains, and it's all really beyond words—especially when I stop to take into account the presence of cow pies, and the hot stink of cow piss, and the fact that all of us smell like curds and whey and live in mortal fear that Little Miss Muffet will come along and eat us.

Dear Don — My father's not feeling well. He told me to tell you that *any time* you want to return to Paradise Falls and help him with the store, he'd make it worth your while.

Dear Barbara — When it comes to a choice between cows and screws, I pass.

Dear Don — Bobby cried tonight. He asked for his daddy. I had to take him to bed with me.

Dear Barbara — Well, better him than Jack O'Connell, right?

Dear Don — I was wrong. I admit it. When a marriage begins, a certain part of a person ends.

Dear Barbara — I'm not quite sure I know what you mean by that, but I think I agree. So I figure the best thing we can do is remain apart.

Dear Don — I love you. You're everywhere in this house. Jack erased nothing. He might as well never have existed. He *is* zero, and he *was* zero. There are chairs where you used to sit, and those chairs still have the outline of you on them.

135

Dear Barbara — You mean my rear end? Jesus Christ, how romantic. Quick—somebody fetch the smelling salts.

Dear Don — When you belittle me, you belittle both of us. Come back. You know you want to.

Dear Barbara — I know no such thing.

Dear Don — I can tell from the tone of your words.

Dear Barbara — That is crap.

Dear Don — Please, for just one day before you die, try not to be dirty.

Dear Barbara — It sounds like a lot of shit to me, but I'll try.

Dear Don — Thank you very much, I'm sure.

Dear Barbara — Hey, I have a lady friend! How about that, huh? Her name is Hannah Bellamy, and she has the Dip-O-Freez franchise in LaBelle, and she makes the best goddamned banana splits in the world!

Dear Don — So you've taken up with some tacky *chippy*. I hope you'll be very happy. Banana splits, my foot. I suppose you're trying to be funny. You know, it's really a shame I've never quite understood your humor.

Dear Barbara — Yes. It really is.

Dear Don — You are insufferable, and I hate you.

Dear Barbara — Well, hang in there, kid. Try to find a Jack O'Connell who'll be able to do you like you want to be done, if you'll pardon the expression.

Dear Don — I will *not* pardon the expression. You are insufferable, and I hate you.

Dear Barbara — Please stop spoiling me with your flattery, you sweet talker you.

Dear Don — Please come home.

136

Dear Barbara — Maybe.

Dear Don — When?

Dear Barbara — I only said maybe.

Dear Don — You know you mean yes.

Dear Barbara — All right.

Dear Don — I love you! I love you! I love you! So when will I see you?

Dear Barbara — Sunday. Saturday night I'm going to say a tearful farewell to Hannah Bellamy, and I suppose I'll get drunk on beer and wine and maybe even banana splits, and then I'll be on my way.

Don and Barbara Pilgrim were remarried on October 11, 1958. The ceremony was performed by the mayor of a little town on the Kentucky side of the Ohio River. The man had a wooden right hand, and Barbara was convinced the thing was made of mahogany. She wondered if any significance should be attached to this—any sort of symbolism or whatever. Don told her symbolism was a lot of crap. He said to her: "We were married by a man who has a mahogany hand, that's all. Don't make it into the end of the world." And then Don and Barbara laughed, and they had at each other in bed. She told him he was better than Jack O'Connell ever had been. He told her he figured almost anyone would be . . . even the man with the mahogany hand. Her father died in 1959, and so Don took over the operation of the hardware store, and he and Barbara were as happy as they ever had been, or ever would be. He told her she was better than all the banana splits this side of hell. He told her it was a wonder they both didn't have bedsores. There even was a night when their son Oscar came into their room to complain about the noise. Numerous photographs from this time still exist. Don and Barbara squint at the camera, and usually they are touching. Hands. Thighs. Hips. It was a time when neither of them wanted to gag because of boredom or aggravation or pain. It was a time when their squinting was honest. It was a time when they faced into the available light. They are frozen and splendid. Those bright days all eventually fell down, but in the photographs there is no hint of anything other than a sort of fine silly picnicked bravery. There is no trace of loss. There is no trace of tiredness. There is no thought given to sweet warm blood forever drained into the abiding earth.

MORE LETTERS

Don and Barbara Pilgrim were divorced for the second time in May of 1972. It was he who wanted the divorce. He tried to explain to her that he was tired, that he needed to be his own man. She never quite understood. She almost understood, but never quite. Pilgrim returned to his family's dairy farm near LaBelle, Ohio, where he designed and built a model train exhibit that he called Railroad City USA. He laid out the exhibit in a rebuilt old barn, and he charged admission. He became greatly respected among model railroad enthusiasts. His former wife remained in Paradise Falls, Ohio, and she died of a kidney ailment in 1974. She and her former husband did correspond, though, and here are excerpts from some of their letters:

Dear Don — How do you like being Casey Jones? Can you hear the train whistles over the mooing of the cows? I expect your relatives think you're crazy. Well, so do I. As a matter of fact, I think you're maybe President of all the Crazies.

Dear Barbara — Nixon got there ahead of me.

Mystical Union

Dear Don — Don't laugh, but I think I've come down with the funniest and most poetic illness. Remember how you used to kid me because I forever was running off to the bathroom to pee, especially when we were having an argument? Well, wouldn't you know it? I apparently have something wrong with my kidneys.

Dear Barbara — Be brave. For whatever it's worth, I love you.

Dear Don — This kidney business is really a terrible bother. I'm forever being hooked up to a machine, and . . . oh well, never mind about *that*. I can write about other things that maybe are more important. Oh, I've been watching a lot of television lately, and every so often marriage is discussed, and I guess there are those who believe marriage is something that has to be worked at. Myself, I always thought it was something that had to be shared. *Working* at a thing sounds like digging coal in a mine. Or delivering groceries. But then what do *I* know? If I knew anything, I wouldn't be living in Paradise Falls, right? I mean, all I do know is that I love you. Even though we can't live together, I love you. Whatever love is. Whatever people feel is. A hayride. A freshman mixer. You join the army, and we write letters and letters and letters. V-Mail. Remember Pearl Harbor. And then the war ends, and we're married, and the boys come. But something is out of alignment, and so we are divorced. And I marry poor Jack O'Connell, God rest his soul. But I divorce him, and I marry you again, and then I divorce you again, and dear me, it surely did become complicated, didn't it? All of it. I suppose this is an ending, and I suppose I ought to be angry, but I don't know . . . I am grateful for the boys, and I am grateful for the days you and I had together, the *good* days . . . of leaves . . . with *me* raking them, of course . . . of laughter . . . Donald Junior and his *fractions* . . . you and the times I think I captured you . . . the times when I was—however briefly—all in the world you needed and loved . . . and so the thing I want to know is . . . why do we end up breaking ourselves apart?

139

Dear Barbara — We break ourselves apart because that's the way we are. Love is fine, and you won't catch *me* criticizing it, but there has to be more, doesn't there? And the more never really was there for us. Still, there's nothing wrong with making a list of the good things. I mean, we never had a really lasting fight, did we? We never had really lasting hatred, did we? But we *did* have really lasting *love*, even if it didn't carry us through our troubles. And that's more than most people have. And at least we've been honest. Something was missing, but at least we acknowledged it. And at least we *touched*, right? Remember what I told you my father said about the same bullshit being beyond the horizon as lies right here in LaBelle? The same mistakes? The same dumb words? Well, he was right, and my life hasn't been all that much, and I think playing God with my little trains is probably the most important thing that's ever happened to me. To *me*. Not *us*. I want you to get it out of your mind that you're involved in some sort of competition. I'm only talking about *myself*, and what has my life been? Cow flop. The war, and the things I saw, the *lunacy* I saw, a lunacy I'll never understand if I live until all the wells run dry. Jim ramming himself into that telephone pole and then sailing like Kitty Litter out over Cape Cod along with my suitcase. Three sons. Good boys, all of them, but they need me about as much as they need two assholes. So here I am with my trains. I want to come to you, but what would be served ? Look, we never should have met. It's not that we were all that unhappy. It's just that there was an *incompleteness*. And incompleteness is worse than hatred or jealousy or anger or any of the rest of that stuff. I love you. Please believe that. But we can't live with one another, and we both know that. First there was the bickering, so Jack O'Connell came along. Then, when all that passed, we just wore out. Or at least *I* did. And you too, I think. Be honest—haven't you ever wanted to lie down and never get up? I know *I* have. So I play with my trains. I stay away from you. Whatever it is I am, I am. I love you, but it's much better if I stay right here. I love you. I love you. I love you. And I thank you for your concern all these years.

Mystical Union

Dear Don — Of course there have been times when I've wanted to lie down and never get up, and the doctor tells me it won't be very long at all before I do just that. Remember me to your trains. Remember me to the cows. Remember me to whatever it is you have that feels something for me. If we could just pick out a certain *thing*, a certain *person*, a certain *day*, a certain *moment* when maybe the lemonade was too sour, or someone's dog was barking too loudly, or there was some sort of bad news on the TV, or one of the babies had made cockie all over the front of your shirt . . . something to *seize* and tell ourselves: *Eureka! Here is the explanation!* But it's never going to be that simple . . . for anyone. So finally we die . . . and we're just as baffled as when we began . . . and what on earth did we *do*? If there *is* an explanation, it's like a pile of knotted and snarled rope, and who knows how to pull it apart? It's all like wreckage, isn't it? Debris. Things scattered everywhere. Refrigerators. Old tires. Oh dear Lord, it *would* have to be my *kidneys*, wouldn't it?

Barbara Pilgrim was fifty when she died. Don Pilgrim was fiftytwo on a certain fall day in 1976 when he was driving on the Indiana Toll Road en route to a model railroad convention in Milwaukee. He stopped at a freeway restaurant, and he went into the men's room, and it was there he discovered he had forgotten his comb. He put a quarter into a machine, and he bent over, and he was about to fish a little plastic comb out of a tray, but something decided to crush his chest, and his heart burst, and he toppled into the machine, bruising his forehead. He slid to the floor, and he sighed, and he was dead. His death was observed by a man named Stephen F. Blumberg, of Southfield, Michigan, who later told a friend the whole thing had been about as exciting as watching a cake fall.

Vasco da Gama & Friend

Look, the truth was . . . Barbara and I liked each other right from the start, right from the first shy crippled little words. We were both sixteen. I had an aunt who taught school in a place called Paradise Falls, which is in southeastern Ohio (I am from a place called LaBelle, which is in *northwestern* Ohio), and I was visiting good old Aunt Helen in the summer of 1940. I think it was the month France fell to the Germans, which would have made it June, and some friend of Aunt Helen's, a woman whose name was Soeder, got her son to fix me up with a blind date. The girl's name was Barbara Sellers. It was a hayride, a YMCA hayride, and you can imagine what a big deal it was. We held hands, and she had braces on her teeth, but she kept insisting I call them "orthodonture." I kissed her that night. It was like kissing a mouthful of dimestore screws and can openers. And I even tried to open her mouth. The Germans had done well with the Maginot Line, and I figured what the hell, I'd be able to open her mouth. But she was stronger than the Maginot Line. She clamped down on my tongue, and the wonder is she didn't amputate it. So then, what with the darkness and the stars and all, I decided to mess around with her chest. The only problem was . . . with the chest she had in those days, I had the goddamnedest time even finding it, and never mind messing around with it. When I finally sort of . . . ah, accidentally stumbled across it, I felt like Vasco da Gama, and I wanted to plant the Spanish flag. Or would it have been the Portuguese flag? Shit. I never can remember. Well, anyway, chest or no chest, she had a quality about her, and she's never lost it. It was a muggy night, and there had been rain that day, and the wagon was out on some back road up near Paradise Lake, and I went to work as hard as I could, and one of my arms was around her, and I said to her: "You have beautiful eyes."

"How do you know?" she said. "It's pitch dark."

"I remember from when it wasn't pitch dark," I said.

"I suppose you think that sort of remark is going to *get* you someplace," she said.

"I surely do hope so," I said.

"Well, you just have another think coming," she said.

I kind of let my hand flop so that it cupped what I figured was one of her breasts. At the same time, though, I looked up. "Nice," I said.

"Yes," she said.

"Stars," I said.

"Right you are," she said. "Very intelligent."

"Now don't get smart," I said.

"With *you*, there'd be a fat chance of *that*," she said.

"If it makes you feel better to talk that way, go ahead," I said. She was wearing a blouse, and my hand wormed its way inside, and the great exploration began.

She didn't seem to notice. She wriggled a little, but she didn't bother with my hand.

I said: "All I meant was, what with all the rain this afternoon, I wouldn't have thought any stars would have been out tonight."

"I guess we're just lucky," she said.

"God blew away the clouds," I said.

"God?" she said.

"Who else?" I said.

"You believe in God?" she said.

"I don't think I got much choice," I said.

143

"You like to talk about deep things," she said. "I never thought I'd have a blind date with a . . . with a *philosopher* . . ."

"Sure," I said. I figured now was as good a time as any. "And with a philosopher who likes to hug and kiss . . ." And I pounced. I kissed her. I seem to recall I missed most of her mouth, but I also seem to recall the screws and can openers.

"Mind my teeth," she said.

"That's a good idea," I said.

"I don't know why *anybody'd* want to kiss *me*," she said.

"What?" I said.

"My teeth and all," she said. "Last week I just about gave Kenny Oliver a cleft palate."

"Don't worry about your teeth," I said. "You're pretty."

"Oh, you're just trying to make out," she said.

"That's true," I said.

"Well, at least you're honest about it," she said.

"I like you a whole lot," I said. I was groping inside her blouse. Honest to God, I was *groping*.

"Last time I was on a hayride, the horse kept making gas," she said. "It wasn't much fun."

"No," I said. "I don't imagine it would be."

"He was an old horse," she said, "and he sort of pooped along, if you know what I mean."

"I think I do," I said.

"A little bit to the left," she said.

"What?" I said.

"If you're looking for what I think you're looking for," she said, "you'll find one of them a little bit to the left."

"Oh," I said.

"Yes," she said. "There."

"Surely," I said.

"You . . . ahh . . . stars . . . you said something about stars," she said. "Ahh . . . what did you mean?"

144

"What?" I said.

"The *stars*," she said.

"Oh," I said. "Yeah . . . the stars . . . I just meant . . . well, that they're pretty . . . the nice night and all . . . I mean, the stars . . . and this wagon . . . and you . . . I mean sometimes I slow down a little and I try to look at the larger things . . ."

She glanced down briefly. "Larger things?" she said.

"Love," I said.

"Oh," she said.

" The . . . ah, the universe," I said.

"Very deep," she said.

"Thank you," I said.

The next day we went walking down by the Paradise River. And we sat you wouldn't believe how primly and properly on the grass. And I spoke to her of I don't know what . . . music maybe . . . grasshoppers . . . the sky . . . chocolate cake. And then, um, she kissed me sort of moist and easy, if you know what I mean. And I wasn't really all that aware of the steel stuff in her mouth. She tells me this was because of her fatal charm. I suppose she has a point. She and I didn't meet again for two and a half years (it was at a Ohio University freshman mixer), but we more or less picked up where we had left off, and now we have three sons, good little fellows all of them, and I look forward to 1952. I work in her father's hardware store, and he's not a bad fellow, and you know something? There are worse things than the old ball and chain. Also, just for the record—her chest filled out real good.

HARRY MCNIECE

Good evening, Mr & Mrs North America & all the Ships at Sea, let's go to press! FLASH! Harry Timothy McNiece, editor of the powerful and influential Paradise Falls *Journal-Democrat*, has decided to pack it in! Kindly do not all yawn at once! FLASH! The woman he loves has left him (and *pssst*, Infidelity Fans, she also has left her *husband*), and she is nowhere to be found! She drove off in her '73 Nova three mornings ago, and she took her three children, and she took the $2,113.44 she and her husband had saved in the Paradise Falls State Bank, and she is *absolutely definitely without quibble* nowhere to be found! It is as though she has been devoured by the skyes! And so FLASH! Harry Timothy McNiece, sitting here in his palatial office deep within the bowels of the powerful and influential Paradise Falls *Journal-Democrat*, has decerded decidded to yield himself to the tender ministrations of Doctor Valium, known as Good Old Val to his legion of admirrers, 5 mg by 5 mg by 5 mg, accompanied by Rolling Rock, of whitch he has bought himself a case as he sits here and types and feals a first draining of his renowned energy! So there is the ultimate FLASH for you, Mr & Mrs North Amiraca & all the rest of you miserable motherfuckers—the DEATH of Harry Timothy McNiece! On account of I loved her, you see! On account of suppose she is dead? On account of did I hassel her tooooo mutch? My Dottie. I had a wife, and Lois was a good women, and maybe she lovved me, but she is stone cold dead in the market, and so I turned to Dottie Washburn, who is blond, who is not yet 30, who feels maybe an

edge of the pain I feel, here at 50 yrs of age, on account of I
got no kid or nobody to give a shit. Um. Beer, and 5 mg on
top of 5 mg on top of I don't remember. Beer is good. Washes
it down. God. Good, I mean. Not God. The God back there
was a typografical error. God: The ultimate existenchial
typografical error. Oh, I want to die. I am not fooling. There
is no theater here. I came to her, and after a time she let me
kiss her, and there were 2 times in a motel, and she said to
me: "Harry, I wish I could say you're as good as my husband, but that would be lying, and we have to be honest,
don't we?" And I said: "Not all the time." And Dottie said:
"Doan't be a hypogridt." And I said: "All right." And then
maybe I think I recall I bawled, and she said: "But we still
can talk." And I said: "But I want your *ass*, too." And I re-
coil I mean I recall I was talking in italics *I was talking in
italics.* FLASH! Hey there, motherfuckers, I believe an
effect is coming to pass! Or if not coming, at least breathing
hard! On account of now I got to put away another 5 mg and
more beer *more beer for the italicized writer here aloan inside the bowels of this place which is like maybe being layered in shidt , huh? eh? wot?* So. Now. Be cal, Harry. Type
CAREFULLY, Harry. When you want to type CALM, type
CALM. Do NOT type CAL. Oh hey, Harry, your love for
this Dottie was love of ass yes, but it also was love of the
truth that she would listen, and so what happens here in
October of 1977 with the leaves so brown? *She leaves town
when the leaves are brown!* So here I am, alone. How do you
get away from bieng alone, from grabbing at your belly on
account of the pain sucks at your gut like a vacuum cleaner? You cannot corral friends, can you. A friend is not a
horse. A friend *is.* A friend cannot be *created.* So the only
place to go from being aloan is the good old 86, so now then
MR & MRS MOTHERFUCKER, WATCH THE KID AS HE
POPS 5 MORE MG! I never drove an MG. Hell, I never
drove anything better than a Poontiac. I'm as Amirecan as

147

appel pi. With an r squared crust & maybe raisins. (You ever raise sins? Big sins from littel sins oftten grow, eh?) Dottie *listened* to me, you see. And she smiled at my little jokes. And finally I bawwled in front of her, and I said I'm 50 and your 29, and its like I want to lick the floor behind you, and I never did a thing, o when I was young everybody said Harry once you get yourself organized youllwrite the great Americannovel, and well all say WE KNEW YOU WHEN (whitch was back at OhioState when the trees were green if you knoww what I mean), but a Paradise Falls boy is a Paradise Falls boy forever, or atleast THIS one was, and MARRIAGE CAME ALONG, and I already had the job here on this paper, and I worked for old George Dilworth until he retired in 1953, me starting out in 1946 as 1 of 2 reporters, or 2 & ½ if you count Wes Snyder, who really was more of a of a of a PHOTOGRAPHER & couldn't write his weigh out of a paper BAG. Hey now, more 5 mg down the old hatch on account of more pain you know????? THE PAIN????? The 5 mg & the beer. Burp. Aaahhh. The releaf of a good burp. So maybe its like Im inside a ball of leather all these yrs, & its wet, & so it shrinks, & it squeezes my flesh until MAYBE THINGS POP OUT, maybe PUS or whatever huh you think? So. Now. Whoa, Harry. Be cal. No, be clam. No, not *clam*. The word is *calm*. Like an old hulk in the Sargasso Sea. Hey, is Paradise Falls the Bermuda Triangle of the soul? What does it have to do with the strange & forever magical hunkered colossal wreck that is Raintree County? My God, how we sukked at Lockridge & Wolfe. There was a fellow used to live here HE WORKED AT STEINFELDER'S DEPARTMENT STORE & HE WAS FRUITY & DAMN IF I CAN MEMBER HIS NAME, but now & then hed talk with me about Lokkeridge & old Tom Wolfy, & we couldnt neither of us understannd why LOKKERIDGE DID HIMSELF IN THAT NIGHT IN HIS GARAGE (but *now* I understand *now* I do *now now now*), &

here writing this is a fat man adrift in selfpity mourning forgotten days (where were you August 6, 1941, Harry you old piece of frogshit you? howcome you dont remember? howcome you got no sense of the valu of the days? is that why you never amounted to a puddle of puke when it came to writing? is that why your column for this hear paper has been like PASTE all thees yrs?), & to mourn forgottin days is to agknowledge the superfficiallity, so lets have moar beer if you please, & my Dottie there were times when I cried & made her cry onaccount of she said the choice Harry betweenn you & my husband is one I cant ever make onaccount of THE PAIN is there no matter whatt I do, 1 kind of pain with him being traded in for anotherkind of pain with you, & WHO TOLD HER SHE SHOULD HAVE SUCH WISDOM????? DID GOD ORDER IT????? This world whitch shall remain nameless has been too mutch for me & did you know I always have been very fond of peanutbutter & jelly sandwitches & Dottie fed them to me????? She placed an ad in the paper & the ad had to do with kittens I think & I followed up on the the ad. Yeh i followed up. i telephoned her & she told me the ad had done just a fine job & all the kittens or whatever had found good homes, & i said maybe we could followup on it, & she said yes yes yes that would be fine, & I ALMOST GOT TO THINKING ABOUT MOLLY BLOOM, & I almost got to thinking she would say yes yes yes I will yes (or whatever it was Molly said), & I almost was thick in the belly YOU KNOW WHAT I MEAN????? o i tell you 5 mor & THE BIG SLEEP WILL SPRED ITS BENEVOLENT BREATH ACROSS THESE FINAL MINITS OF YRS TRULY, 5 mor mg is all thats necessary, god damn shit i dropped the little fuckers THERE WILL BE A SLIGHT PAUSE IN THIS PROGRES- SIVE & NO DOUBT ENNOBLING DETERIORATION WHILST YR FAITHFUL CORRESPONDENT CRAWLS UNDER HIS DESK & SCOOPS UP ALL THE DOCTOR V

PILLS HE CAN FIND, now, here, be calm, be a clam, o i got
it, & pop goes the tab from YET ANOTHER can of ROIL-
ING ROCK, gulp, glup, glub, & if a man were to beet his
arms against his chest long enough & hard enough HE
EVENTUALLY WOULD BEAT HIS CHEST PLUMB
AWAY, EH PARTNER, & HIS GUILT WOULD CAUSE
HIS ARMS TO COME OUT THE OTHER SIDE, WHICH
PROBLY WOULD MAKE HIS SHOALDERS & HIS
HEAD FALL OFF NOT TO MENTION HIS ARMS THEM-
SELVES (IT IS ROLLING ROCK; IT IS NOT ROILING
ROCK; WHO THE FUCK IS READING THIS COPY?????),
so then see the rgeef? geref/graff/greef/grief? SO THEN
SEE THE GRIEF????? see that I have pizzed aweigh the um
the um the potential until all that is left is a fat bag of fuck-
ing gas who causes a young woman sutch dizztrezz that she
leaves her hubby—*and me—and me—AND me* (no amper-
zand here)—& goes off with the kids & the monie to do
Godd knows what Godd knows where, & when she was with
me the last time she said I CANT STAND IT HARRY FOR
GODS SAKE CANT YOU & TOM LEAVE ME
ALOAN????? & o i should of left her aloan in the first place
ON ACCOUNT OF I AM A VAIN POSTURING NINNY
WHO PLAYS AT BEING A RUINED HULK THE WAY
SOME PEOPLE PLAY AT BEING DRUNKS, USING THE
GAME AS A WEAPON ON ACCOUNT OF I NEED SYM-
PATHY OR ASS OR WHATEVER!!!!! So there is the ultimate FLASH for you, Mr & Mrs Motherfucker. The ultimate flash FLASH flash is i never knew what i was or what
i felt. The ultimate flash FLASH flash is when i was a boy i
used to sit aloan at the fairgrounds & watch the sun come
up & there was a girl named BARBARA SELLERS who
found me out, but she never said anything, & then a whoal
long time later i brought day lilies to her grave, on account
of day lollies lullies lillies reminded me of that morning
sun, & its all sweet isnt it????? ONLY CAN IT BE BE-

LIEVED????? only can i find one thing in my life thatwasnt theatrical o o o o o how many of these litttlle 5 mg fuckers do i have to take????? only, while reading this, i see the uppercase I becomes the lowercase i for no reason other than as some sort of um DRAMATIC ILLUSTRATION, & goddam even my PAIN is theatrical. i want to sleep. iwanttoslep. o i think i killed my dottie. i think she & her kids are in a dittch. her husband tried to knock me down, & i let him. he came hear & he knocked me down & i said YES YES YES I WILL YES & he said what????? & i said if Molly can be fucked i can be hit. i said discipline i said yes all my life ive needed discipline ooooo discipline mea cupla i mean mea culpa WHAT EVER HAPPENED TO THE SIXTH DAY OF AUGUST IN THE YEAR 1941????? (i am heartily sorry & now pls forgiv me but i am at last very VERY sleepy) so this ought to be enou

KENNY OLIVER

He would buy a girl a gardenia, and carefully he would insert it in her hair, and he would smile and tell her she was beautiful, and perhaps she was. His name was *Kenny* Oliver. He never was known as *Kenneth* or even *Ken*. He was skinny and he had a benevolent urgency, and his name just about *had* to be a diminutive. His face was freckled and sharp, and his hair was sandy, and surely it was meet and right that he was a Kenny. He was barely five and a half feet tall, and so he had a way of bouncing on his tiptoes, and perhaps there was something hostile and frenzied within him. But he never permitted it to emerge, or at least he never permitted it to emerge publicly. His father was an engineer for the C&O, and his mother had briefly been an Episcopal missionary in southeast China, but she'd not been all that interested in lice and starvation, and so she had returned to Ohio, and within a year she had met and married Edward Oliver, and he was a good man. Kenny was born in 1924, and he was the Olivers' only child. Edward and Nancy Oliver doted genially on their son, and they reared him in an atmosphere of easy and freckled good will. And there was a time . . . it lasted perhaps three or four years . . . when Kenny was acknowledged to be the best dancer in Paradise Falls. And it didn't even matter if the girl loomed over him, or even if she moved as though God had attached lead sinkers to her toes . . . Kenny grinned at her, and he never lost the beat of the music, and he *led* her, and he *held* her, and later she would gather her girlfriends to her, and she would whisper fondly (the words coming through giggles and warm saliva) of his *personality*, of the quick and competent way he had of not holding back, of dreamily capitulating to the music, the beat, the sweet ritual. He wore bow ties and checked shirts, and he was forever teeth, and he would snap his fingers and narrow his eyes, and he would permit himself to be transported by the music of the Hocking Valley Chieftains, or the Paradise Falls Jazzcats, or any of the other barely competent bands that labored through the shoals and hazards of the various ersatz Dorsey and Goodman arrangements their leaders had picked up mostly from listening to the radio or playing phonograph records. But it was not the *barely competent* music Kenny Oliver heard. It was the *real* music, edited by his ear and his mind and perhaps even some sort of impatient knot in his viscera. He spoke of this one time to his favorite girl. Her name was Barbara Sellers, and he said to her: "I mean, this is *Paradise Falls*, Barbara, and only a dumbbell would expect the best. But I got *brains*, after all, and so I can make myself not hear what I'm hearing and hear what I want to hear. Does that make any sense?"

Mystical Union

And Barbara Sellers, who was just as skinny as Kenny Oliver and every bit as benevolent (if perhaps not as urgent), said to him: "Of course it makes sense, and it's one of the reasons I love you." She was fifteen, and Kenny was fifteen, and she kept insisting she loved him. They had been hugging and kissing for about three years, and Kenny wished she did love him, but he didn't believe she did. She had braces on her teeth, but she was not afraid to smile, even when the sunlight was bright and the glint of her smile was nearly enough to scorch the eyeballs. He would bounce on his quick happy tiptoes, and he would blink at her smile, and sometimes it brought moisture to his eyes, and so he would hug her, and they would kiss, and he would manage now and then to insinuate his tongue around and under and through the braces. And he would moan. And Barbara would moan. And there were three times when she allowed him to touch her between the legs. The third time took place the night of the Paradise Falls High School Class of 1942 prom. Her dress was yellow, with white dots and silvery jimmies, and he had bought her a purple orchid, which didn't go with the dress too terribly well. But Barbara did not complain. As a matter of fact, she actually jumped up and down when she opened the corsage box. She had Kenny help her pin the corsage to the neckline of the dress, which meant his hand brushed against her bosom. Her father and her mother and her two younger sisters stood in the Sellers' front room and watched the ceremony, and one of the sisters . . . Rosemary . . . actually wept a little. And in point of truth Mrs Sellers' eyes were not altogether dry either. Kenny of course danced with Barbara that night, but he also danced with every other girl in the Class of '42 (and *four* of them were *colored*, for heaven's sake!), and it was later . . . much later . . . in the back seat of his father's '38 Ford (Kenny had parked the car on a bluff near the hamlet of Earlham, and the bluff afforded a fine view of

both the Paradise River and the morning sun) . . . as
dawn came in a diffident smear from behind the hills
. . . that Kenny was able to reach up Barbara's golden jimmied skirt and tug aside her panties and explore the fine
moist little muff between her legs. And she spread her legs
and guided his hand. And he tried to unbutton his fly with
his free hand. But Barbara said: "No." And Kenny said:
"Please?" And Barbara said: "I can't." And Kenny said:
"Yes you can." And Barbara said: *"No."* And she was crying. Oh, not as loudly as her sister had cried, but loudly
enough, especially there in the back seat of that '38 Ford.
And Kenny tried to move his hand (or his middle finger actually) back and forth, or up and down, or whatever it was a
person was supposed to do. He and Barbara were virgins,
and maybe he was hurting her. The thing was, he'd never
written any books on the subject, and maybe he was *tearing*
her; maybe he was making her *bleed.* So he withdrew the
finger, and he said : "I'm sorry." And Barbara said: "There's
nothing to be sorry *about.*" And Kenny said: "Then what is
it? Are you sad?" And Barbara said: "Of course I'm sad."
She had been in a sprawl, but now she abruptly sat up and
pushed Kenny to arm's length. And she said: "I'll be going
to Ohio U, and you'll be going to that business college in Columbus, and this is like an *ending*, you know?" Kenny did
not reply. Instead he closed his eyes. Math had been his
best subject at Paradise Falls High, and he wanted to study
to be an accountant. He shuddered, then opened his eyes
and said: "But Athens is what? maybe seventyfive miles
from Columbus? It's not like one of us is going to be off on
the moon." He tried to embrace Barbara, but she slid back
from him, and her head moved from side to side, and she
said: "I . . . we got the class picnic yet. And we'll be
together all summer—if you don't get drafted. But then,
well, one thing'll lead to another; you just wait." And Kenny again closed his eyes. Most of the guys in the Class of '42

already had enlisted, but Kenny had not. The reason was simple—he was afraid. In the army, it really didn't matter how good a dancer a fellow was, did it? And benevolence didn't count for owl turds, did it? All that mattered was how well you *sliced* the enemy like maybe the enemy was a *chicken* squawking in a *corner* and you were coming at it with a *hatchet*. And so he said to Barbara: "Are you mad at me because I haven't joined up?" And Barbara said: "No. Of course not. That's your business." And Kenny said: "Then what's wrong?" And Barbara said: "Don't push at it. Please. I mean, don't you *understand* what we *are now* is different from what we *were* and we'll never *go back* and it's all *finished* and I want to cry because it's all like the Arabs have come along and taken away our tent and we're in the cold and we're going to have to be brave forever and answer for what we do without having a mama or a papa to run to, without being able to *dance it away* or *smile it away* or *tell a joke* or *run* or *giggle* or *fall on the ground*?" And Kenny said: "I don't understand." And Barbara said: "You do too. Or at least you understand enough." And a week later Kenny took Barbara to the class picnic, and they hugged and kissed down by the river, and she permitted him briefly to suck her left nipple. But that was the end of the hugging, the kissing and the other things she once inaccurately had called love. She went away that fall to Ohio U, and Kenny took a room in Columbus and attended the business college. He didn't have much fun, though. He was a *civilian*, and few girls would dance with *civilians*, and, well, um, so in May of 1943 he enlisted in the Marines. He spent more than a year and a half in the South Pacific, and he killed dozens of Japanese, and he was discharged in October of '45 with the rank of first lieutenant. He never was as afraid as he had thought he would be. He corresponded infrequently with Barbara, and it was a month before Kenny's discharge from the Marines that she married a man named Don Pilgrim. Kenny returned to his genial parents, and occasionally he encountered Barbara on the street. She smiled at him, and she visited with him, and she told him he would have to come over for supper some night. But the invitation never formally was extended. Kenny was polite with her, but what he wanted to tell her was: Jesus, how can we talk like this when I've *touched* you? He went to work as a teller in the Paradise County National Bank. He attended many dances, and he still wore bow ties and checked shirts, and they became his hallmark, and his freckled amiability made a great many people tell him he reminded them of Henry Aldrich. But how many fucking Japs had Henry Aldrich killed, huh? Kenny's mother died in 1951, and his father died in 1963. Kenny never had married, and in 1966 he left Paradise Falls and took a job as the chief bookkeeper for a cement firm in Vincennes, Indiana. He moved on to Okmulgee, Oklahoma, then Alexandria, Louisiana, then El Paso, Texas. He last was heard from in the summer of 1977, when he mailed a Return Postage Guaranteed card to a woman named Marilyn Cooley, who was arranging the thirtyfifth reunion of the Class of '42. The card bore Kenny's signature and a check inside a square labeled SORRY, I'LL NOT BE ABLE TO ATTEND. The postmark was smudged, but it appeared to be Corvallis, Oregon.

THE AMBERSONS & BARBARA SELLERS

The 1942 Paradise Falls High School senior picnic was held as usual at the Elysian Park, and the Ambersons were among the chaperones. He taught English and coached the school's track team; he was fortyfive, but he still was able to run the mile in less than five minutes. His wife, Anne, was a trifle plump, but there was a sort of efficient and straightforward prettiness to her, and she was . . . to put the proposition as simply as Amberson could . . . the only woman he'd ever loved. They had three children—two boys and a girl—and the older boy, Henry, had enlisted in the army. Anne Amberson called Henry her Always Boy. His birth had caused her enormous pain. Amberson knew she was aware that she perhaps loved Henry too much. He also knew she was aware that there was little she could do about the situation. Pain was pain, and its defeat needed constant acknowledgment . . . at least as far as Anne Amberson was concerned. Now, while chewing on celery and radishes and feeling a loginess spread inside his belly and his chest, a homely loginess to be sure, a loginess brought on by perhaps one hot dog too many, one spoonful of baked beans too many, one swallow of Coke too many, while sitting with Anne at a picnic table and watching the various members of the Paradise Falls High School Class of '42 as they hollered, as they ran witlessly in a pickup softball game, as boys and girls paired off and giggled and held hands, as a sort of frail twilight haze drifted in from the northwest, as the moist early June green of the grass and the trees lay all sticky and tumescent everywhere around them and extending out, out beyond their field of vision, as Amberson wriggled a bit uncomfortably and chided himself for being too *philosophical* and *profound* at what was essentially a silly and trivial time, now, here, despite the absurdity, despite the gas within him, despite what he liked to think of as his good sense, Amberson permitted himself to feel what was almost a sort of bereavement. Oh, there they all were, those young people, and the ritual of the class picnic was a sight more important to them than it should have been. It almost was a ritual of death . . . the death of childhood, of this particular sort of yipping and running, the clasping of hands. Nearly all the boys had enlisted, and they would be

157

gone within a month, and now and then Amberson heard one of them shout something to the effect that those goddamned Japs had just better *hang onto their assholes* when the guys of the Paradise Falls High Class of '42 came after them. And Amberson exhaled. And he glanced at his wife. And she knew what he was thinking, and so she nodded. And eventually he said: "It's a little morbid, isn't it?"

"I suppose so," said Anne Amberson. "If you look at it a certain way."

"A year from now, when the kids from 'fortythree are out here, maybe one of *these* kids will be dead."

"Yes," said Anne Amberson.

"But it's more than the war," said Amberson.

"Yes."

Amberson was a small man, and he wore spectacles. He removed them, and he began cleaning the lenses with his handkerchief. "For most of them," he said, "there'll never be better days than these have been."

"I don't like to believe that," said Anne Amberson.

Amberson shrugged, concentrated on cleaning the lenses.

"One of them could become president," said Anne Amberson. "Who are you to consign them to the wastebasket . . . the, ah, the scrap heap . . . so casually?"

"I'm not talking about wastebaskets," said Amberson. "Oh, most of these, ah, kids will be fine. They'll have babies, and they'll vote in all the elections, and they'll turn out just about the way you and I have turned out. Which I don't think is bad. Because, you see, I honestly believe we are living the sort of life we have been *ordained* to live. And it isn't bad at all. But don't you see that for some people the ordaining could be aggravating? The lack of choice, I mean?"

"What are you trying to say? That if you'd had a *choice* you wouldn't have married me?"

Amberson sighed. "No," he said.

"Then what *are* you trying to say?"

"That maybe we are lucky. That maybe we are *very* lucky. That most people can't . . . ah, come to terms as well as we have."

"You mean surrender?" said Anne Amberson.

"No," said Amberson. "I mean precisely what I said. I mean *come to terms*. I mean *we* were born for this kind of life . . . this town . . . the park . . . the trees . . . all the rest of it. But how many people can say that?"

"All right," said Anne. "I understand you. But, well, look . . . they're *having fun* . . . I mean, *listen* to them . . . *look* at them . . ." And Anne moved an arm in a sort of swoop. The grass was smeared now with the shadows of trees, and the sunlight nicked at the softball players as they dotted in and out of it, and now and then they were splattered by it, and perhaps a trace of enervation had crept into their voices. "It is a sweet twilight," said Anne, "and they'll look back on it with a sort of comfortable nostalgia. Is that so bad? Is it *death?*"

Amberson said nothing.

"Well?" said Anne Amberson.

Amberson blinked. A girl named Barbara Sellers walked past. She was small, and her features were bony, but she had a splendid smile, a smile awash with a reckless overbite, a smile that extended itself into her eyes, which often were moist. She was holding hands with a boy named Kenny Oliver, and she turned her splendid smile on the Ambersons, but she did not speak to them. She and Kenny Oliver walked behind a picnic shelter, and Amberson supposed they were looking for a place where they could hug and kiss. He glanced at his wife and said: "I like her a great deal."

"I know," said Anne.

"She is the best, the most sensitive pupil I've had since I don't know when."

"Yes."

"Those two essays of hers that were published in *National Scholastic* . . . they ere excellent, weren't they?"

"Of course they were."

"And I've tried to encourage her to write more."

"I know."

"But she doesn't seem to hear what I am trying to say to her."

Anne Amberson folded her hands.

"Barbara Sellers has *talent*," said Amberson.

Anne Amberson nodded.

"But something about this life will tear it down. Pressures. Something."

"Because writing would make her appear . . . strange?"

"Yes," said Amberson.

"That is a large indictment," said Anne.

"I suppose so."

"Here, on such a pretty day, such a terrible thing to say."

"I apologize," said Amberson, "but it is what I feel."

"Then why have *we* been so blessed? Why are *we* able to live within all this?"

"I don't know. Maybe a day'll come when we'll both have the leisure to examine the question."

"Perhaps so," said Anne.

"But don't bet on it," said Amberson.

"I won't," said Anne.

Amberson had guilts. Everyone had guilts. There were days when he didn't care a scintilla whether he penetrated the awareness of even one pupil. There were days when he was overcome by some sort of frozen and inexplicable grief. Still, his life had not been much of an ordeal, and he was properly grateful. But what of that girl, that Barbara Sellers? Nathan Hale had been the subject of one of her essays. Her cat had been the subject of the other essay. She had written of them with grace, style, in her own voice. But the

160

magazines would fall away, and the type would corrode or
be melted down, and it would be as though she had deliberately pressed a pillow over her face. She would marry Kenny Oliver. Or she would marry *someone.* The smile perhaps
would remain, but she would be devoured by what? statistics? custom? vows? fear of loneliness? And so her capacity
would shrivel, and her talent would rust away like an old
oil drum. And Amberson shook his head. And now the twilight was an enormous palm. And cries carried thinly. And
this Barbara Sellers, this miracle, no doubt now was embracing Kenny Oliver, and was grace involved? was style
involved? was her own voice being heard? Amberson looked
at his hands. He looked at his wife. She smiled at him. He
smiled. He listened to the cries, the sounds of leaves, the
river, God, laughter, history. And he told himself there really was nothing he could do, and he probably was better off
worrying about his heartburn. So he covered his mouth,
and he belched, and his tongue was flooded with an after-
taste of sweet baked beans, courtesy of the Class of '42.

LOIS MCNIÈCE

Lois McClatchy was tidy. Her feet were small and careful, and her words were precise, and much of her flesh was
translucent. She had three older brothers, which meant she
spent her girlhood as though she were imprisoned within a
circle of Conestoga wagons, and her brave brothers were
beating off wild Indians, not to mention careless seducers.
The most belligerent of her brothers was the oldest, whose
name was Dan. He was enormous, and his breath often
came all green and hairy, and he said to her: "I know what
they *want*, these guys who come sucking around you . . .

on account of they all want the same thing, and I know that on account of I'm the same like they are. Like when I'm with Leona Brownell, I'm *just exactly* the same. You ought to see me. You'd laugh fit to split, and that's a fact. I mean, I get to snorting and I get to pacing the dirt like . . . well, never mind . . . maybe you can guess what I mean, huh? It's that blond hair of hers. Godalmighty, Lois, it's like I want to fly to the moon . . . I'd probably weigh about twelve pounds, but I'd have a smile on my lips, believe you me." And then Dan tried to be serious, and he told Lois a man was no sort of man at all if he let his baby sister be, ah, led astray by the first smoothtalking jasper who came down the pike. And so he and her two other brothers, Larry and Bucky, maintained their careful vigil. They never asked Lois what *she* thought of their behavior, and she never had the nerve to volunteer an opinion. She was barely five feet tall, and she weighed barely ninety pounds. She was born in 1930, and her father and mother were plump, amiable, hardbreathing and harassed. Her father, Leo T. McClatchy, was a lawyer, and it was his good fortune that one of his sisters . . . Aunt Louise, a formidable woman, pigeonbreasted and amply wattled . . . had married into the Soeder family, which was one of the most prosperous in the county. As a result, Leo McClatchy received enough Soeder legal business (plus legal business from people who for one reason or another wanted to get on the good side of Aunt Louise's husband, Hans Soeder, a grain merchant) that the McClatchy family was able to survive the Depression. The McClatchy home was on Meridian Avenue; it was low; it had undergone several additions; it lay at the top of a shallow hill in a sort of mottled slump, streaked by sunlight and the forever agitated shadows of leaves and bending branches. The house abounded with books and the smell of books, dust and the smell of dust. Mrs McClatchy genially allowed as how all the dust was too much for her, and so she let it go. As a result, Lois sneezed her way through most of her girlhood. But Papa would not relinquish any of the books. He had inherited them from his father, who had been a professor of rhetoric and English literature at Kenyon College. "My boyhood constituted the best time of my life," said Leo T. McClatchy, "when I had *serenity*, when I felt myself awash in *ideas* and *noble emotions*, when I was able to grasp the world around me and understand its configurations. *Now*, though, how can I or anyone else understand configurations? Here I am, an Episcopalian with a Catholic name, and I suppose it hasn't hurt my law practice all that much, and I suppose I ought to thank the Lord for small favors, especially my sister's fortunate marriage to good old Hans, him and his grain business. But I'm sorry; I keep having a feeling that I've missed a train . . . and I keep having a feeling that I've fallen down while trying to chase it . . . and I have scraped my face on little stones, and my clothing is torn, and my dignity is forever a thing of the past." But then Leo T. McClatchy smiled. He liked to talk with his daughter, and he insisted she was the apple of his eye, and he would sit with her in the front room, and invariably he would say: "But don't listen to me. My complaining is all a lot of nonsense. I keep behaving as though the world has just missed having another Clarence Darrow in its midst. Which is a lot of the proverbial baloney. I am what fate and my nature have decreed me to be; I do not have the capacity to be a tragic figure. I am a small-town lawyer, and not a very good one, but at least I am not a bank robber or a Nazi or a pederast. So I shall settle for what I am. And anyway, what I might have been really is moot." Another smile. When in doubt, Leo T. McClatchy always smiled. He died of a sudden stroke when Lois was sixteen. The stroke took him while he was smiling. He was about to bite into a slice of breaded veal cutlet, and his smile was gentle, and then his face dropped onto his plate, and he died with meat and mashed potatoes and peas and gravy pasted to his forehead and his chin and his cheeks. Lois was given sedatives by the family doctor, a man named Groh, and she also was given sedatives two years later, in 1948, when her mother died of a liver malignancy that caused the poor woman to jaundice and just about glow in the dark. That was the year Lois was graduated from Paradise Falls High School. She was valedictorian, and she spoke to hardly a soul (her valedictory speech at commencement was barely audible, even over the public address system), and it was her brother Dan who took her to the senior prom. He bought her an orchid corsage, but he did not dance with her. He had fought on Okinawa, but he did not know how to dance. Still, this wasn't all that terrible, since Lois didn't know how to dance either. She attended Ohio State, and she was graduated in 1952 with honors in mathematics, science and education. By then all her brothers were married, and Larry and Bucky had moved with their wives to Columbus. But Dan and *his* wife still lived in the place on Meridian Avenue, and so Lois obtained a teaching job at Paradise Falls High School and moved in with them. Dan's wife was a large girl whose maiden name had been Martha Sibbisan, and she already had given him a son, and she told Lois she planned to give him four more children. "All I've ever wanted to be is a baby machine," said a grinning Martha Sibbisan McClatchy, "and I hope you can stand the noise." And Lois, who still was a virgin, smiled, plucked at her collar, told Martha she was sure everything would be just fine. And Lois never was a bother. She always did her own laundry, and she even ironed her panties. Martha could not get over this. There were times Martha laughed, and of course Lois reddened. There also were times Lois was unable to sleep, first because of the sounds of the baby, then because of the sounds Dan and Martha made as they vigorously sought to manufacture another

baby. And they were successful, and it was another boy.
And they were successful again, and it was a third boy. And
Lois pressed her fists against her temples. Occasionally,
though, she would touch herself. The walls of her room
were bare. She seldom wore jewelry. Occasionally, though,
she *would* touch herself. Yes. Occasionally. She lost her
maidenhood in 1961 when she was thirtyone. She was
raped . . . or at least she saw it as rape . . . by a man
named Harry McNiece, who was editor of the Paradise
Falls *Journal-Democrat.* He had a room over Hoffmeyer's
Restaurant, and he spoke to her of William Butler Yeats,
and he gave her Chablis to drink, and then his *mouth* was
on her—his *mouth!*—and she was larger than either of
them had any reason to expect, and later he said: "It certainly wasn't as difficult as I thought it would be." And Lois
said: "*Difficult?* What are you trying to *say*—that I'm
easy?" And Harry McNiece smiled, embraced Lois, kissed
her cheeks, then said to her: "I was talking about the physical thing . . . your, ah, *dimensions.* Look, have I ever
shown you any disrespect? You know I haven't. You also
know I do love you, after my fashion, whatever that is. And
you know I'll never be all I wanted to be. College, I mean.
My, ah, lost youth. The intimations of Wolfe and Lockridge
and Yeats I had when I was younger. You are a realist,
Lois, Which is one of the reasons you're such a good math
teacher. You don't waste your time with dreams and pos-
turings, and those highschool kids instinctively *understand*
that. Maybe it has something to do with your tight little
voice. Or the way you move. I'm not really sure. But, at any
rate, you *do* make an impression on them; you supply *neatness* and *logic,* and they *want* neatness and logic, even
though they don't know they do. And that goes for me, too.
Marry me, my love. Place my days in some sort of sweetly
orderly sequence." And Lois said: "All right." And Harry
McNiece said: "Really?" And Lois said: "It felt sort of good,

you know?" And her fingers dug into Harry's belly, and he groaned, and she used her mouth on him, and her cheeks puffed with warmth. Dan approved of the marriage. "McNiece is a little weak, I think," said Dan, "but I expect *you'll* straighten him out, won't you? If my little sister puts her mind to a thing, it happens, doesn't it?" The wedding was attended by all three of the McClatchy brothers, their wives, their total of ten children, the entire faculty (and faculty spouses) from Paradise Falls High School, plus Mr and Mrs Hugo G. Underwood (he owned the *Journal-Democrat),* plus Harry McNiece's widowed father (who for years had operated a newsstand and candystore next to the Ritz Theater), plus even the pigeonbreasted and amply wattled and now quite elderly Aunt Louise Soeder. Lois had three miscarriages in seven years, and Dr Groh told her she never would be able to come to full term, and so she had her tubes tied. She and Harry bought a house on Spring Street, and she kept a flower garden. She attended teaching conventions and seminars held in such places as Columbus, Toledo, Chicago, Cleveland. She was appointed to chair the math department at Paradise Falls High School. And she resumed the occasional touching of herself. And occasionally she masturbated herself with a Water-Pik shower massage device. Her husband spoke to her, and he smiled at her, but at the same time he vanished. She decided the house on Spring Street was too large, and so she talked him into buying a smaller one on Meridian Avenue. It was nextdoor to her brother's place, and she and Martha visited back and forth. She remembered to smile at her husband, and he remembered to open doors for her. Had she been raped that first time? Probably not, but she always wondered. And she always wondered what transgression she had committed to earn herself such pain. And it was a pain that finally became physical, and in 1975 she died of liver cancer, the same disease that had taken her mother. She was fortyfive, and she neatly arranged herself at the end, and she glowed, but her hair had been combed by a nurse, and so at least she was tidy, which meant her sense of order was not offended. It was quite logical, by the way, to iron panties. If they were ironed, they would lie flat in a dresser drawer. Harry McNiece wept over her, and she only wished she had the strength to tell him not to make such a foolish spectacle of himself.

LLOYD PILGRIM & BARBARA SELLERS

Old Lloyd Pilgrim fished the paper pouch of Red Man from a pocket of his overalls. He carefully opened the pouch, then looked up, frowning.

Barbara Sellers grinned. "Oh, go right ahead," she said.

"I am much obliged," said Lloyd Pilgrim. He twisted off a substantial chunk of the tobacco, opened his mouth, placed the chunk inside, then slowly began to chew. His mouth was flooded with the sour brown juice of tobacco, and he leaned back a little, and he felt some of the tightness go out of his legs. He was sitting on the davenport in the front room, and he was not used to sitting in the front room, but Daisy had insisted. Daisy was his wife. She was out back in the kitchen, where she was fixing supper. All told, five persons lived here—Lloyd, Daisy, two of their sons (Jim and Lloyd Junior) and Daisy's father, old Mr Polk, who had been a maintenance of way foreman for the New York Central and now was retired. Lloyd and old Mr Polk got along remarkably well. They had the same opinion of wars and politicians and oratory. They saw it all as bullshit. In point of fact, Lloyd saw just about everything as being bullshit, and he was convinced there was no place a person could go to escape it.

"I tried it once," said Barbara Sellers.

"Pardon, ah, what?" said Lloyd Pilgrim, startled.

"Chewing," said Barbara Sellers. She was nineteen, close to twenty. She was fragile, and she had uneven teeth, but she was pretty enough.

"Oh," said Lloyd Pilgrim.

"It was Mail Pouch, though, not Red Man. This boy and I . . . his name is Kenny Oliver . . . well, he and I were at the Paradise County Fair of, ah, 1938, which meant I would have been fourteen, and anyhow, we went out behind the swine barn and he dared me, and so . . . well . . . ah . . ."

"You took him up on it? And you got sick?"

"That is correct," said Barbara Sellers. She wriggled. She hugged her belly. She made a face, and most of it was teeth, clownish and moist. "I don't know how you *do* it."

"Practice," said Lloyd Pilgrim.

"I *expect*," said Barbara Sellers.

"Been doing it since I was a boy," said Lloyd Pilgrim. "Used to chew in school. Got the teacher real aggravated."

Barbara Sellers was perched on a straightbacked chair. "I imagine so," she said.

"When I wanted to spit, she wouldn't let me go to the window. She made me swallow."

"*Blushhhh*," said Barbara Sellers, hissing, making another face—teeth again. "Heeeesssshhhh."

"My sentiments exactly," said Lloyd Pilgrim. "The only thing is, when you swallow as much juice as *I* have, you get so you either like it or you die."

"That surely must be a fact," said Barbara Sellers. She nodded. She folded her hands in her lap. She unfolded her hands. Her fingers moved in spasms. She gnawed at the inside of her lower lip, then said: "Don and I know what we're doing. It'll work out all right. You'll see." She nodded. "No question about it," she said.

Lloyd Pilgrim nodded, chewed. In a moment or so he would have to open the front door and spit out across the porch railing. He hoped this girl didn't mind a little cold air. It was January of '44, and it was the coldest January he could remember. He was fortythree years of age, and so he had passed through a decent sight of Januaries, but none as bad as this one. He and Jim and Lloyd Junior worked here, three hundred acres, all in dairy cattle, just outside a little farming community called LaBelle, in northwestern Ohio not all that far from the Indiana line. It was flat country, and nothing came between the wind and a man's flesh.

"Don says you never call him Don," said Barbara Sellers.

Lloyd Pilgrim nodded. "I always call him Donald. I didn't name him *Don*. I named him *Donald*. If he wants to call himself *Don*, that's fine; he can call himself the Duke of Windsor for all I care. Myself, though, I call him Donald. I tried to talk him out of letting himself get drafted, do you know that?"

"Yes," said Barbara Sellers. "He told me it was a short conversation, though, and he said you didn't make any real fuss when he let you know he was bound and determined."

Lloyd Pilgrim shrugged. He stood up and crossed the room. "Excuse me," he said. He opened the door. Snow swirled on the porch. He spat a syrupy stream hard and accurate, and it vanished over the porch railing. Quickly he slammed shut the door and returned to the davenport. "Hope you didn't get too much of the cold air," he said.

"Well, it certainly was *refreshing*," said Barbara Sellers.

"Mean to tell you," said Lloyd Pilgrim. "Cat froze to the sidewalk other day."

"So Mrs Pilgrim was telling me. The poor thing. Ah, the *cat*, I mean. Not *Mrs Pilgrim*." Barbara Sellers hesitated,

169

smoothed down her skirt. "But, um, it did live. And I expect it still has eight lives to go, if you can believe what's said about cats."

Lloyd Pilgrim was silent. He felt what was probably a rage, and it was in his belly, and finally he said: "Nuts."

"Pardon?"

"I'm sorry. I don't mean to talk nasty, but I don't believe much of anything. I don't even believe much about this war. I think it's all a lot of *talk*, you know? I mean, all right, a lot of people are dying, but why should Donald have to be one of them? Jim and Lloyd Junior got farm deferrals. Donald could of had one, but he let himself get drafted. How come?"

"I think he believes the war is important," said Barbara Sellers.

Lloyd Pilgrim said nothing. Don . . . *Donald* . . . had attended Ohio University with this girl. She was from a place called Paradise Falls, down in the southeastern part of the state, and her father was in the hardware business. She and Donald were *engaged.* They had arrived yesterday from Paradise Falls, where they had spent the first three days of his furlough. She had been as cheerful as a pig in warm mud, and she said something to the effect that it was so cold it would be a miracle if the bulls didn't turn to steers. And even Lloyd Pilgrim had laughed at *that* one, as he had to admit. And so now it wasn't so bad to be alone with her. Donald had gone off to the depot with Jim. He had said something about wanting to watch a train or two. The main line of the NYC went right through LaBelle. The Water Level Route itself. Donald always had loved trains. He and Jim probably were sitting in the car right now, and by God maybe they would just about freeze to death, but by God they would *see a train.* Donald was the youngest, and there had been times when he and his mother had played tag in the front yard. Everyone said they were crazy, but

170

they didn't seem to care. (Lloyd Pilgrim supposed there were all sorts of things hidden inside his wife. He supposed there were all sorts of things hidden within all men's wives. Just as there were all sorts of things hidden within all *men.* Needles. Raw places. Aggravations. A tight locked cage layered inside with dead forgotten laughter. Ghostly bullshit. Derelict dreams, webbed and crazed.)

The girl had been looking at the floor. She suddenly brightened. "Oh! I forgot! Your sister sends her best. She told me to tell you her bad shoulder seems to be coming along just fine. She is a nice woman, Mrs Keppler is. And a good schoolteacher, I'm told. And I have *that* on *very good authority.* You see, there's a little girl lives next door, and her name is Penny Hook, and she's in the fourth grade, and Mrs Keppler is her teacher, and Penny just *dotes* on Mrs Keppler, and believe me, Penny Hook is not an easy person to please. I mean, she's so fussy she won't eat raisin bread unless you cut off the crusts."

"Helen married an automobile salesman," said Lloyd Pilgrim. "Both my sisters married automobile salesmen. Lord God Almighty. Well, anyway, she and Fred Keppler went off to East Chicago, Indiana, and then he was killed when his machine was hit by a trolley, but at least she had her teaching certificate to fall back on, and that's how come she wound up in your home town. She didn't have a child, but at least she had a certificate—and she's gotten through the bad times better than I would of thought."

"And it was because of her that Don visited Paradise Falls. And we met on a hayride. Oh, it was a silly time. He was a blind date and all. And I wore such braces on my teeth you wouldn't believe. In those days, though, I called them 'orthodonture,' on account of I thought the word wasn't so crude, la de da, tra la."

Lloyd Pilgrim exhaled. He chewed. "Don't lead Donald to expect too much."

171

"Pardon?"

"Don't lead Donald to expect too much," said Lloyd Pilgrim. "There's only . . . um, there's *limits,* you know?"

Barbara Sellers said nothing.

"The world is hard," said Lloyd Pilgrim.

Barbara Sellers sighed, plucked at her skirt.

Lloyd Pilgrim made several more trips to the front door, and stains from the tobacco juice spread in a semicircle out beyond the porch railing. Then Donald and Jim returned from the depot, and they had *seen a train,* and Donald went to the girl and hugged her, and he told her the train had been a grand sight, and he told her he would live forever. She hugged Donald, and her hands clawed at his upper arms, and old Lloyd Pilgrim watched them, and the layered forgotten laughter remained undisturbed, and he was only fortythree, and he could not understand why he was falling into the habit of thinking of himself as *old* Lloyd Pilgrim.

The Ambersons

It was a brilliant February afternoon, layered with mounded and untroubled snow, but Ohio US 33-A was scummy with ice, and so Amberson drove cautiously. But then he always drove cautiously. He always did just about everything cautiously. He was nearly fortyfour, and he was an English teacher and the track coach at Paradise Falls High School, and he didn't suppose he was the most exciting human being ever to have popped from the Mind of the Lord, but on the other hand whom had he ever really harmed? He and his wife, Anne, had been married nearly twenty years, and in that time he had been unfaithful to her just once, and she probably had been unfaithful to him never. She had given him two sons and a daughter, and there never had been any reason to question her. Even the thought of questioning her was enough to make Amberson shudder. His own rather sorry little infidelity had taken place in the summer of 1938 with his late brother's widow. There had been only the one occasion, and the woman had insisted that Amberson had performed an act of great generosity. Amberson was not so sure, however. Could lust be explained away that easily? He wished he knew. Oh, there were a great many things he wished he knew. Or perhaps "understood" was a better word. Hester Ridgely, for example. Here, on this brilliant February afternoon (it was a Saturday, and the year was 1941), Amberson and his wife were returning to Paradise Falls from a village called Hebron, where Hester Ridgely's funeral had been held that morning. Hester, a spinster, waxy of flesh, with a cluster of wens on her neck, had taught social science at Paradise Falls High School for thirtyseven years until her retirement in 1939. Amberson had been in charge of Hester's retirement party, and she had been presented with a lapel watch and a suitcase. She had wept, and she barely had been able to stutter out a sort of speech . . . a clutch and gabble of words having to do with her gratitude to all her fine friends on the faculty. Then she went to Hebron, which was not far from the Buckeye Lake amusement park. She spent the final two years of her life in Hebron—and it wasn't even two full years, in point of fact. She stayed with a younger sister, the fat and talkative widow of a man who for many years had been a mechanic in charge of keeping in repair the park's various rides . . . rollercoasters, ferris wheels, merrygorounds and the like. Hester's right lung collapsed a few months after she moved in with her sister, and then Hester suffered a number of strokes that incapacitated her to the extent that she was able to do little other than open and close her eyes and occasionally utter a

single dark and secret syllable, something on the order of
bluh or *ach*, something no one was able to understand. Amberson and his wife learned all this from the fat and talkative sister, who was happy to meet them, who told them Hester often had spoken warmly of them—*before* the strokes, of course. And the Ambersons smiled. And they thanked the woman for passing along the information. They both had liked Hester, even though she had been a classically traditional and sometimes wearisome old maid, and they wondered why the Lord had seen fit to put her through such a hellacious final ordeal. The funeral was attended by nine persons, and Hester was buried in a cemetery that was on a frozen little hill within sight of the Buckeye Lake rollercoaster. Now, in the car, as Amberson drove gingerly on the slick brick pavement of 33-A, his wife said: "It's as though Hester lived her entire life in a paper bag."

"That's a good way to put it," said Amberson. "A very good way."

"Are you as depressed about this as I am?"

"Yes," said Amberson.

"And it's not just that she's *dead*. It's that pitiful funeral. It's that sister of hers, that sister with the *mouth*. Can you imagine how it must have been for Hester at the end, paralyzed the way she was and unable to get away from all those *words*?"

"It could not have been pleasant," said Amberson.

"Those poor homely spinsters who come and go and nobody notices them . . . dear God . . . dear God . . . what did the faculty give her, a lapel watch and a suitcase?"

"Yes," said Amberson.

"I expect she never used the suitcase except for the trip to Hebron."

"I expect not," said Amberson.

Anne Amberson shook her head. "Well, as long as the

world is full of Hesters, I won't have to worry about you when you go to work. You're not about to be seduced, are you?"

". . . no."

"As long as they have wens and all."

". . . yes."

"As far as I can recall, about the only pretty teacher who comes to mind is that *flirt*, that *Regina Ingersoll*, and she went away a long time ago, didn't she?"

"Yes. She resigned in the summer of 'twentyeight."

"Oh? Really? Do you have the date memorized?"

Amberson shrugged.

"Was . . . hey, was there ever anything between you and her?"

". . . no."

"I don't like the way you said that. Something happened, didn't it? The way she went around *batting* her *lashes* at anything that was male. And *showing* her *knees*. She taught French, correct? Oh, I just *bet* she taught French. So please tell me what happened."

"Nothing happened," said Amberson.

"You don't sound very convincing."

"I'm sorry."

"Did you *want* something to happen? Did *she* want something to happen?"

"I don't believe so. Not really."

Anne Amberson glared at her husband. "What sort of answer is *that*?"

Amberson sighed. "All right," he said. "All *right*. Listen closely now to my grand confession. I believe the story is at least a little amusing. But I don't imagine you will." He hesitated. The car skidded a little. He sucked at his lips, held the wheel tightly, brought the car back under control. The tires crunched, and the Paradise County fields were heavy with the snow, heavy and severe, blank. Finally he said: "It was Halloween of 'twentyseven, and Fred Boyd gave a party. You were visiting your sister, remember?"

"No. I can't say as I do. But I'll take your word for it."

"Thank you. Just about all the faculty was there . . . Hester Ridgely . . . everybody . . . including that . . . that *vamp*, Regina Ingersoll."

"And something happened between the two of you?"

"In a sense. You see, we danced, and then we sat on a davenport, and we talked of this and that, and she told me she once had been married, but the marriage had been a disaster. The reason was that . . . ah, she and her husband . . . you see, he was too large for her. And so she finally got around to asking me. She finally did, yes indeed."

"Asking you? Asking you what?"

"The size of my penis," said Amberson.

"What?"

"She wondered whether perhaps we would be able to connect."

"What?"

"But nothing came of it. I wouldn't tell her. I was very suave and controlled."

"Why are you smiling?"

"Am I smiling? Well, if I am, remember—when you're smiling, the whole world smiles with you."

"Stop that!"

"Oh," said Amberson. "I apologize. But it all was such a long time ago, and Regina Ingersoll hasn't been heard from since June of 'twentyeight, so what difference does it all make?"

Anne Amberson was leaning forward, and she was gasping, but now her voice was under control. "I don't think it's funny at all. I think it's disgusting. But you were flattered, weren't you? You'll probably carry the memory of it to your grave, won't you?"

Amberson hesitated. Finally he said: "I suppose I will."

"It's outrageous," said Anne.

"It could have been worse," said Amberson.

"What?" said Anne.

"Hester Ridgely could have asked the question," said Amberson.

"*Hester Ridgely?*" said Anne.

"If *that* had happened, I wouldn't be here now. I would have expired of the shock. *Here Lies Howard W. Amberson, God Forgive Him.*"

"Very funny," said Anne.

"I hope so," said Amberson. He shrugged. He supposed Regina Ingersoll would never from now on exactly be his wife's favorite topic of conversation. He was correct. The Ambersons lived for more than thirty years after his Regina Ingersoll confession, and Anne Amberson never did laugh. Amberson, though, did at least smile. And there were times when a trace of what? nostalgic lust? drifted across his mind and perhaps his belly. He never was unhappy with the memory, and Regina Ingersoll flourished forever in his heart.

Don Pilgrim & Barbara Pilgrim

I was there in that hospital room when she died. It was the first day of August in the year 1974, and she was just fifty, and I sat at the foot of the bed, and I didn't say anything. She wasn't hearing anything anyway, so there really wasn't much sense for me to of spoken up. She wouldn't of heard a thing. I loved her. I still do. Hell, she was my Barbara, and she brought me to understand the taste of sweet things. I think about her a whole lot. Surely I do. I only been married twice, and she was my wife both times, and I swear to you: I'll kick the shit out of anyone who says I don't love her . . . even now, when all that's still standing of her is the memory of her.

It was her kidneys, and they sort of fell away, you know? A longdistance telephone call came from her sister Phoebe, the old maid, and Phoebe said: "Maybe it would be decent if you came to see her for one last time. Maybe she would recognize you. I mean, she always *has* talked about you. And she always *has* seemed to care. I don't know *why*, but maybe it's not my place to ask the question."

"That is probably correct," I said.

Phoebe hung up without saying anything else. Good old Phoebe.

I packed a grip and started the drive down to Paradise Falls. I live near a little place called LaBelle, which is in northwestern Ohio not far from the Indiana line. Paradise Falls is nearly catercornered across the state, and so the drive was more than two hundred miles. What with good weather and the interstates and all, I made the trip in less than three and a half hours, which was humping it, and no shit. A man my age shouldn't own a Mustang, but I do, and the goddamned thing goes like hell, and it doesn't guzzle as much gas as you might think.

I drove straight to the Paradise Valley Memorial Hospital, and I had to piss like you wouldn't believe. I couldn't even wait to get inside the hospital, and so I pissed right out there in the parking lot. I pissed against the left front tire of a '71 Mercury. Or at least I started to, but then I heard a sort of whistling. I looked around, and some guy was headed straight for me. He was sort of scratching himself and looking at the sky, and so I managed to zip up and stroll away. Sure enough, he got into the '71 Mercury. But he hadn't noticed the piss that was smeared on the tire, and he drove off. And I nonchalanted myself all the way into the hospital, where I stopped in a men's room and finished the business at hand.

Both of Barbara's sisters were in the room with her. Phoebe, the old maid (big tits, a heavy face), gave me a look that made me think maybe I had a dead fish hanging from my collar. The other sister, Rosemary Cross, was bawling. And so what else was new? Rosemary Cross bawled when a newspaper was torn, for Christ's sake. Her husband was hugging her. He was a milkman, and he didn't have much of a chin. Remember Andy Gump? Well, there was old Andy, but Rosemary had married him, and I think she loved him, and I think she still does. And I suppose *he* loves *her*. At least he puts up with her bawling. And you know, she wouldn't be a badlooking woman (big tits, blond hair, good skin) if she ever managed to shut off the waterworks.

Barbara was breathing with her mouth open. Her eyes were closed. She had been unhooked from the dialysis machine. I sat down. Rosemary came to me, and her tears spilled on my lap, and she told me it was only a matter of time. I nodded. She touched one of my hands and squeezed it. Again I nodded. I squeezed back. What the hell, the woman was a goddamned pain in the ass, but she meant no harm. I sat a little forward in my chair. Barbara and I had been exchanging letters ever since our second divorce, which had taken place two years earlier, and I knew she was more or less resigned to this fucking *thing*, this *death*, and she'd written to me of grief, of bafflement, of schemes and explanations that were *invisible*, you know? We had come down a long road together . . . and apart. We divorced once because she was crawling into bed with an asshole named Jack O'Connell, who was the worst fucking windbag and phony in Paradise County. We divorced the second time because, ah, Yours Truly ran out of gas. I went back to LaBelle, and I lived on my brother's dairy farm, and I built myself a big HO model railroad layout, and I called the whole shooting match Railroad City USA, and I charged admission, and I made a little money, and I *hurt*, and I thought a whole lot about her, and I loved her (and I still *do,* God damn it), but it wasn't enough. Which was why I'd left her in Paradise Falls. She'd wanted to go with me to LaBelle, to do anything I wanted to do, but there'd been no way. What do the doubledomes call it—attention span? Well, how come so many of us got attention spans that are so short they can't even last a lifetime? Jesus Christ. Shit. You think I don't feel sorry about what happened? You think I don't twist myself like a goddamned paper clip? Hell, I twist myself like beyond anything you've ever known, I expect. Barbara and I had three sons, and she could outfuck any six women I've ever known, and she always was *graceful,* you know? she always *moved well,* you know? she always had *this grin,* you know? she always *tried to make the best of things,* you know? But I finally left her for good, and on account of my trains, on account of I'd never had *shit* that had been *mine,* you know? Sharing is good. Love is good. But is it so bad just to take one thing and not share it with a goddamned soul? Some *dream* maybe? Some halfassed *notion*? Well, anyway, bad or not, it's what I chose to do, so we divorced the second time. But we did correspond. And I tried to make her understand what I saw as incompleteness. And she tried to make me understand pain. I've saved all her letters. And at the end, when for maybe a minute she was conscious and she was able to speak, maybe to us or maybe to God, and at the *very* end, when she looked at *me* and spoke her *very* last word, she was echoing a letter she'd written to me. The letter had used the word "*debris.*" I don't understand. Why "debris?" Oh sure, she was baffled. So am I. But she could of talked about the boys. Or she could of talked about apples, cats, kisses, the sky. But instead it was finally necessary that the finally necessary word finally necessarily had to be "de-

bris." So then what did all our years mean when *that* was
the word that came from her at the end? I mean, we *did*
laugh. The times in bed *were* good, and let the sky fall if I'm
lying. Does it all come down then on *me*? Did *I* knock down
the walls and rip out the floors and tear apart the furniture? Was I all *that* selfish when I went off to LaBelle that
last time and built my layout and sat over the trains like I
was the Great Lord Jehovah and wouldn't let her help me?
How come hardly any of us has enough space inside to take
care of all the things we're supposed to take care of? How
can we share and how can we be ourselves? How can we not
spread all this fucking *pain*? How come there is so much
bullshit? My father warned me about bullshit when I was a
boy. Jesus Christ. Shit. God damn it.

Oscar and Bobby, two of our boys, showed up, and they
kissed their mother. But they and Cross, the milkman, had
gone to the cafeteria for coffee when Barbara opened her
eyes and spoke for the last time. She looked at Phoebe, and
she looked at Rosemary, and she looked at me (I think), and
she said very clearly: "I . . . I mean, I've never even had a
chance to think of myself as being old. How come I'm being
torn down before I'm ready? I mean, isn't that enough to
baffle you right out of your pants?"

I tried not to look at her. I dug at my right thumbnail
with my left thumbnail.

But *she* looked at *me*.

My back was stiff, and finally, what the hell, *I* looked at
her.

Her lips drew back from her teeth. "Debris," she said.

I said nothing.

And she said nothing more. She looked at her sisters, and
that fucking Rosemary was howling, and even tough old
Phoebe was sniffling a little. Then Barbara looked at me
again. This time I did not look at her. The word had been
said, and the word was "debris," and it was the goddamned

181

last word, and no other words were necessary. I expect she died easily enough. I say this even though I don't know exactly when her breath stopped. All I did was sit there, and I don't recall that I blinked, and then Barbara wasn't blinking, and a doctor came in, and Oscar and Bobby came in, and Andy Gump Cross came in, and the doctor fussed over Barbara, and then he told us she was dead, and Rosemary whooped and carried on like the goddamned Martians had invaded. Barbara's mouth had fallen open. The doctor closed it, and he closed her eyes. *She'd* spoken to *me*, but *she* wouldn't of heard *me*. I really believe that. I have to. Otherwise, what sort of a man is it who would just sit there and say nothing? Later, when the men came from Zimmerman's Funeral Home, I recognized one of them. I'd pissed on the left front tire of his '71 Merc. I wanted to say to him: *Hey, asshole, I know something you don't know.* But I didn't say anything. He was young, and I supposed he was new. Otherwise, I surely would have remembered him. I figured he was fresh from some embalming school, just a kid from who knows where, trying to make a buck. I wanted to hug him, and God damn it, that is a fact. (Barbara had been ticklish, and we would giggle and thrash in bed. Her teeth had been crooked, but at the same time they had been sexy. She really *had* wanted to help me with the HO layout. But I wouldn't let her. Did I do the right thing? Jesus, I don't know! I don't! I don't! *How large can pain be?* Jesus! Jesus! Sexy buck teeth. Honest to God. She had kept the grape arbor trimmed, and she had been fond of ice cream. But she died seeing and saying "debris." Days, babies, love, voices, and it all comes to *debris*. Shit. Hey, could there of been something else she'd wanted to say to me at the end? Was that why she stared at me? If so, Jesus Christ, what could it of been? What's missing here? Who in the goddamned hell will answer for all of it?)

Tom Washburn & Harry McNiece

Tom Washburn walked into the *Journal-Democrat* offices after the paper had closed down for the night. But Harry McNiece, the editor, still was there. He was sitting loosely behind his desk. He was fifty, and Tom Washburn was thirty, and Tom Washburn went to him and said: "Stand up."

"Surely," said Harry McNiece, rising. "Yes. Yes. Yes. I will. Yes."

Tom Washburn hit Harry McNiece in the belly.

Gagging, Harry McNiece slumped to the floor. He shook his head. Finally, blinking, he looked up and said: "Yes. Yes. Yes. I will. Yes."

"She's gone," said Tom Washburn. He was speaking of his wife, Dottie. She and Harry NcNiece had been friends, maybe lovers. "She took the kids, all three of them, and she withdrew all our money from the bank, and she drove away in the Nova."

"Yes. Yes. Yes. I will. Yes."

"What?"

Harry McNiece nodded. "If Molly Bloom can be fucked," he said, "then surely I can be hit."

"What?"

"I need discipline," said Harry McNiece.

"Shit," said Tom Washburn. He pulled Harry McNiece upright, then slammed him down in his chair.

"Discipline," said Harry McNiece. "All my life I've needed discipline."

"What? *Discipline?* And who's *Molly?* I'm talking about

Dottie, you fucking sack of shit you. She's gone. She's taken all the kids."

Harry McNiece nodded.

"What'd she do? Leave *you* a note too?"

Again Harry McNiece nodded. "She . . . she left it here while I was out to lunch. The gist was that she was sorry . . . but there was a certain . . . inadequacy . . . "

Tom Washburn looked around for a chair. His eyes were warm, and his fist hurt, and there was an immense weariness in his knees, the backs of his legs; he felt knotted, thin of breath, and maybe his brains had been shoved off to one side. He found a swivel chair, pushed it next to where Harry McNiece was sitting, then flopped down. "She was fine until *you* came along. You and your *what?* your *ideas?* your *words?*"

"I was only trying to give her an . . . option . . . "

"And so you hurt her . . ."

"I suppose," said Harry McNiece. He belched. He covered his mouth. "Excuse me very much," he said, "but I've spent most of the afternoon over at the Sportsman's."

"No shit," said Tom Washburn. "You mean to tell me you're drunk? Well, how about that. I never would have guessed it."

"Yes . . . I am indeed drunk . . ."

"No *shit.*"

"I believe I detect . . . sarcasm . . ."

Tom Washburn exhaled. He glared at Harry McNiece, whose face was fat and blotted, whose belly hung over his belt, whose vest was undone and whose necktie had been pulled loose. "You really look like a fucking bargain," said Tom Washburn.

"Is . . . *nattiness* . . . required at a time like this? Would it . . . ah, would it please you . . . would it be, ah, better . . . if, ah, I toddled off to my place and . . . ah, took a shower and changed my clothes?"

Mystical Union

"Who's Molly?" said Tom Washburn.

"A character in a book," said Harry McNiece. "A very long book, and I don't think it would make much sense to you. So, ah, pay no attention to what I said."

"A *book*," said Tom Washburn. *"Shit."* He shuddered, shook his head. Harry McNiece had been stopping at the house for about a year, and Dottie had been feeding him peanut butter and jelly sandwiches and giving him milk to drink, and they had spoken to each other of *books*. Among other things. And all the time Tom Washburn had been working like a nigger . . . and *with* niggers . . . at the Paradise Falls Clay Products. He had found out about all this, and he had confronted Dottie with it, and in effect she had told him to go to hell. She had told him no, she would *not* stop feeding the peanut butter and jelly sandwiches to Harry McNiece; she would *not* stop giving Harry McNiece the milk to drink; she would *not* stop discussing *books* with him. And she had told Tom no, nothing *wrong* had taken place between her and Harry McNiece. And she had told Tom he had just better believe her, or she would move out and take the kids. And Tom had fallen apart, and he had wept, but Dottie had refused to back down. That had been in the summer, and now it was October, and a note was wadded in Tom's shirt pocket, and the note read:

Dear Tom — Harry and I have made two attempts at being lovers, but they haven't worked out too well. So he cannot be my choice. No matter how well he talks and how many good things he and I share, if he cannot satisfy me, then I am no woman. You, though, who CAN satisfy me (and surely you know that), cannot speak to me. So then what remains for me but to take the kids and go away? I love you. I also love Harry. But how in the name of God can I keep existing as though someone has dropped me into a folded umbrella? If I am trapped, then I must untrap myself. Please, I

beg you, don't try to track us down. There may be a time
when I return, but it has to be MY time, when my head is on
straight, when I'm comfortable with whatever my space is.
Do you know what space means? I don't mean OUTER space.
I don't mean Star Wars. I mean SPACE. Please try to understand.

Grunting, Tom pulled out the note, unwadded it, handed it
to McNiece.

McNiece read it and nodded.

Tom watched him.

McNiece reached inside his jacket and handed Tom
another note. "Mine is not so lengthy," said McNiece, "but
the statement is precisely the same." Now McNiece's voice
and words were calm, and he did not in the least appear to
be drunk. (His voice and words were so calm they almost
were hollow—the way computerized voices and words were
hollow.) The note to McNiece read:

> Dear Harry — As we both now know, the element we
> thought might be lacking is truly lacking. So I must leave
> you. I must leave Tom as well. I am taking the children, and
> I am truly sorry. Truly. Truly. Truly. There. Five trulys in
> one paragraph. So please believe me.

Tom looked at McNiece. "What happened? Couldn't you
get it up?"

"I could get it up," said McNiece, "but it just didn't *do* all
that much once it *was* up."

Tom began to shake. He made fists. He opened the fists.
He pressed his palms together. "We're talking about *my
wife*," he said, and his voice came unevenly. "We're talking
about *you* and my wife. Jesus. And we're talking about your
cock. Jesus Christ, I ought to . . . I ought to . . . cut it
off . . ."

McNiece shrugged, said nothing.

186

"You don't *care*, do you?" said Tom, hugging himself.

"Not a bit," said McNiece.

Tom began to cry. He unfolded his arms from around his chest. He pressed his palms against his eyes.

McNiece said something inaudible.

Tom's palms came away from his eyes. He blinked at McNiece. "She was a good wife until you came along, you sonofabitch. An old fart like you, and you see a piece of nice twitching twat, and her not yet thirty, and you fill her with bullshit, and now she's gone, and God damn you, I ought to . . ." Tom's voice fell apart, and he bent forward.

McNiece touched him on a shoulder.

"Why me?" said Tom.

"Maybe I should kill myself," said McNiece.

"What?"

"Maybe she's dead. Maybe she's had an accident. She and the children."

"Jesus . . ." said Tom, weeping.

"I wanted her, but there was more . . ."

". . . more?"

"The talk. Rhetoric. We would talk of music and trees and Edgar Allan Poe. And we would talk of Alma Mahler. Who also married Gropius the architect. Who also married Franz Werfel. Dottie had great respect for Alma Mahler. Great interest in Alma Mahler."

"Alma who?"

"Never mind," said McNiece. He stroked Tom's shoulder. "Alma Mahler was only part of it. I believe we also spoke of sealing wax. Pumpkins. Dreams."

Tom glared up at McNiece. "And *I* got no dreams?"

"I don't know," said McNiece. "You're the only one who knows that."

"I got *lots* of dreams. For her. For the kids. For myself. College. Vacations. Security."

McNiece said nothing. He continued to stroke Tom's

shoulder, and Tom let him. A few minutes later McNiece also was weeping. He then tried to embrace Tom, but Tom stood up and ran out of the office. McNiece killed himself three nights later, and Dottie came home four nights later. She had telephoned the *Journal-Democrat*, and she had been told of McNiece's suicide. Tom promised her there never would be a folded umbrella. She put the kids to bed, and she told him yes, yes, she knew all about it. She smiled, but her eyes were gummy. Tom stripped her, and he shoved her onto the bed, and he mounted her, and she was dry as sticks and paper and broken concrete. But he was enormous, and he didn't *give* a shit, and he flooded her, and so much for the sticks and the paper and the broken concrete, right?

MYSTICAL UNION

My father didn't believe in much of anything. That doesn't mean he wasn't a good man. Actually, he was a hell of a man. The only thing is, he put most of the world in one basket, and the label on that basket read BULLSHIT, and I wonder if maybe he was being a little too harsh. Myself, though, I guess I agree with him more than I don't agree with him. I went to Ohio University for a while, and maybe this'll shock you, but I never really had all that much use for what I suppose most people would call pure knowledge. Professors. Books. Diagrams. Logical progressions. The sky and the goddamned stars. I say the hell with the sky and the goddamned stars. I say let them be whatever they want to be. We can admire them, and we even can be a little scared of them, but that doesn't mean we have to let them grind us up. Whatever we are, we are. Small, big, whatever. So why bounce ourselves against things we can't control?

Mystical Union

Education and all that sort of stuff are terrific, as long as a person keeps them inside a scheme he can understand. I come from a place called LaBelle, Ohio, which is a wide spot in the road up in the northwestern corner of the state, not far from the Indiana line, and one day my father took me to the New York Central depot and showed me the tracks and the horizon, and he tried to put it in my mind that maybe if we all stopped trying to deal in things that are beyond us, well, maybe then we would appreciate what we have. I mean, life is the way we live it—and that's enough. The stars are fine. Hooray for the stars. But who in the name of Jesus Christ Almighty can explain a human being? Blood. Bones. Spirit. Heart. Gas. Maybe I'm crazy (what the hell, I suppose I ought to go take a long nap in a rubber sheet), but you know what I want out of *my* life? I want to know what *I* am. Which is why I divorced Barbara the second time, and if that's cruel, I'm sorry. You see, I never have given a damn about *Einstein's Theory,* and I never have given a damn about *Democrats* or *Republicans* or *Hitler* or *wars* or *politics* or *history* or any of *that* crap. And I never have cared squat about *concepts* or *abstractions* or all those damned *words* those professors at Ohio University kept trying to jam up our asses like knowledge was the great . . . I don't know . . . the great suppository of life. What I wanted really to know was whether I could take whatever it was I had and bring it in on one person, and maybe share the small things *human beings* share, *and never mind the stars,* then maybe I'd understand how come the electric particles or whatever it was that came to form Don Pilgrim caused him to get involved with Barbara, marrying her twice, meeting her on a goddamned dumb hayride in a place called Paradise Falls, Ohio, then meeting her again at a freshman mixer at Ohio U, passing through two and a half years of war and all the time *thinking* about her, *wondering* about her, wanting to *taste* her, running it all through his

189

mind and his balls how she would *be* when he finally got together with her on their wedding night. And then came September of '45, and he married her, and she was great. And he wasn't so bad himself. And there was love. And the lovers lived in Paradise Falls, where he worked in her old man's hardware store. But the love eventually wasn't enough. So she went to bed with an asshole named Jack O'Connell, and she divorced me. Then she divorced O'Connell because he couldn't get it up, because he'd always been a fucking phony windbag from the word Go. Then she wrote me a mess of letters, and the letters got the best of me (and memory got the best of me), and so I married her again. And the second time maybe it was better. But still, finally, it all gave out. I just plain got tired. I needed something else. Rest from all the aggravation. I don't know. Marriage is an oath, right? Well, the oath never changes, never becomes tired. But the people who take the oath do become tired. And all the time the oath is staying the same. Which means maybe people don't break oaths. Which means maybe oaths break people. I worked my ass off for her and the boys. The life of a hardware store isn't all that full of thrills, and I complained about it, but I never backed off, you know? When I said I'd do a thing, I did it. But finally, in the spring of '71, I sat in the kitchen with Barbara one evening, and we drank coffee, and I said to her: "We're both too tired."

She looked at me. She was fortyseven, and she was thin and perky, and I still thought of her as being pretty.

I had sort of rehearsed the words, and so I got them going. "Love . . . humor . . . shared days . . . look, the boys are grown, and I appreciate all the good times, but I just don't want to be married anymore . . ."

"I did it to you, and so now you're doing it to me," she said.

"You mean Jack O'Connell?" I said.

190

"Of course I do . . ." she said, and she was biting the edge of a hand. She was crying. Just like that. She was able to speak, but she *was* crying, and her tears came in maybe what you'd have to call a smear.

"Forget Jack O'Connell," I said. "Jack O'Connell was a goddamned clown. I'm not trying to get back at you. All I'm saying is that some people—you and me, for instance— aren't built for the long haul."

"I'll die without you," she said.

"Sure," I said. "And prunes'll grow in my nose. You're not about to die. God put you together with bricks and steel pins, and you know it."

"You're tired of me . . ." she said.

I stood up. I went to the refrigerator and banged a fist against the door of the goddamned thing. "I'm tired of this *life!*" I said. "Don't you understand?" I went around the table and I took her by the shoulders and pulled her to her feet, and she was crying louder now, and I hugged her, and finally I said: "God damn it, do you know what I want to do?" I kissed her hair. I said: "You know what I *really* want to do? I want to go back to LaBelle and build a railroad. How about that, huh? Lloyd has a barn that he's going to tear down, but he'd save it if I asked him, and I'd take it over and buy a whole lot of HO equipment and build me the finest layout in the state, and maybe I'd even charge admission, and maybe I'd call it Casey Jonesland or Railroad City USA. I've always loved trains. Good old trains. I mean, to put on one of those blue striped caps and sit at all the knobs and dials and watch the little trains and the crossing gates and press the whistle buttons and throw the switches . . . my God, now there is something that catches at my *blood*, you know? Yeah. It would be like I was God, you know?" I let go of her. I backed away maybe a step, maybe two steps. I don't know. It doesn't matter.

She pressed fists against her eyes.

I stood flatfooted. I said: "We're all entitled to dreams, aren't we? Gingerbread cottages. Bread crumbs. Yellow brick roads. Whatever. Maybe some are more ridiculous than others, but—"

Her fists came away from her eyes. "But where . . . where did all the good things go?"

"It's not a question of good things. It's a question of tiredness."

"I love you."

"I love you too," I said. "But I'm not talking about *love*. I'm talking about *tiredness*."

"And you want to play God with toy trains . . ."

"Yes," I said.

"And without me . . ."

"I have to do it by myself," I said.

"Why?"

"Because then I can concentrate on it," I said.

She came to me. She sort of clawed at my shirt, and then she leaned against me. She spoke carefully. "I could help you," she said. "I could take pipe cleaners and twist them so that they came out looking like little animals. Some plaster of paris, and presto, I'd make you a little sheep . . . or a chicken . . ."

"No," I said.

"That's cruel," she said.

"I suppose," I said.

"Please?" she said.

"No," I said.

It was May of 1972 when we were divorced for the second time. Now it's Christmas of '73, and she's come down with some sort of kidney trouble, and I don't suppose she'll last long. She is in Paradise Falls, and I am in LaBelle (and Railroad City USA is doing fine), and I want to visit her, but I don't. I can't see how anything would be served. What the hell else could be said? All that crap about sharing and electric particles? I think the best thing for us to do is stay put. Barbara and I were married the first time in an Episcopal ceremony, and here's a nice little quote for you. It comes from the *Book of Common Prayer,* and it says marriage is *an honourable estate, instituted of God, signifying unto us the mystical union that is between Christ and his Church.* End quote. The words that grab me are "mystical union." Mystical union. Oh, you bet. And it all sure mystifies the shit out of me. Barbara always yelled at me for saying things like that, but I just can't help what I feel. I mean, loving and getting along—the difference is bad enough, and the goddamned pain is bad enough. But then along comes tiredness. And a whole lot of sad flat remembered *BULL-SHIT.* And so here I am, and the little trains go around and around, and I am mystified, mystified, mystified.

JACK O'CONNELL & MISS EVANS

I am *spatted,* you see. Yes *indeed.* My creases can pierce an oak plank, and my pecker can beat an elephant to death—as perhaps you could attest, eh? My name is *Jack O'Connell,* and I am *thirty years of age,* and I am a graduate of Oberlin College, and would you like me to recite Byron for you? encapsulate the life of Ulysses S. Grant? argue either side of Malthus? analyze the London symphonies of F. J. Haydn? I am, you see, no vapid ninny, and I indeed feel sorry for you if you believe I am protesting too much. This is *1936* after all, and we possess too much psychological wisdom to be deceived by the rhetoric of windbags who protest too much. Therefore, if I *understand* the danger of excessive windbaggery, how can I *indulge* in the practice? The notion is patently absurd, wouldn't you say? I mean, look at me. See my teeth? Note the evenness? And note the firm thrust of my jaw? Oh yes, smile if you like. And if your mind wants to call me an ass, that is its privilege. Ah, but the catch is . . . I *understand* how absurd I might seem to some people. So it's not as though your mind's laughter never has been noted by me. But you see, it does not matter to me that there are those who misunderstand. As long as I smile, as long as I am properly *spatted* and as long as I am fully cognizant of *my* mind's powers of retention and invention, and as long as I know that the thrust of my personality gives me an impressive aspect, then I shall continue to be the person I am . . . a man of *confidence*, a man of *taste* and *feeling*, a man who recognizes no Depression. Ah, but wait, when I call myself a man of confidence, I do not mean to call myself a confidence man. You see, I am terribly aware of the subtleties of the language, and at all times I *exercise* my mind and force it to be *precise*. So when I say man of confidence, take it as "man of confidence" and not "confidence man." Would you like another drink, Miss Evans? Oh, we have plenty of scotch. To ask Jack O'Connell if he has enough scotch is akin to asking the Pope if he has enough incense. More ice? All right. Splendid. Here we are. I must say I am very pleased that you have come to my place, and I do hope you were not too scandalized when I spoke a little while back of my, ah, pecker. However, since our meeting *has* evolved into what I can only describe as a moment of intimacy, I assume you'll be able to bear with any occasional lapse of taste on my part. And surely twenty dollars does serve to ease much of your discomfort, doesn't it? In these times, how often can a young woman such as yourself earn twenty dollars in an evening? Our meeting surely was fortunate, wasn't it? I am, you see, quite lonely, and not everyone is as willing to hear me out as you have been. You apparently possess natural courtesy, don't you? Despite your, um, *profession*, there is more than a touch of breeding within you, isn't there? I admire breeding. Oh, not that *I* have all that much, but I have observed it in others. After all, one can hardly have attended Oberlin *without* observing it. But I do not want to mislead you. My antecedents are not grand. I was born and reared in the town of New Lexington, which is the seat of Perry County. My father, Thomas C., owned several coal mines, and they did more than tolerably well until '29. Within two years, though, my father had gone bankrupt, and two years ago he died of a bloodvessel ailment. My brother Patrick and I support our mother. Patrick, or "Pat," as nearly everyone calls him, remained in New Lexington, where he married a girl named Nancy McCoy, and they already have two children. I have been living here in Columbus since '31, and I always have been gainfully employed. I am an appliance salesman, you see. Oh, not that I want to spend *the rest of my life* as an appliance salesman, but Old Man Depression has forced us to make do with whatever we can find, isn't that so? Actually, though, things are looking up for me. I have been offered a position in a store in Paradise Falls. You know where Paradise Falls is? Oh, good. Well, at any rate, it has a store called Steinfelder's, and I shall be working at a higher commission, with a higher draw. Oh yes, a higher draw, which means money one can *draw* against *commissions*, if you grasp that. You do? Well, good for you. But understand please, I'll not be spending the rest of my life in Paradise Falls. If New Lexington wasn't large enough for me, then neither will be this Paradise Falls. Do you understand the nature of dreams and ambition? Do you understand the poetry that can suffuse the human spirit that is fulfilled? So therefore, because of that wish for a completeness in my life, I wear spats. And my teeth are splendid. And my jaw is firm. Not that Columbus has been any bed of the proverbial roses. Far from it. In the five years I have lived here, I have had my share of heartaches and disappointments. But I have remained *spatted*, you see, and I have unleashed my mighty pecker with happy regularity, and you'll never find *me* down in the dumps, and that is a guarantee. Was I down in the dumps back in the bedroom with you? I was *good*, wasn't I? You felt *reamed*, didn't you? *Reamed* and *creamed*, correct? I am no simple *customer*, am I? No *client* to be *serviced* as though I were a *Chevrolet*, correct? Surely, from the way you cried and carried on, there was some sort of emotional commitment, wasn't there? Oh, of course there was. Why do I insist on asking a question to which I already know the answer? So do not think of me as being defeated. Do not think of me as being—what was that? A little bit of a freshening, did you say? Of course. It would be my pleasure. Here now, a little scotchywotchy, a little ice, and we have built you a fine drink. No, please do not cover yourself. I enjoy the color of your nipples, Miss Evans. Where is the painter who could capture such a pinkness? Reubens would pass out from frustration. He favored women of generous proportions. Indeed he did. Ah. Such nipples. And the way your lovely pale throat works when you swallow your scotchywotchy . . . um, such a sensual pleasure I am given. And surely one such as myself deserves sensual pleasure, eh? When one is constantly *spatted*, when one strives so urgently, when one's smile and one's jaw are forever at the ready, is not that person occasionally entitled to relax? My father used to say to me: "Jack, if you keep looking at the bright side without seeing what the rest of life is all about, the chances are you'll burn out your eyeballs." I loved my father . . . surely I did . . . but I did not subscribe to his pessimism, and I *do* not subscribe to his pessimism, and I never *will*. It is imperative, especially these days, to face squarely into THE BRIGHT SIDE. They are three words that are written in capitals across the eye of my mind . . . THE BRIGHT SIDE. You and I, Miss Evans, surely up to now the world has little noted us, but does that mean we must accept *obscurity* as our ultimate and unalterable *lot?* I say *no!* I say let my rejection of obscurity *thunder* like *boulders* in a *cave!* I say—what? How's that? More scotch? Of course. Help yourself. I say we are *without limit!* I still strive, you see, to *sound my barbaric yawp* from the *rooftops of the world!* Whitman. A paraphrase. To apply poetry to the truths of the world . . . ah, how rewarding. So mark this, Miss Evans. Mark that one day the world will hear from John K. O'Connell. Mark that 1936 will not be forever. Mark that the future will explode for all of us like a fat tomato in the hot sun. Hello? Do you hear me? Yes? Well. Ah. Your grip, you see. Your grip on the glass. It seemed a trifle loose for a moment there. Are you feeling all right? Oh, good. I wouldn't want to think that I've *altogether* exhausted you. As a lover, I always have striven to be a gentleman and not a brute. It perhaps has something to do with my *spatted* nature, wouldn't you agree? My father said to me one day: "Jack, you probably could talk your way through a concrete wall." And I said to him: "Is that some sort of implied criticism?" And he said to me: "No indeed. It's only a sort of speculation, that's all." I have many times thought back on that little conversation with my father, and I do believe he was expressing a degree of envy. At any rate, *I* choose to interpret his remarks that way, and he isn't here to defend himself, is he? Ha! Ha! Ah, but he was a fine fellow, and Patrick and I were fortunate indeed, as was our mother. She crochets now. She occasionally speaks of Ireland. She writes me little notes. She uses an indelible pencil. She has faith in my ambition. She says to me: "Anything you think you are, fine, as long as it pleases you." Oh, Miss Evans, she is as good a woman as my father was a man. I am fortunate. Oh, I am lonely as well, but perhaps that is the price one must pay when one prepares for fate to intervene and point the finger. So then I do thank you—ah, Miss Evans? Miss . . . um, Miss Evans . . . your drink

197

. . . oh, don't worry about the carpet . . . it's not all that clean . . . come here . . . please try to stay awake . . . my pecker awaits . . . *what?* I beg your pardon? Did you say *sleep?* Do I understand that you're saying I'm some sort of—why, you bitch. You filthy fucking bitch. You whore. God damn you. Wake up. I said wake up. This is the most discourteous behavior I've ever . . . oh, you bitch you. Dirty. You . . . you *like* being cruel? Dear baby, don't fall asleep. Please? I'm sorry. I shouldn't have called you names. Please don't fall asleep. Please listen. Please. Please?

WIFE & MOTHER & ALL THAT STUFF

The words are pretty. The marriage words. But marriage isn't words. When a baby sucked at my breast, it wasn't sucking *words.* I mean, a marriage is, um, chemicals. Um, blood. Um, ways of talking and thinking. Oh, all right—so nothing I'm saying is all that new. But to some people it's never understood at all . . . the sort of people who look on marriage as some sort of what? social contract? something to do when you're twentyone or so and it's June and your pants are so hot you're afraid to sit down for fear of scorching the upholstery? But there's a lot more to marriage than, um, flaming underwear. Oh, not that I am such a deep thinker. God forbid. I always more or less have been a conventional person, and never mind my three marriages. But at least I have made an *effort,* do you know what I mean? And I say this even though I never really was much more than what my world told me to be. And that hurts. Which I admit. In all my life, I have loved only two men. One is my husband, Don. My *current* husband, I suppose I should say.

Mystical Union

This is 1960, and heaven knows what 1961 will bring, correct? But forget Don for a few seconds, okay? I want to discuss the other man I loved, and maybe I still do love him. His name is Howard W. Amberson, and he teaches English and coaches the track team at Paradise Falls High School. He is a persnickety little man, and he has a sort of precise way of talking that is. Sort. Of. Very. Deliberate. Like. He. Is. Biting. On. A. Wal. Nut. He was my English teacher in my senior year, which was 1942, and I suppose there were kids who laughed at him behind his back. And I suppose there are kids who still do laugh at him behind his back. But I don't believe there ever have been too many, and I know *I* never was one of them. I *loved* him. He seemed to be (and he probably still is) a *complete person*, as though he had himself all sorted out. And you know what he used to say to me? He used to say I had a gift for expression. Huh. I don't know where he got *that* idea, but anyway, he said to me: "Barbara, whatever you are never will come along again. Don't just let it slide." And of course his voice was calm and precise, as though maybe he were reciting a column of figures. But there was nothing *cold* in him. It was just his *way*, and maybe it had something to do with why I loved him. I always have been impressed with people who are precise. Don't ask me why I married Don (and *twice*, at that!), who is about as precise as mashed potatoes, but I expect Don is the exception that proves the rule. *Mr Amberson* , though . . . well, *Mr Amberson* made me feel *important*, and I knew he wasn't lying to me—on account of that would have been a betrayal of his precise nature. He believed in me, can you imagine such a thing? Why, he even had three of my class essays sent away to *National Scholastic* magazine, and *two* of them were *published*. One was about Nathan Hale, and the other was about our cat. And it was all very well and good, but I don't know . . . in those days it was more important that I took exercises to develop my chest. That was the way the world was, and that's the way the world *is*, correct? A girl has to develop her chest. If she has a good chest, she is *popular*, and she will find a *husband*, and what else is there? Yes. Yes. Chests. Yes. Chests and husbands. Yes. Chests and husbands and, oh *my* yes, babies. I loved Mr Amberson, but he was hollering down a rainbarrel, and so nothing came of my, harrumph, literary career. Instead, I conformed. I toed the good old line. Oh sure, I've been married three times, but then nobody's perfect, right? But anyway, husbands and babies. I want to discuss one husband and three babies. I want to discuss Don and the boys. In 1945, shortly after I was married, I read an article in *Redbook*, and that article said babies provided the cement that kept a marriage together. Well, Don thought it all was a lot of baloney, and we had I don't know how many arguments, but finally the babies came, three in three years, and they all were boys. First Donald Jr, born June 10, 1949. He was able to do fractions by the time he was five. Then Oscar, born October 9, 1950, and named after my father. Don never has liked the name. He says it makes Oscar seem like some sort of sissy dress designer. Fortunately, though, Oscar loves football, and he's bigger than all his playmates. And then finally, on December 1, 1951, Bobby came along. He is the handsome one. He isn't even quite nine years old yet, but already there isn't a little girl in Paradise Falls who hasn't swooned and just about wet her little panties over him. But the boys are all good boys, and Don and I are proud of them. Still, the thing about cement is it's not enough. The thing about cement is a person can get her feet stuck in it. Three boys in three years, and then, wowee, world, old Barbara was put to work for fair. Diapers. My God, diapers. Sandboxes. Swings. The time Oscar swallowed the turpentine, and we took him to the hospital in Lancaster, and the doctor said: "Oh no, ma'am, there's no way in the world this little fellow will live." But Oscar did live. How do you live with turpentine in you? Well, don't ask me. Ask Oscar. Huh. Well. And then our happy home always needed to be dusted. Still does, for that matter. Dusting and ironing. Sheets. I don't know why, but all my life I've *ironed sheets*. It's a waste of time, I know, but *some* people are brought up to *iron sheets*. Maybe it has something to do with a person's religion. I don't know. The washing machine. The vacuum cleaner. And then little boys. *(No, you can not burn Tommy Hungerford at the stake, young man, and you put down those matches this instant. and what's that in your other hand? That can, I mean. Lighter fluid? Oh, my God. My God.)* Little boys. *(What are you doing there with yourself? Shame on you. The devil will get you. You put your hands on yourself, you'll stick to yourself until the moon turns to peanut butter. Only bad people do that. Bad nasty little boys with minds that are like a cesspool and hands that have warts all over them.)* Little boys. My goodness, how come I was never told about all this? Little boys. Dear me. *(Oscar, why are you sticking Bobby's head in the toilet? What's the matter? Don't you like him? Get his head out of the toilet right this minute.)* Oh, and all the times I've shopped for groceries. The squeezings. The balancings and weighings. Crisco. Produce. Peach season, so we eat peach pies until we're spending half our days in the bathroom. I mean, for me peaches have an effect, and that's a fact. And they have the same effect on the rest of the family. And, hey, while we're discussing domestic life, how about leaves? Do you think my sainted husband, the King of the Hardware Store, ever rakes them? Fat chance. He is too *tired*. He *works* too hard. And after *all*, he has too many *screws* to count. So there I am, the glamorous Mrs Barbara Pilgrim, mother of three, raking away like someone's hired flunky. Raking the leaves and burning them. But then of course there *is* the odor. Thank the Lord for the odor. At least it gives me something to *breathe* while I do his work for him. The odor of leaves. High in the nose, correct? High in the nose while King Donald takes himself a nice snooze. Wonderful. Leaves and diapers. Cockie. Yech. Hang out the wash, Barbara. Tote that ironing board, Barbara. Dust the furniture, Barbara. Popsicles and pot roasts and eggs and milk and the annual Easter ham. Dishes. Clean, dirty. Dirty, clean. *Do* it, Barbara. *Clean* it, Barbara. *Lug* it, Barbara. *Discipline* them, Barbara. Think of how you're *cementing your marriage*, Barbara. Oh, my. Oh, *my*. The turpentine . . . Oscar, the poor dear, screamed and gagged, and he should have died, and I wiped wet sticky stuff from the corners of his mouth, and the doctor and old Don told me everything would be all right. Sure. Fine. But what did *they* know of the *juices*, of the *love*, of the *warmth*, of the way my flesh had been torn, of the way they had shaved me, of the way each time the doctors had been just like Don and this new doctor, the turpentine doctor, telling me nice and bland and smiling how everything would be all right. But I screamed anyway because I *hurt*, because when you're a kid no one says how large the pain will be, how long the days will be, how they know nothing at *Redbook*, how after a time no matter *how* it is, no matter *how* strong is whatever you feel, no matter *how* you . . . you . . . you *gut yourself* because of what you call love, it all begins to slow down. The days . . . oh, God . . . oh, my God . . . the *days* . . . the flat straight days of . . . irons . . . and formula . . . and Lincoln logs . . . flat and straight and dry . . . oh, yes. I mean, sidewalks and tea cozies and gossip and funerals and scoldings and Ritz crackers and lumber yards and the feel of a fresh cold slippery honeydew. Roofs. Aerials. You turn on the TV, and there's Uncle Miltie, which means it's Tuesday night, and good old Don is laughing away, laughing and scratching, drinking beer and sort of digging at his nose. And the marriage has been cemented. *Sure* the marriage has been cemented. You *betcha*. And mornings are like a sky dripping buttermilk. And pigs sing like canarybirds. And the hills are made of green cheese. And so all right. *All right.* Jack O'Connell came along. And we found a motel in Lancaster. And he read Byron to me. And eventually Don and I were divorced. And I learned the hard way (or maybe the soft way is a better way to say it) how empty and pathetic Jack really is. So Jack is gone, and I'm married to Don again, and it's not so bad. Don hasn't changed, and I still rake the leaves, and the boys make a lot of noise, but at least I know my limitations. The line exists, and I see it, and so I toe it. There are times when I want to call on Mr Amberson and apologize to him. But those times are not frequent, and I expect they'll become even less frequent. But none of this means I hate myself. Actually, if push came to shove, I think I would classify myself as a reasonably nice person. Not strong, you understand, but certainly reasonably nice.

OSCAR SELLERS

Oscar Sellers was born in 1890 in the Hocking County village of Orbiston, which in those days was a busy and filthy mining community. His father put him to work in the mines when he was twelve, and he ran away from home when he was thirteen. He was accompanied by his younger brother, Willie, who was eleven. Their father, who had been a widower since 1896, was fond of beating them with his belt, and finally one night . . . when the man was particularly drunk and his rage and grief had taken all the tightness out of his bones . . . the brothers attacked him front and rear, knocking him down, kicking him until he was senseless. They took all his money, which amounted to four dollars and change, and Oscar left behind a note that read:

> The next time we see you weal all bee daid & even then itll be too soon yr sons OSCAR & WILLIE.

The boys walked out of Orbiston, and they walked out of Hocking County, and a week later they were working in a livery stable in Paradise Falls. The livery stable was a great deal better than the mines had been, and no one beat them with a belt. They attended school when they could, and they slept on pallets near the horses. They changed their clothes and bathed when they could. The stinking warmth of the horses was comforting when the nights were cold. Oscar opened a savings account at the Paradise Valley Farmers' & Merchants' Bank in 1904, and both he and Willie contributed to it. By 1909 they had saved a thousand dollars, and they both were expert at taking care of the new motorcars, or machines, and they were acknowledged to be perhaps the best mechanics in the county. By then, most of the livery stable's business was given over to motorcars, and the owner, a Mr Fridley, had given the brothers several pay increases. Oscar and Willie had moved into two rooms over Dill's Saloon, and for amusement they drank, and now and again they visited old Irene Maxwell's notch parlor on Mineral Avenue. They did not know, though, whether they wanted to be motorcar mechanics all their lives. Oscar was especially uncertain about this. It was the dirt . . . the grease and the oil and all the rest of it . . . that bothered him. In 1910, or perhaps 1911, he got to thinking that perhaps Paradise Falls could use a new hardware store. He first spoke to Willie of this on a June day in 1911 when they journeyed back to Orbiston to attend their father's funeral. The old fellow had fallen into a rock quarry, smashing himself into a sort of porridge. Oscar and Willie whispered together as their father's coffin was being lowered into the earth, and Willie agreed that a hardware store seemed like a pretty good idea. That was the nice thing about Willie— he went along. In 1915, when Oscar and Willie had three thousand dollars in their savings account, they approached Leon D. Walls, president of the Paradise Valley Farmers' & Merchants' Bank, and Oscar told the man of their plans. Leon D. Walls smiled, and he told the brothers he admired their spunk. He allowed as how they were excellent risks, and in January of 1916 the Sellers Bros Hardware Store was opened on Main Street next to Steinfelder's Department Store. Oscar was drafted in 1917, and he suffered a shrapnel wound in his chest during the Argonne fighting. He also suffered a severe case of gonorrhea, but the mercury treatments were successful, even if they did hurt like hell. The girl's name had been Solange, and oh well, no man could expect to face all risks successfully. In early 1919, when Oscar came home, he discovered Willie had increased the store's profits almost by half, and he congratulated his brother, who grinned and told him shit, anyone who hadn't made money from the war was just plain goddamn unconscious. Willie was married later that year. The girl was heavy, but she knew how to laugh. Her name was Frieda Klopfer, and she and Willie drowned in 1920 when a sudden summer storm capsized their canoe on Paradise Lake. Oscar ordered an enormous tombstone for them, and under their names and dates he had the stonecutter inscribe the two words WE LAMENT. And Oscar said to himself: Good old Willie. And Oscar said to himself: Shit. He began spending sixteen and eighteen hours a day in the store . . . or at least until Kathleen Strawn came along. That was 1922, when he was thirtytwo and she was nineteen. She was fragile, and her chin was pointed, but her smile came so quickly it was as though all the teeth on this planet had simultaneously decided to bathe themselves in the sun. She told Oscar she couldn't bear it that he was so lonely, that he worked so hard. She told Oscar her parents cared as much for him as she did—in a different way, of course. And then she giggled, and she kissed him, and he wanted to burst, and so he and this Kathleen Strawn were married in April of 1923, which also was the month he paid off the last of the bank loan. Their first daughter, Barbara, was born in 1924. Their second daughter, Phoebe, was born in 1927. Their third daughter (and last child), Rosemary, was born in 1928. Oscar then groped through decades of tintinnabulations and the odors of powders and perfumes. His wife opened herself to him as often as he desired. The Depression came and went, and the store survived. Oscar drank beer and gained weight, and he became aware that he was having a bit of trouble with his breath. Barbara was his favorite daughter; she seemed to respond to things, to take note of the world. She often would speak to him of dogs and tea cozies and the Eastern Star and the sounds of locomotives. She reminded him a great deal of her mother; she would lean forward when she spoke; she would touch; she would project a sort of tumbling breathlessness in which the ends of words sometimes were gulped and therefore became unintelligible, but at the same time were lovely, soft, free of boredom or worldliness. Rosemary, on the other hand, never said a word from one day to the next. Or at least so it seemed. When she did make sounds, they usually had to do with weeping. She wept in church. She wept at the picture show. She wept when she stood before sunsets. She was tall and blond, splendidly bosomed, and her features were softer than her mother's or Barbara's or Phoebe's. Actually, if it weren't for the incompleteness that was revealed in all her weeping, she probably could have been more than simply conventionally pretty. She was seventeen when Barbara was married to a man named Don Pilgrim in 1945. She was herself married the following year . . . to a

206

young fellow named Durward Cross, who delivered milk. He was chinless, but he was the first young man to propose to her, and of course she married him. To have done anything else would have made her weep. Her father thought she was crazy, but he said nothing. He did not believe in interfering in other people's business, even if the other people were his daughters. As matters turned out, Rosemary and her chinless husband had five children, and they remained married forever. Oscar Sellers' middle daughter, Phoebe, never did marry, though. She borrowed money from her father and opened a place called the Astor Beauty Shop, and it did well, and she paid back every cent of the money, plus interest. She bought a house, and she filled the house with caged birds, and you never heard her complain. Oscar Sellers couldn't understand her, and neither could Kathleeen Sellers, and eventually they gave up trying. So Barbara it was for Oscar Sellers—and he also liked Barbara's husband, Don Pilgrim, who sometimes cussed too much but was goodhearted and willing to help operate the store. Oscar Sellers wanted Pilgrim eventually to take over the store, and at first everything was fine. And the young couple even gave Oscar Sellers three good rambunctious grandsons. But then something dry and tentative and uneasy lay down in front of Barbara and her husband, and they tripped over it. And Pilgrim lost his temper, telling Oscar Sellers the goddamn hardware business wasn't worth the powder to blow it up. And then Oscar Sellers found out Barbara was seeing a man named Jack O'Connell, who was an appliance salesman and who talked too much and who probably was full of shit up to his eyeballs. Oscar's wife, Kathleen, died of a stroke in early 1956. She was just fifty-three. Maybe it had something to do with Barbara's divorce. Kathleen was watering her indoor plants, and something exploded in her brain. Barbara divorced Pilgrim a little later that year. Then she married O'Connell, and Oscar took O'Connell to the Sportsman's Bar & Grill and laid it out that the sonofabitch would have to shape up. A great many beers were put away by Oscar and O'Connell, and O'Connell told Oscar everything would be just fine. But there was something blank and astonished behind O'Connell's eyes, and Oscar did not believe a word of what the man said. And that night, lying alone in bed (he did not like lying alone in bed; he did not like cold sheets; he did not like silence; he did not like closing his eyes and thinking of the pain a particular woman must have felt when her brain had exploded), Oscar Sellers allowed as how his daughter Barbara was a goddamned fool. But he said nothing to her. He did not believe in being pushy. She divorced O'Connell in '58, and Oscar never learned why. It probably was just as well. By that time his breath hurt, and he said to himself: Maybe it's something I caught when I was in the mines however many years ago that was . . . or maybe it's from the shrapnel . . . who knows? Barbara remarried Pilgrim later in '58, and Pilgrim returned to the store. Oscar died of emphysema in August of 1959, and Barbara was with him, and Pilgrim was with him, and Rosemary was with him, and Durward Cross was with him, and Phoebe was with him, and he saw Solange, and she was watering the indoor plants, and Willie was beating him with a belt, and the warmth of the horses made a person forget their stink, and now sound drained from Oscar Sellers, and now sight drained from Oscar Sellers, and only a sort of numbed regret remained, and then it also was gone. And then came embracings, and all the fine appropriate words were groaned and murmured, and on the tombstone of Oscar Sellers was inscribed the single awful massive lovely mighty word: FATHER.

Barbara O'Connell & Jack O'Connell

"Jesus Christ," said Jack O'Connell, "my hands are cold."

"I'm sorry," said his wife.

"It's *July*," said O'Connell, "and my *hands* are cold."

"Jack . . . dear Jack . . . oh my God . . . "

"July," said O'Connell, "and my hands are cold, and all I can think to do is swear. I'm supposed to be articulate, remember? That's one of the reasons you married me, isn't it? All my *talk*, right? Jack O'Connell and his *poetry*, right? *Blah blah blah*, right?"

". . . yes," said Barbara O'Connell.

O'Connell cupped his hands over his bare crotch. His teeth began to click.

She embraced him. "It'll be all right," she said. "We'll work at it, and it'll all be just fine. You just wait."

"No," said O'Connell. "All the blah blah has caught up to me."

"That's stupid," said Barbara O'Connell. "You've never had trouble before."

"The more I think about it, the worse it becomes. Do you understand that?

"Yes," said Barbara. "I think I can."

"It's like stage fright."

"You don't have to be afraid," said Barbara to her husband. "I'm not your enemy." She pressed her face against his chest. She was smallboned, fragile, with small high breasts, and her voice was breathy, ingenuous. She took one of his hands and she rubbed it against her belly and she said: "You kiss my belly well. You always kissed it well, and you still do. You are my friend, and I am your friend, and there is nothing we cannot do for one another . . ."

O'Connell's eyes were wide and white and dry. He was a large man, and he was an appliance salesman, and he had a reputation for arrogance. "The world should see me now," he said. "Jack O'Connell and his blah blah."

"What?"

"In case it has escaped your attention, there are those who think I am an overbearing horse's ass. Well, they should see me now . . . Mister Limp of 1957 . . ."

"Don't say that. You're only making it worse."

"There's no way in the world I can make it worse," said O'Connell. "This is really the ultimate irony for the bullshitting seducer, isn't it?"

Barbara changed the subject. "The *boys*," she said. "Maybe it's the boys. Maybe their presence inhibits you. Oscar *does* make a lot of commotion. He can't help it, but he does seem to keep stumbling into things." Barbara hesitated. She knew Jack didn't like to discuss her three sons by her first husband, but what on earth else could she do? She and Jack had been lovers for years before she'd divorced her first husband and married him, and he'd never had any difficulty *then*. He had read Byron to her. He had been sweet. He had indeed been eloquent.

"Please," said O'Connell. "Please let's not get into the boys and all that. I mean, I never even had them *pass across my mind* just now. I was thinking only of you, of your breasts, your . . . there . . . yes, right there . . . your belly . . . I mean, how easily and willingly you always lubricate for me . . . Jesus, Barbara, Jesus, how come, for a man who quoted *Byron* to you when he was courting you, all I can think of to say is *Jesus*? And how come my *hands* are so cold? What's happened to my *blood*? Are my sins freezing me to death?"

"Hush," said Barbara.

"No. No. I can't. I mean, *I love you,* and tonight . . . yes
. . . tonight all the signs were right, weren't they? We
even drank wine, didn't we? But not too *much.* Not to ex-
cess. Red wine and easy talk. Red *meat.* And I sat at the table, and felt myself *grow,* and it was as though right *then* I
could have done it. So why can't I do it *now*?"

"I love you. Please hush. Please."

"No," said O'Connell. He rubbed himself. "Look," he said.
"Look. Look. Look. Nothing. The proverbial act of trying to
get the proverbial blood from the proverbial turnip. Zero.
You ought to throw me over the side. You ought to make me
walk the plank."

". . . no."

"But you *will,* you know. You'll have to. What else can
you do? Stock up on bananas and candles?"

"Please don't talk that way," said Barbara, weeping.

O'Connell hugged her. He held her as closely as he could.
"I don't know what it is," he said. "We've seen so many people . . . the minister . . . that doctor in Columbus . . .
what's there left for us to do? call a meeting of the United
Nations? I mean . . . ah, my God, Barbara . . . what
are we supposed to *do*? kill ourselves over this thing?"

Barbara snuffled away the sound of her weeping. "Hush,"
she said. "Now, now." She lay partially on top of her husband. She reached down and touched his limp cock.

"No," said O'Connell.

"Yes," said Barbara.

"No . . . no . . . you know what you're doing?"

"What?"

"You're making my *feet* cold *too.* First my hands, now my
feet. Jesus, Barbara. Please. Oh, dear Christ."

"God," said Barbara, and she rolled off her husband. She
swallowed. She was wheezing. Her arms came up, and she
laced her fingers behind her neck, and she glared at the
ceiling. The wallpaper was decorated with Doric pillars,

and their significance was not lost on her. She was after all a *college graduate*, and she'd needed only three years instead of the usual four, and she'd almost made Phi Bet.

"A lover who doesn't love . . ." said O'Connell.

"You're my *husband*," said Barbara. "Something will *happen*." She glanced at O'Connell and smiled. This was the same smile she'd displayed for him when she'd believed the words. But now she no longer believed the words. A time comes. A certain specific corner falls away, and the object then is beyond repair. The wine and meat had been perfect. The conversation and the laughter had been beyond reproach. The boys all had been sent to their Aunt Phoebe's house. They loved their Aunt Phoebe, and they had been delighted. Aunt Phoebe's house was full of caged birds, and the boys enjoyed the sounds of the caged birds. Oh, everything had been most auspicious, but still that certain specific final corner had fallen away, and the shattered things now were too numerous, and so it was just as well that the structure be demolished. Barbara made a dry whistling noise through the openings between her teeth. She shrugged. O'Connell kissed one of her arms. He kissed one of her elbows. "Thank you," she said. "Thank you. That's very nice."

"All right," said O'Connell. "I'll keep trying."

"Of course," said Barbara. She made another dry whistling noise through the openings between her teeth. O'Connell had been a superb lover before their marriage. Her first husband, Don Pilgrim, had been too rough. But Jack . . . ah, that Jack . . .

"I love you so much," said O'Connell.

Barbara nodded. She and O'Connell were divorced in February of 1958, and she remarried her first husband in October of that year. There followed times of work and laughter and an ultimate awful pain. O'Connell died of an embolism in 1971. A year later Barbara divorced her first husband for the second time. There would appear to be as many final corners as there are days. She died in 1974, and she never understood a thing having to do with O'Connell's failure. Don Pilgrim was with her when she died. She looked directly at him when she spoke her final word. It was: "Debris." Then she felt her eyeballs fall away, and that was the end of her.

WORLD WAR IX

Donald Theodore Pilgrim and Barbara Eugenia Sellers were married in the Grace Episcopal Church, Paradise Falls, Ohio, the morning of Saturday, September 8, 1945. He was just discharged from the army, having served as an infantryman in the European Theater of Operations. His family's home was on a dairy farm near a place called La-Belle, which was up by the Indiana line, but he had agreed to come to Paradise Falls and work in a hardware store owned by his bride's father. The way Donald Theodore Pilgrim saw it, the life of a hardware store was superior to a life of cows. A week later, after a short honeymoon in French Lick, Indiana, the newlyweds had their first home-cooked breakfast together, and Barbara fixed him eggs, pancakes, sausage, juice and coffee. He told her she would turn him into a dirigible, but she smiled and said that never would happen. Then, embracing him and kissing him, she said: "We'll be different, won't we?"

"You betcha," said Don Pilgrim.

"And you don't *really* mind coming to Paradise Falls?"

"No."

"Your family is very nice, but I just couldn't live among all those cows . . . and that *mess* . . ."

"Okay. I understand."

"Thank you," said Barbara.

"Precious," said Don, "whatever *you* want, *I* want."

"We'll need to have lots of babies."

"Pardon?"

"Yes," said Barbara, smiling. "You'll work hard, and I'll be a good mother, and everything'll be fine. You'll see."

"Well, I'm not so—"

"I was reading in *Redbook* just the other day how children can cement a marriage. If we have little ones, how can we break apart? How could we be that cruel to them? Could you be that cruel?"

"I guess not, but I think maybe you and I have got to make it on our own."

"Well, the children will be part of us. I mean, it wouldn't really be proper if they had somebody else as their father, would it? I don't want to have to put an ad in the paper: 'Wanted, one breeding companion, preferably white, references required.'"

"That's not funny," said Don.

"It wasn't supposed to be," said Barbara.

The evening of Monday, April 8, 1946, the Pilgrims had a supper of wieners and mashed potatoes and sauerkraut. There had been rain all day, and Barbara had been caught in it, and it had made her hair an absolute disgrace. In addition, she was a little vexed with her husband.

He frowned at her. "What's wrong?" he said.

"What day is today?" said Barbara.

Don shrugged. "I don't know."

"It's our seventh monthaversary," said Barbara.

"Oh."

"Well, don't *faint* . . ."

"I'm sorry."

"You really ought to remember things like that. They're important to women."

"Well," said Don, "there was some sort of bollix at the store, and somehow we received four hundred axes."

"And that explains why you forgot our monthaversary?"

"I hope so. I mean, we got enough axes to chop down every tree in Paradise Falls and behead all the Democrats."

"I wouldn't be surprised," said Barbara.

Don frowned at his plate. He looked around. "How about some mayonnaise?"

"I will *not* give you *mayonnaise* on your *wieners*. It's not *good* for you."

"I like mayonnaise on my wieners," said Don. "Mayonnaise on a wiener is an old Pilgrim family custom. All my life I've had mayonnaise on my wieners. A wiener is nothing without mayonnaise on it."

"Fooey," said Barbara.

The Pilgrim family automobile was a ramshackle '38 Plymouth coupe. It was in such bad condition by early 1947 that Don was spending most of his free time working on it. He and Barbara discussed the subject at breakfast Sunday, February 16, 1947.

"We ought to get a new car," she said.

"We can't afford a new car," said Don.

"We could if you let Papa help with the payments."

Don glanced away and said: "Fuck Papa . . ."

"What did you say?"

"Nothing," said Don, speaking quickly. "Not a word. It's just that I don't want to hear about *Papa*. It's enough I got to work in his goddamned hardware store."

"When we were married, you said you wanted to. You said you preferred it over cows."

"Hell," said Don, "I'd prefer the Ohio State Penitentiary over cows."

The subject of children became paramount in the summer and fall of 1948, and one evening Barbara marched into the front room, where Don was listening to the radio, turned off the radio, seated herself on the sofa next to him and said: "One of these days we're going to have a baby."

"Yeah," said Don. "So we can *cement* the marriage."

"Right."

"Some woman I know told me all about it. She'd read an article in *Redbook*."

"That is correct," said Barbara.

"The pitterpatter of little feet. Giggles. Screams in the night. Puke on the rug. Sometimes I think Jim had the right idea. One keg of beer. One pickup truck. Boomo."

"Don't be morbid."

"Well, this hardware store life isn't exactly laying me low with its excitement. Do you know how many kinds of screws there are? Ah, never mind. Any minute now you'll accuse me of talking dirty. Sometimes I . . . ah, well, the thing is . . ."

"The thing is what?" said Barbara.

"The thing is . . . my God, how do we keep it from just sort of drying up? I mean, I love you . . . but your body . . . there's nothing about your body I don't know, and—"

Barbara slid back from her husband. "That's baloney, Mister Donald Pilgrim! There's a *lot* about my body you don't know! And there are *some* things you've *forgotten*! You hear that? *Forgotten!* I mean, like what was sweet and secret . . . well, it's sort of all slipped your mind . . . the first things . . . the first feelings . . ."

Don stood up. "What am I supposed to be? sixteen all my life?"

"Why not? And anyway, what are we talking about? an old car that is turned in because its wheels fell off and its *frammis* won't, um, *evacuate* anymore? Love isn't a thing that's *turned in*! I *love* you, Don!"

"Go ahead! Hum it! We can jitterbug to it!"

Barbara stood up. "And what about that fifty dollars?"

"What?"

"That chartered plane! A Piper Cub! You and a Piper Cub and an unscrewed urn, and out went your suitcase, tra la, like money didn't mean a thing to you!"

"Jim was my brother, and it was my fifty dollars!"

"Cape Cod! My Lord, he was crazy! And *you* were crazy *too!*"

Don was backed against a door. "Right! Crazy! I loved my brother, and so I was crazy!"

Barbara was backed against a piano bench. "Couldn't you have just scooped him out?"

"What?"

"Maybe with a spoon or something?"

"Oh my God!"

"Well, can't I even ask a civilized question?"

"*Civilized question?*" howled Don. Then he made fists. He forced down the level of his voice. "All right," he said, "I'll let that pass . . . but, ah, what's all this about sweetness? Don't you think I understand the sweetness? Of course I do. But what about . . . what about *bullshit*, Barbara? I've told you how my father took me to the LaBelle depot and spoke to me of bullshit, right? And maybe I sort of grinned at the time, but it all was *true*. I mean . . . screws . . . wrenches . . . *your* father and I doing an inventory of softball bats . . . *softball bats* . . . and catchers' mitts and fuses and nails and pliers and saws and even brooms . . . *brooms* . . . here I am, living a life up to my ass in *brooms* . . . and it was *my* choice . . . it was either *brooms* or *cow flop* and so I chose *brooms* . . . but I . . . well, I saw something at the edge of the brooms, the *life* of the brooms, something warm and loving, something that wouldn't be fussing at me because I like mayonnaise on my wieners and because I can't afford a new car every sixty days and because I spend fifty dollars on account of I love my brother and want to do what he wanted me to do. Look, I just—"

217

"Stop it!" screamed Barbara. "I don't want to hear a prose poem! I love you, God damn you! Is it all so difficult to understand?"

"Hey, the lady cussed!"

"You're goddamned right I did! And I'll do anything else to show you I love you!"

"Ah, get off my back!"

"I'm not *on* your back!"

"The hell you're not! Look, I've done what you wanted! We live here with the brooms and all! What more do you want me to do?"

"What?"

"You heard me!"

"I want a baby!" screamed Barbara, weeping.

"To *cement* the marriage?"

"Yes!"

"What if I get you some *real* cement instead? I can get it for you at cost! I happen to work in a hardware store!"

"That's not funny!"

"It wasn't supposed to be!"

That conversation took place the evening of Wednesday, October 20, 1948. Barbara Pilgrim gave birth to three sons in the next three years. As of 1978, the oldest, Donald Jr, was a journalist in Ottawa, where he had fled in 1970 to escape the Vietnam War. The second son, Oscar, was a high school football coach in Fort Wayne, Indiana. The youngest, Robert, was an ordained Episcopal priest.

PHOEBE SELLERS & MRS FRANKLIN

Phoebe Sellers was fifty in 1977. She never had married, but it wasn't as though she'd not had opportunities. Even at fifty, she knew there were men who would be only too happy to marry her, but at her age why should she take the bother? An occasional lover was enough for her. She lived alone in a house that was full of caged birds . . . canaries, parakeets, parrots . . . and they and the occasional lover gave her all the company she required. And *actually*, considering what she *did* for a *living*, she surely didn't need a lot of *talk* in her spare time. As owner and operator of the Astor Beauty Shop, she was absolutely *inundated* with talk, and so in her private time she needed really nothing more than the sounds of the caged birds. And she clucked at them. And she smiled. And she told them they didn't know how lucky they were. And her smile went away, and solemnly she spoke to them of cats. And they blinked at her. And they pecked. And they chattered. And she told them they were the Elect of the Lord.

One summer day she was trimming the hair of a Mrs Franklin, whose husband was the Paradise Falls postmaster, and she said: "I really don't mind at all." The statement came from nowhere; it simply exploded like a cheap balloon full of dry forgotten breath, and the explosion really wasn't that much of an explosion. Rather, it was a sort of tired grunt.

"Pardon?" said Mrs Franklin. She was perhaps forty, and she believed she resembled Julie Andrews, and so she always insisted that her hair be shaped to her skull and cheekbones.

"I'm sorry," said Phoebe. "I don't know what I meant."

"Which isn't like our Phoebe Sellers," said Mrs Franklin. "What?"

Mrs Franklin smiled. "Well, you're not exactly a *cringing butterfly*. There are a lot of us who admire you a great deal—do you know that?"

"Admire me?" said Phoebe. "Who admires me? Should I run for office? Is that what you're trying to say?"

"*No.* Now don't be *silly.* It's just that a lot of us old married . . . us old married *stickinthemuds* . . . well, we like your *style.* You don't really give a hoot about much of anything, do you?"

"I give a hoot about myself. I give a hoot about this business. And my nieces and my nephews."

"But *I'm* talking about *pressures,*" said Mrs Franklin.

"Pressures?"

"Marriage. Children. All the pressures we have to . . . ah, *confront* because we're told it's never right to be lonely . . ."

"But being *alone* doesn't mean a person has to be *lonely,*" said Phoebe.

"Oh," said Mrs Franklin.

"Remember my sister Barbara?"

"Of course I do."

"Well, she was married three times, and twice to the same man, but she maybe was the loneliest person I've ever known. She had three sons, and she spent all the good years of her life *handcuffed,* you know? And then the doctors came along, and they hooked her up to a dialysis machine, and then she was in the ground, and how much did she ever have? If we could bring her back, if we could tell her she could do it all over again, do you think she *would?* Do you think she would be *that* crazy?"

"Do *you* think all married women are like your sister?" said Mrs Franklin.

"I don't know," said Phoebe. "And I don't want to find out. All I do know is that Barbara never was all she could have been. Myself, maybe *I'm* not all *I* can be *either,* but at least I'm failing on my *own* terms. Barbara . . . oh, that Barbara . . . good grief, she could *laugh* . . . and she knew how to *write little things* . . . she, um, *valued breath,* you know? She always was *open to things,* you know? And so

220

she's fifty years old, and her kidneys give out, and she's been married three times, and at the end, when she is in the hospital, you know what her exact last word is? It's 'debris.' I am with her, and I hear it *very distinctly.* I mean, this is *Barbara* . . . Barbara and all her *laughter* . . . but at the very end nothing crosses her mind except some crazy picture of . . . *debris* . . ."

"Very nice," said Mrs Franklin.

"What?"

"My hair, I mean."

"Hair?"

"The way you're doing it," said Mrs Franklin, nodding toward a mirror. "The trim has such a nice balance."

"Oh."

"You're really very good at what you do."

"Thank you," said Phoebe.

"I didn't mean to interrupt."

"That's all right," said Phoebe.

Mrs Franklin hesitated. Then, staring straight ahead, she said: "That was a lie. It's just that enough is enough."

"What?"

"I didn't want to hear any more of it—talk of *debris*, I mean. Such a terrible word. Makes me think of wars and earthquakes."

"Yes. So then why did you bring it up?"

"Pardon?"

"*You* brought it all up, Charlene Franklin. You and your talk of *pressures*, of *married women*."

"Oh."

"If you didn't want to listen, you shouldn't have come pussyfooting around the subject in the first place."

"Yes. I expect you're right. I'm sorry."

"Sorry doesn't make it," said Phoebe.

"Pardon?"

"The whole world is sorry," said Phoebe. "If you don't want to hear what you don't want to hear, then don't open your mouth."

"Really, Phoebe, you don't have to be so . . ."

Phoebe carefully set her scissors on a counter. She walked around in front of Mrs Franklin. "I'm finished," she said. She frowned at Mrs Franklin's hair. "You look fine," she said. "You can go now. You can get the hell out of here, and I don't care if you ever come back." Phoebe's voice was measured and quiet. "I mean that, Charlene. I mean every word of it, and I don't want you thinking I'm going to change my mind."

There was no color in Mrs Franklin's face.

"Please go," said Phoebe. "There is no charge."

Mrs Franklin stood up.

Phoebe helped Mrs Franklin out of her smock, and Mrs Franklin was shaking. Mrs Franklin went out of the Astor Beauty Shop without looking back. Several women frowned at her. Phoebe managed to get through the rest of the day without any further ugliness. She stopped at Hoffmeyer's Restaurant for a dinner of chicken and peas and mashed potatoes and coffee and rice pudding. She walked home. She fed her caged birds, and she talked to them, and she said: "Oh yes, do make noise, make all the noise you like. But don't ask *me* for *truth*. But unless you *want* it. The next one who turns away from me, I'm going to fetch a knife and cut a throat. That will put an end to at least part of the commotion, won't it?" Then Phoebe sat alone at a front window. She sat alone. She sat. She sat and sat. She sat, and she rested a cheek against the pane. She sat, and she blinked at automobiles and listened to dogs. She sat, and after a time touched herself. She went to the telephone and called a man named Norman Starr. He was ten years younger than Phoebe, but he cared for her a great deal. He told her he would be right over. She thanked him. The caged birds squawked and sang. The caged birds beat their wings, ruffled themselves, pecked, strutted.

AL & THE LITTLE FELLOW

Maybe you don't know Willits. Hell, I don't expect hardly nobody knows Willits. If it wasn't for the Skunk Railroad, probably nobody outside fifty miles of Willits would know the place. But the Skunk Railroad has put Willits on the map—kind of, at least. I mean, the Skunk Railroad runs east from Fort Bragg to Willits, and in Willits it connects with the Southern Pacific. It's quite a tourist attraction, that old Skunk. It real name is California Western, and it was a logging railroad in the old days, bringing lumber from the Fort Bragg sawmill out to the rest of the world. Oh, there still is a freight train runs on the Skunk just about every night, but I don't imagine the tracks'd still be there if it wasn't for the tourists. Ah, great God Almighty, the tourists; I expect they come from all over the world so they can ride the hairpin turns and listen to the steam engine of the Super Skunk and look at the redwoods and think maybe of Paul Bunyan or whatever the hell it is tourists think of. Oh Jesus, flowered shirts. Cameras. Kids howling. In the summer, Willits is just about like your typical Disneyland whenever a Skunk train arrives, and the tourists fan out, and they look for film and postcards and maybe little varnished chunks of redwood that have WELCOME TO WILLITS CALIFORNIA & THE REDWOODS burned or stenciled on them. Oh sure, it's all a rip, but who cares? If people want to be ripped, who the hell has a right to stop them? Me, I stay out of the way. I am seventyfour years of age here in this month of September in the year 1977, and I

tend bar in a little joint I own right near the Skunk depot
and the place where the Skunk joins the SP, and I'll serve
you beer, and I'll serve you a shot with your beer, and I'll
serve you chili and onions that'll tear out the lining of your
belly, and I'll even serve you Polish sausage sandwiches, although there are them who have told me the goddamned
things ought to carry a warning from the Surgeon General
of the United States. But never mind the food. I want to tell
about a certain little fellow who was in my place a few days
ago. He was interesting—to me, anyway. He sure God was
more interesting than most of the trash I get for customers.
He was maybe five and a half feet tall, and he wore an old
gray suit that had narrow lapels. Most of his hair was gone,
and the little he had lay in strings, with a sort of reddish
tint. He was maybe fifty, maybe sixty. Hard to tell. He wore
a bow tie that was clipped on, and he had freckles, and his
teeth weren't good. He was carrying a cardboard suitcase
when he pushed open the door and came ambling in. The
Willits railroad depot also is the bus station, and he'd just
gotten off the southbound Greyhound, the San Francisco
express. He was grinning when he came in. Danny Easter
and his girlfriend, old Frieda Rule, were sitting in a booth,
and they were playing a Dolly Parton record on the juke-
box. Damn if I can remember which one it was. At my age,
everything sounds just about the same, you know? Well,
anyhow, the little fellow's *ears* just about *flapped* when he
heard the music, and the first thing he done was set down
the suitcase and start to dance. Honest to Christ, why
would I lie to you? The little sonofabitch *danced*, and his
hips went north and his ass went south, and he grinned at
me, and he grinned at Danny and Frieda, and finally Danny took his hands off Frieda's tits long enough to applaud.
And so did Frieda applaud. And so did I. What the hell, how
often is it that some goddamned Fred Astaire comes dancing into the Bear State Cafe in Willits, California? And so I

bought him his first drink, which was straight Old Crow, no chaser, ice on the side. He sucked ice as he drank, and he told me the bus had been too hot; something had gone wrong with the airconditioning. He said his name was Oliver, and he said he originally was from Ohio, and he told me he was a bookkeeper, and a damned good one. "I was up in Corvallis," he said, "and now I'm on my way to the City of the Golden Gate—there to seek further fame and fortune."

"Further?" I said, and maybe I grinned a little.

The little fellow snickered. "Further," he said. "I am a veteran of World War II, and I am a hero. I was a first lieutenant in the Marines, and I received two Bronze Stars, and I killed a whole lot of those dirty Japs, you know?"

"Good for you," I said.

"Do you remember that war?" he said.

"Sure I do," I said. "Indeedy. The war years I poured more liquor and beer than I ever have before or since."

"You think I'm a dancer *now*," he said. "You should of seen me *before the war*."

"How's that?" I said.

"There wasn't a girl in Paradise Falls who wouldn't have given her eye teeth to of danced with me," he said. "You know that talk about niggers having natural rhythm? Well, there hasn't been a nigger on the face of the earth who ever could of *held a candle* to the kid here." And he pointed a thumb at his chest, and he laughed, and his bow tie wobbled like a goddamned cork in the baby's bathwater. "Barbara Sellers was my favorite, but then she had to go and marry the wrong guy. She . . . hell, I don't know . . . I don't want to talk about it. I mean, what with all the years . . . old age . . . whatever . . . I mean, maybe she's dead by now, for all *I* know . . . oh, damn it all anyhow . . . the past . . . "

I nodded. "Us old farts maybe comb through the past too much," I said. I saw his glass already was empty. I poured him a good one, a double. Old Crow isn't all that popular in the Bear State Cafe, and so I can afford to be generous with it. I looked past him, and Danny was rubbing Frieda's tits again. I grinned at them and let go a tongue fart.

Frieda laughed. "What's the matter with you, Al? You got no respect for Love's Young Dream?" She was maybe forty, and Danny never would see fortyfive again, and she wore a white sweater and a black vinyl micromini, and her outfit maybe had been on sale the week before in the Army & Navy store in I don't know where, maybe Eureka.

Danny let go his own tongue fart, and then he and Frieda hugged, and it was like maybe they were kids in a barn.

I smiled at the little fellow. I said: "Whatever was real back then . . . well, it gets to be like Danny and Frieda over there. Sooner or later the floor sort of gives way."

The little fellow drank. He sucked ice. "Barbara and myself started kissing when we were twelve. And I taught her to dance. Which was like being taught the violin by old Heifetz. But then the war came, and she went off to one school, and I went off to another school, and finally I enlisted, and it got so a day without a dead Jap was like a day without sunshine, you know? Hey, where'd I come up with that—a TV commercial? Anita Bryant?"

"I believe so," I said.

"I don't hardly anymore know what's real," he said. "I mean, what's me and what's a TV commercial? Jesus, most of the Japs were too scared shitless to surrender. I think they'd been told we would cut off their balls. And you know, maybe we would of."

"I bet you remember it all real good, don't you?" I said.

"Yessir," he said. "Little Kenny Oliver, wouldn't hurt a fly, likes to dance, and he winds up being a Gyrene, rough as a cob. Surely is a peculiar world."

"Correct," I said.

"I think about her all the time," he said. "Even now. Even

226

after all these years. It's maybe why I keep moving around. If I move, things pass; they distract me, you know? I don't have to sort of *hold my breath*, you know?" Then a quick grin. "But I *am* a goddamned *bulldog* of a bookkeeper, and I got the references to prove it. Never a dissatisfied employer, and that's a fact." He finished his second drink. "The man at the station tells me there won't be another bus for the City of the Golden Gate for I believe he said seven hours. So I got a whole lot of time, right?"

"Right," I said.

He drank. Skunk trains came and went. Tourists marched along the sidewalks, but they all were the family trade, and none of them stopped in the Bear State Cafe. I looked outside and I saw flowered white shirts. The little fellow spoke of inflation. Danny and Frieda came to the bar, and the little fellow bought him a Coors' and her an Oly. The little fellow kept looking at his lapels, and he kept shooting his cuffs, and he kept adjusting his bow tie. From time to time he listened to the sounds of the tourists. The family trade. Americans. Patios and swimming pools. McDonald's. I think maybe Danny and Frieda and the little fellow and myself are the last survivors of a way of living that's been all chewed up, you know? The little fellow put away maybe a dozen drinks, but he didn't speak of his family. A man who rides the buses from here to there to the next place, the last thing he speaks of is his family, am I right? He was fine when the next bus came along, and he needed no help—with his suitcase or his balance or anything—when he crossed to the station. Danny and Frieda and me agreed his capacity was a fucking miracle. The Skunk Railroad, by the way, is called the Skunk Railroad because back in the '20s it had diesel cars that stunk so bad you could smell them coming before they were in view. I don't know why I bring that up. Maybe on account of there's so much in this goddamned *world* you can smell before it's in view.

227

Like throwing in the towel and the sponge and the kitchen sink and your balls, right?

DOTTIE WASHBURN & HARRY MCNIECE

"I suppose it all comes down to mutuality," he said.

"Mutuality?" said Dottie.

Harry nodded. His full name was Harry McNiece, and he was editor of the Paradise Falls *Journal-Democrat*, and he was fifty. "Of concern," he said.

"Mutuality of concern . . . " said Dottie.

"Does that sound too much like *Love of Life*?" said Harry.

"Of course not," said Dottie, "but I'm married, and —"

"And you're twentynine and I'm fifty?"

"Please stop harping on that."

"I have to. The years are there. I can feel them. Believe me, I can feel them. Every one of them. They're like boulders, you know?"

Dottie touched one of his hands. He was sitting across a kitchen table from her. It was her kitchen, and he had stopped by for a peanut butter and jelly sandwich and a glass of milk. He was a widower. He had no children, and he lived alone in a small gray frame house over on Meridian Avenue. He had been stopping at Dottie's place for perhaps a year. Her husband worked at the Paradise Falls Clay Products, and she had three children. She loved her husband, but perhaps she also loved Harry McNiece, and sometimes perhaps she was aware of boulders of her own.

Harry glanced down at the place where her hand was touching his. "Thank you."

"For what?"

"The hand," said Harry. "The touch. Jesus Christ, Dottie,

228

I love you, and you make the best goddamned peanut butter and jelly sandwiches between here and Zanesville, and . . . ah, shit . . ."

Dottie squeezed Harry's hand.

"God damn it," said Harry, and tears were squirting from the inside corners of his eyes, and they squirmed along the sides of his nose. He inhaled. He wiped at the tears with his free hand. He said: "I want something to happen, don't you . . . don't you understand? I mean, peanut butter and jelly sandwiches are fine, but how much of all this backing and filling can I . . . can I be expected to put up with?"

"I don't know," said Dottie.

"But we both understand years, don't we?"

"What?"

"Generations. Days. Time. Calendars. Reunions. Babies. Custom."

"What?" said Dottie. She figured she knew what he was trying to say, but perhaps it would be better if he spread it all out . . . for himself as well as for her.

"God damn it," said Harry. "I want to *touch* you."

"You already have."

"That's not what I mean."

"We talk," said Dottie. "And I'm touching you *now*. And there's a real connection. You read books. I read books. We discuss what we read. And our minds touch, don't they? Of all the people in town, you're the only one who makes me feel as though I'm in touch with more than Q-Tip swabs and the Welcome Wagon. I love you too, Harry, you turkey."

Harry's head moved from side to side. He said nothing. His eyes were out of focus. He was a large man, and his flesh was loose.

"Look at me," said Dottie.

Harry's head moved from side to side. Side to side.

" . . . please," said Dottie.

He sighed. He looked at her. "I don't suppose I'm much of

229

a man," he said. His eyes still were out of focus. "At my age, all this nakedness. I ought to have more wisdom . . . I ought to have more . . . control . . . "

"Hush," said Dottie.

Harry looked away from her.

"But what about *me?*" said Dottie.

Harry said nothing.

Dottie had known Harry McNiece for years. His wife had taught math at Paradise Falls High School. Dottie had known Harry McNiece the way one knows the milkman, or a checkout clerk in a supermarket. But then, about a year before, she had stopped in at the *Journal-Democrat* to place a classified ad having to do with some kittens she wanted to give up for adoption. Harry McNiece took the ad, and he smiled, and he told her she looked like a gift of heaven. It was a warm day, cloudless, coruscating, and she was wearing her bright yellow pants outfit. She was blond, with a square face and immense blue eyes, and she knew the bright pants outfit flattered her. She told Harry McNiece no one ever before had called her a gift of heaven, and she told him she always would be grateful to him. *He* told *her* great God, it was a newspaperman's duty to report the truth, and that was all he had spoken—the truth. Two days later he called her, and he told her he wanted to know whether the classified ad had brought results. But she knew better, and it wasn't long before he began stopping in for the peanut butter and jelly sandwiches. She would shoo the kids upstairs or into the front of the house, and she and Harry McNiece would discuss F. Scott Fitzgerald, or King Tut, or the symphonies of Gustav Mahler. So then came a love. Probably not the love she felt for her husband, but *something.* Yet now, looking at this flaccid and distraught Harry McNiece, she said: "What are we supposed to have—some sort of brief encounter? Did you ever see that old movie on television? Of course you did. Everyone has. Trevor Howard and Celia Johnson, right? Gentle and delicate, right? And at the end everyone weeps, right?"

Harry looked at her. "Yes," he said.

Dottie nodded.

Harry nudged at his eyes, but nothing was left of his tears. "Yes," he said, "I saw the movie. And everyone wept. Fine. I know that. Just like old Harry here before you, old Harry replete with a loving peanut butter and jelly sandwich, everyone wept. All right. All right. All right. Fine. So we weep for things that cannot be. But what about *moments*, Dottie? Brief encounters. Whatever. What about *right now*, Dottie? What the hell do you expect me to be, some kind of goddamned *stick* rolling across a dry sidewalk? *I love you.* What do you want me to do? Organize a *committee* that'll *certify* it?"

"And I love you too," said Dottie.

"That's not what I mean," said Harry.

"All right," said Dottie.

Harry withdrew his hand from under Dottie's. "What's that supposed to mean?"

"It means all right, the thing is under consideration."

"Really?"

"Really," said Dottie.

"So I'm supposed to wait?"

"Yes," said Dottie.

Harry nodded. He stood up. He said nothing.

Dottie glanced down at her fingernails. Several of them were frayed. She patted at her hair. She should have washed it this morning.

Harry let himself out the back door.

She watched him cross the yard, past the grape arbor and the sour cherry tree. She rubbed her tongue against the insides of her teeth. The kids were upstairs, and she heard them sing and yell and gurgle and stir as they awakened from their naps. She thought of boulders. She opened a hand and placed it against her belly. She said to herself: What am I doing? trying to press away a hurt? She exhaled. Her husband would be home in a few hours, and he would smell of bricks, and tonight the family would have wieners and beans for supper. She thought of Harry, and she thought of Gustav Mahler. Gustav Mahler's widow, Alma, had married Walter Gropius, the architect. And then she had married Franz Werfel, the writer. Good God, what a woman she must have been. Dottie closed her eyes. *She* was Alma Mahler Gropius Werfel, said Dottie to herself. And *me*, I'm Dottie Washburn, and my husband works for a brick and tile company. Now one of the kids was banging something on the upstairs floor. Perhaps it was a skateboard. Dottie opened her eyes. She thought of *moments*. She thought of *time*. She knew she would be dead for more time than the mind of the world was capable of imagining. The mind of the universe. The mind of everything. She supposed she was ridiculous. She supposed this place was ridiculous. But perhaps she had a small option. Foolish, yes. As anachronistic as a 1913 calendar, certainly. But there it stood, and the skateboard banged, and she supposed she would have to do something about the noise, and she ached.

DON PILGRIM & JIM PILGRIM

Don Pilgrim, who was home on furlough, sat in the family's '37 Hudson with Jim, who was the older of his two brothers. It was January of 1944, and last night a blizzard had smacked across the flat fields, and the morning sunlight made the fields whitely explosive, full of little shoots of speckled light. The car was parked next to the LaBelle,

Ohio, depot of the New York Central, and there were no
sounds other than the sound of its idling engine. Soon,
though, there would be a larger sound. A train would come
along. Trains always came along. This was the *main line* of
the New York Central, and it had *four tracks.* The *Twenti-
eth Century Limited* and all *sorts* of grand trains went
through LaBelle. Only one local a day in each direction
stopped there, but a person nonetheless had a glimpse of the
grand trains. Don had loved trains all his life. There were a
great many things he loved—including playing tag with his
mother, which always had astonished the other members of
the family. He knew he would be sent to Europe when his
furlough ended, and he supposed he would take part in the
Second Front invasion everyone was talking about, and
maybe he would be shot to death or blown up or whatever,
and maybe . . . yeah . . . he was feeling a little sorry for
himself. He smiled. He was sitting on the passenger's side.
The car swayed and rattled. Jim had kept the engine running so the heater would function and he and Don wouldn't
freeze to death. "Sure was a pisscutter of a storm," said
Jim. He was tall, and cords twitched in his cheeks. He had
been deferred because he was a farm worker. The Pilgrim
family had a large dairy spread . . . three hundred acres
. . . just outside LaBelle. Jim and Don's other brother,
Lloyd Junior, had chosen deferral. Don for some reason had
chosen to allow himself to be drafted. He had been attending Ohio University in Athens, and he had been taking
agriculture courses, and they had bored the living shit out
of him. He supposed he just wasn't cut out for farm life. He
supposed he just didn't give a good God damn about cows
and never would. He grinned, grimaced. The white reflected sunlight hurt his eyes. Again Jim spoke: "It's been a bad
winter so far. Worst I can remember. Cat froze to the sidewalk the other day."

"How's that?" said Don.

"You remember old Mrs Cutler over there on Toledo Street?"

"Surely," said Don.

"Well, she's got this orange cat, and the other day the damn thing got itself stuck to the sidewalk."

"And it *froze*? I mean, it *died*?"

"No. Hell, no. Mrs Cutler ran out of her house with a teapot full of hot water, and the hot water melted the ice. I expect the cat was ascared just about half to death, but I hear it wasn't hurt none. She scooped it up, pried it loose or whatever, and she wrapped it in a bath towel, and she fed it warm milk. I get all this from Frank Staggers, who got it from his wife, who got it from Mrs Cutler herself."

"Sounds like you're talking about the clap," said Don, grinning.

Jim snorted. The windshield was steamy. He swiped at it with a sleeve.

"You really do like her, don't you?" said Don. "And I don't mean Mrs Cutler."

"If you mean your Barbara, sure I do. I wouldn't of said so if I hadn't. None of us would of said so. We ain't the sort. You ought to know that."

Don nodded. He was engaged to a girl named Barbara Sellers, and he had brought her here to visit his family. She had attended Ohio University with him, and she lived in a place called Paradise Falls. Don had spent the first three of his seven furlough days with her and her parents in Paradise Falls. This was the second of the three furlough days they would be staying with his people. They had journeyed from Paradise Falls to LaBelle by train and bus and train again, and Barbara had been exhausted, but she had smiled for his family, and her talk had been breezy, and everyone apparently had liked her. He didn't suppose she was the most beautiful girl in the world (she was too skinny, and

her teeth were too prominent), but what the hell, since
when had anyone ever mistaken him for Robert Taylor? He
and Barbara had been brought together nearly four years
earlier by his widowed aunt Helen, who taught school in
Paradise Falls and had enlisted the aid of a woman named
Soeder in fixing up Don as Barbara's blind date on a YMCA
hayride. In 1942 he again encountered Barbara—at a Ohio
U freshman mixer. They were engaged shortly before he
was drafted in March of '43. If he didn't love her, then he
didn't love anybody, and he never would. She could taunt
him. She could snap her overbite at him. She could laugh at
him. But none of those things mattered. There were times
when she ran from him, when she howled at him and told
him he was a goof and a nincompoop, that he talked too
much and took too much for granted, that he was dumb old
Don the Cowman as opposed to Piers the Plowman. But
Don didn't give a shit about those times. All he knew was
that perhaps he had made a connection. He was not even
yet twenty, and there still were times when he cut himself
shaving, but connections were important to him. He figured
he never would know a hell of a lot about the universe or
God, but maybe someday he would know at least a little
about Barbara Sellers, who he hoped would be Barbara Pilgrim as soon as this goddamned war was over. (To be a man
was to understand limits, correct? Don's father, old Lloyd
Pilgrim, believed this. He had taken Don to this depot a few
years earlier and he had pointed to all the horizons and he
had spoken of bullshit, telling Don there was no escaping it,
and it existed everywhere just as fully as it existed in La-
Belle. But what had he really said? that there was only so
much we could attempt? that we were held back by humanness? that it forever narrowed our view of the world? that
bullshit—or frailty or whatever—was as common as air
and spit and there was no sense trying to push it away?
Which meant it all came down to limits, correct? Limits.

The edge of a flat earth. *Danger: Beware of Falling Off.)*

"I hope I do so good one of these days," said Jim.

"What?" said Don, blinking.

"I hope I get me a girl good as Barbara. A girl who laughs. Nothing like a girl who laughs, I always say. And she's got a real *sassy* laugh, you know that?"

"I surely do," said Don, grinning.

"The way she *marched* into the front room, and her smile just about melted the goddamned floorboards. I mean, she even made *Pop* grin. How many times you ever seen *him* grin? If you was to count them on your fingers, you'd have fingers left over, and you know it. But she sets down with him, and she pats him on a knee, and she tells him it's so cold she wouldn't be surprised if all the bulls has turned to steers, and old Pop, all of a sudden it's like he's swallowed a goddamned bale of hay, and maybe even with a pitchfork sticking out of it."

"Yes," said Don. "It surely was a sight."

"So don't worry about her and us. Everything's hunky-dory."

Don nodded. "I appreciate that." he said.

"So the thing you got to do now is watch out."

"What?"

"So you don't get yourself shot."

"Won't happen."

"Well, you take care."

"Yes sir," said Don to his brother. "That I will."

"We love you, God damn you," said Jim.

"Thank you," said Don. Then, after a hesitation: "I think."

Jim grinned a little. His corded cheeks twitched.

Don leaned forward, brushed steam from the windshield. He saw smoke. A train was coming from the west. He rolled down his window and leaned out. Cold air hit him like knives. The hog was a K3, a 4-6-2, and it was hauling mail cars, and it was moving real smart, like goose shit through a tin horn. Don knew all the hog—locomotive—designations, and he could describe a hog from a distance the way some people could describe birds. He decided to get out of the car. He said nothing to Jim. He hopped down from the '37 Hudson and slammed the door behind him, and he was aware that Jim was rolling up the window. He breathed with his mouth open, and his breath came all clouded, and it was sucked away. The train came, cacachucketa, cacachucketa, cacachucketa, and sure enough, the hog *was* a K3, and the drivewheels were awash in steam, *cacachucketa, cacachucketa, cacachucketa*, and there was one terrific ultimate blast of the whistle, and then the hog thundered past, and Don waved at the fireman, and the fireman waved at Don, and the mail cars thudded over the rail joints and the switches, *cacalucka, cacalucka, cacalucka*, and then the train was gone . . . the rods, the cocks, the wheels, the valves, gone in a clatter. Don's eyes were hot, and he watched the train vanish against his father's awful dreaded horizon, and he returned to the '37 Hudson, and he climbed inside, and he said: "I'll see that again."

"What?" said Jim.

"Everything," said Don. "There will be no dying for a while. I promise that."

"Hot damn," said Jim.

HANNAH BELLAMY

Maybe you remember my father. His name was Spaulding (Spud) Carr, and he pitched for the Giants and the Phillies and the Dodgers from 1916 through 1928. He was a lefthander, and I have talked with old men who batted against him, and they tell me he threw the best spitter around. When you hit the ball, it sounded like a rotten plum . . . or at least that's what the old men say. And I don't suppose they'd lie about it. I mean, why would they lie about it? Oh, I can understand why people lie, but not when there's nothing to be gained from it. Ah, well, anyhow, Papa was in the big leagues thirteen years, and he and Mama had just one child—Yours Truly, Hannah Annabel Carr, born August 11, 1922, in the good old City of Brotherly Love. I've always liked the ring of my first two names . . . Hannah Annabel . . . Hannah Annabel . . . and I even liked the way my name sounded when I married that bastard Luke Bellamy . . . Hannah Annabel Bellamy . . . Hannah Annabel Bellamy . . . like little silvery decorations on a sleigh, right? Merry Christmas, right? The bells of Hannah Annabel Bellamy. Bing. Bang. Bong. Tinkle. Tinkle. Dear me, such a name. Too bad Luke turned out to be such a shit. Oh, well. Into each life some shit must fall, right? But *anyhoo*, getting back for a sec to my origins, my father was the illustrious Spud Carr, who won 111 games and lost 134 in his perhaps less than brilliant career, and my mother was a little Michigan girl whose maiden name had been Frieda Haller. She and Papa were from a place called New Hamburg, which was down near the Ohio line. He didn't have fifteen cents to call his own when a sore arm ended his pitching days, but Mama's family was well fixed, and I spent my girlhood in relative comfort in good old New Hamburg. Mama's father was an undertaker, and he insisted Papa get an embalmer's license and help out. This just about killed Papa, but he didn't want to be beholden to Grandpa Haller, and so he lent a hand—if you'll pardon the expression. We lived over the funeral home, and I got so I didn't like Papa to touch me. I couldn't help it: I just *didn't*. I *tried* not to let it bother me, but I couldn't just behave as though all the fathers in the world had hands that stank of formaldehyde and God knows what all else. Mama died in 1936 after an ovarian cyst turned cancerous. She was embalmed by a man named Dillard, who was brought in from Monroe. Papa then began to drink, and he kept telling me I hated him. He kept asking me how *I* would like it if the world had judged *me* to be washed up at the age of thirtyfour. I tried to explain to him that there were more things in the world than baseball and whiskey. But he wouldn't listen. Luke Bellamy listened, though. He was a young embalmer Grandpa Haller had hired away from a place in Detroit. He was twentythree when he came to work for Grandpa Haller; he had a jaw that put me in mind of Dick Tracy, eyes that put me in mind of Mandrake the Magician, a mouth as juicy and kissy as Gable's, a body all compact and muscular and utterly without belly. Well, seeing as how I was sixteen at the time, I don't imagine that it'll come as any particular shock to you that he had little trouble getting into Yours Truly's bloomers and making off with her precious and previously untouched treasure. That was 1938, and our first time was on the floor under a stand in the room where the coffins were on display. Later he actually had the nerve to say that in the midst of death we had been in life . . . after a manner of speaking. But do you *know* something? *At the time* I *laughed.* I was little smileyfaced Hannah Annabel Carr, and I had had my fuel pump cleaned out for fair, and it had been the greatest thing since the invention of saltwater taffy, and my God, right then I would have laughed if a *dead troll* had been *nailed* to my *belly.* I mean, when it came to *silly,* the kid here knew no peer. A few weeks after this event, a man came out from one of the Toledo papers, and he and Papa spoke together for about half an hour. A few days later Papa received a clipping, and the headline read: WHERE ARE THEY NOW? And the first paragraph read: *Spaulding (Spud) Carr, the former spitballing lefty who*

once dazzled National League hitters with his masterful as-
sortment of breaking pitches, is now engaged in a less lively
profession than baseball. He makes his living as an under-
taker. And the story went on to make various puns and
wisecracks about Papa having been a livewire, about the
dead ball and the lively ball, et cetera, et cetera, and I'm
sure you can fill in the blank places. Papa became drunk as
soon as he read the story, and he remained drunk for four
days. It wasn't long afterward that he began to hallucinate,
and even when he was sober. He got to believing that he
was managing the New York Yankees, and he insisted everyone call him Marse Joe McCarthy. Again and again he
told us he was sorry he had to play Babe Dahlgren for Lou
Gehrig, but Lou's health really was bad. Still, the *rest* of the
team was doing fine, wasn't it? Rolfe, DiMaggio, Selkirk,
Crosetti, Dickey . . . ah, what a great bunch of fellows,
what a pleasure to manage them. Papa was sent to a state
hospital in the late summer of '39, and three years later he
died of some sort of congestion in his arteries. By that time,
as perhaps you might expect, I had long since married the
dreaded Luke Bellamy, and Grandpa Haller (who really
was fond of me; he claimed I made him smile) had loaned
Luke enough money to open a funeral home in a place
called LaBelle, which was down in Ohio just below the line.
By *that* time, the undertakers were calling themselves "funeral directors," and so I gave good old Luke the name of
Cecil—after Mr DeMille, of course, as in Cecil B. I told
Luke he ought to wear a beret and a scarf whenever he laid
someone out or arranged flowers or made sure everyone
signed the Condolence Register. He didn't think I was being
particularly funny, but then neither did I. You see, by that
time I didn't really think Luke was all that amusing. Oh, I
still enjoyed having my fuel pump cleaned out by him, but I
did *not* enjoy the fact that maybe half the female population of LaBelle enjoyed having *its* fuel pump cleaned out by

him. It's a wonder he got any sleep, and that's a fact
. . . what with all his corpses and all his women. Oh, sure,
I know—a stiff prick has no conscience. *But there is a limit
to everything.* Especially when five or six of those damned
women would telephone him every day. So finally what I
did was: I beat him up. In July of 1943 along came a very
warm evening, and the windows were open, and I was lying
alone in bed, and I was fanning myself with the hem of my
nightgown, and old Don Juan came in at about midnight
from one of his late house calls, and so what I did was: I
jumped out of bed and told him to put up his dukes. When
he didn't, I slugged him right on the button. Blam, down
went the Great Lover, just like that. Oh, he was in good
shape all right, but only for one activity. I hauled him to his
feet, and I threw a glass of water in his face, and I began
beating on him, and he didn't even have enough sense to
cover up. We were divorced in early '44, and he received a
commission with the army Graves Registration people, and
I haven't seen him since, and if I never see him again, it'll
be too soon. The funeral home went to me in the settlement,
and I sold it to a man named Bonds. I always had been a
good cook, and so I opened a little restaurant out on 20-B. It
did well, and I sold it at a good profit in '54. Then I bought
two hamburger stands, also out on 20-B, plus a little place
that later became the first Dip-O-Freez franchise in northwest Ohio. It was at about that time I met Don Pilgrim, who
had been living in a town called Paradise Falls but had divorced his wife and had moved back to his family's dairy
farm near LaBelle. There was no bullshit to Don. He told
me he was too old for bullshit. He told me I had a good body
on me, and he wanted it, but he was damned if he would indulge in a lot of dumb highschooly backing and filling. If *I*
wanted *him*, fine. If I didn't, okay, the clouds weren't about
to turn to stone. Well, that sort of direct approach had been
tried on me before (I mean, when a woman has been di-

vorced for thirteen years, *all* approaches have been tried on her . . . as long as she doesn't have pimples on her ass, warts on her tongue or seven ears), but there was something about the steady way Don looked at me that caused me to fall down and let him wreak his will. I own a splitlevel ranch out by the Purina mill and what are now known as the Conrail tracks, and he liked to lie with me and hold me and listen to the trains. He spoke to me of his father, and he even spoke to me of his kids and his former wife, and sometimes he just about cried. So, what the hell, it was no particular surprise to me when he returned to her in '58. That was that . . . or so I thought. But that *wasn't* that. He divorced her again—in '72. And again he returned to LaBelle, only this time he took an old barn and filled it with toy trains and opened an exhibit and called it Railroad City USA. And he and a nephew named Ralph ran the thing. And I helped out now and then. I had turned into nine miles of bad road, and that is the truth, but then Don was no bargain either, so it all wasn't so terrible. We both knew the truth of ourselves, and we were able to laugh about it, and so the nights in my splitlevel ranch were better than you might believe. There were . . . and are . . . china bunnies on the dresser. There was . . . and is . . . a framed photograph of the 1922 Philadelphia Phillies on the wall over the little mantel in the front room. My father is third from the left in the rear row. He is the one with the narrow face. Did I love Don Pilgrim? Well, he never really gave me any reason not to, and so I suppose that means I did. He was fiftytwo and I was fiftyfour when he died of a heart attack in the fall of 1976. Two years earlier, he had watched his former wife die. Nobody watched *him* die, though, since the great event took place in the men's room of a restaurant on the Indiana Toll Road. He had been in the act of buying a comb from a machine. He had a mess of relatives, and they all attended his funeral. He'd been laid out, by the way, in

the Bonds Funeral Home, which once had been the Bellamy
Funeral Home, where I'd lived with that godawful Luke.
Talk about your bread upon the waters. Well, *anyhoo*, it
was a smooth clear morning when Don was buried, and I
stood at the LaBelle Township Cemetery next to a woman
named Phoebe Sellers, who had come up from Paradise
Falls. I hadn't ever met her before that day, but we hugged
each other when the prayers were over. It turned out she
was a sister of the former wife. She told me he had been a
good sort of fellow. I agreed, and then we both bawled, and I
said goodbye to her. I looked up and saw a big black swoop
of Canadian geese. They were gray too, and they were very
large. I walked away as quickly as I could. No. You probably don't remember my father. You'd have to be real old,
correct?

BARBARA PILGRIM & KATHLEEN SELLERS

My last conversation with my mother took place the
morning of the day she died. That was in January of 1956,
and I was in the process of divorcing Don, and Mama and I
sat at her kitchen table, and we drank hot chocolate, and
my three little boys were running and whooping down in
the basement, and Mama smiled at me and said: "I wish I
knew what to say to you. I really do. But there's been nothing in my life that's—"
I shook my head. "Shush," I said. "Don and I just
. . . well, we just don't get along . . . and now with Jack
O'Connell in the picture, there's no sense . . . well, ah,
you know what I mean . . ."
"I suppose," said my mother. She was fiftythree years of
age, and her maiden name had been Kathleen Strawn. She

was small, and her chin was pointed, and she was thirteen years younger than my father. She had lots of teeth, same as I do, or at least she had lots of *large* teeth, same as I do, and she had a quick grin that displayed them very well. Now she presented me with that grin, and she said: "How does it feel to be sitting across a table from a woman who's living where she wants to live and doing what she wants to do?"

"Ah, what's that? Are you, ah, trying to rub it in—about Don and me, I mean?"

Quickly my mother frowned. "No," she said, "I wasn't talking about *that*. I'm sorry. I didn't mean for you to take it that way. All I was trying to say was . . . all I *am* trying to say is . . . *look* at me . . . how come I'm so lucky?"

"Lucky?"

"Yes," said Mama. "I really do love your father, you know. After all these years, I still can laugh at his old jokes, and I'm solemn when he wants me to be solemn, and there even are times when . . . well, you know . . ."

I smiled. "Please, Mama, no *confessions*."

"But it's a *nice* confession," said Mama. "Why, only the night before last we . . . well, we had a very good time."

"*Shush*," I said. I still was smiling.

Mama's hair was gray and fine. She patted at it. She was wearing a blue dress and a white apron. The kitchen and the dining room abounded with potted plants, potted ferns, indoor vines (the sort that trailed from enormous old cast-iron stands). Mama often had told me she liked to breathe the odor of the plants and the ferns and the vines, especially at *this* time of the year, what with the cold and the snow and all. And now she said: "It's all like my plants. My ferns and vines and whatever."

"What?" I said.

"When your father and I . . . *touch*, it means we're alive, same as seeing the green of the plants and the ferns and the vines means *they're* alive. Nothing like being alive, I always say."

"I agree," I said. "Well put."

"Now, *Barbara*," said Mama.

"Sorry," I said.

"Drink your chocolate."

"Yes ma'am," I said. I lowered my eyes with what I hoped was enormous contrition. I drank my chocolate. I giggled. I was thinking of my mother and my father. I was trying to picture whatever it was they *did*. I suppose all children do that sort of wondering about their parents, and I suppose I was a little embarrassed. Finally I looked up at Mama and said: "I'd be surprised, wouldn't I?"

"Surprised at what?" said Mama.

"At whatever it is you and Papa do," I said.

Mama grinned. "You are a *caution*," she said.

"*I'm* a caution?" I said. "Well, *I'm* not the one who's *bragging* . . . "

"We should talk about something else," said Mama. "My green things. This is Tuesday, which means they'll get a good watering. In the wintertime, what with this gas heat, there's hardly any humidity *at all*, do you know that? Which means I have to make sure everything gets its drink."

I looked around. "Hey, plants and things!" I hollered. "The drinks are on the house!"

"Absolutely," said my mother.

Then we were silent for a time. We sipped at our chocolate, I thought of Don, the man I was divorcing. I thought of Jack, the man with whom I had been sleeping. There was a motel in Lancaster, and Jack read poetry to me when we went there. Or at last *some* of the time he read poetry to me. I supposed I loved Jack, even though I would miss Don. Oh, Don swore too much, and sometimes he made jokes when nothing really was funny, but he had been a good father to the boys, and he had done well in his job at my father's hardware store. Now, though, Don was in the process of returning to his family's home, which was in a little farming community called LaBelle, away up in the northwestern part of the state. And I knew I would miss him. Oh, he could be insensitive, and he seemed to have no *idea* how remorselessly routined our life together had become, but he was not a *bad* man, and there were times . . . really, and never mind Jack . . . that I wished Don and I had been able to come to an understanding. But that sort of thing requires a great deal more than a mousily vague and vaporous *wishing*, and I never really passed that stage. Jack kept getting in the way . . . Jack with his mouth and his hands and his poetry.

It was my mother who finally spoke. "In my day," she said, "I expect things weren't so complicated."

"Maybe they weren't," I said.

"All I knew was I loved your father," said Mama, "and it didn't matter a speck that he was thirtythree and I was twenty when we were married. That was 1923, and in 1923 you said a thing straight out, and that was the end of it. I told your father I couldn't bear it that he was so lonely, that he worked so hard. I called him Old Sobersides, and I really *did* hint that I wanted to marry him. You see, that sobersided Oscar Sellers was—and is—a man of, um, *strength*. I'm lucky to have him for a husband, and you're lucky to have him for a father, do you know that?"

"Yes."

"The world went away from me," said Mama.

"What?"

"*It* got complicated, but *I* stayed the same. Wars. Atom bombs. All of it. Nearly thirtythree years. Lindbergh. A third of a century. Roosevelt. Frank Sinatra. How many days? ah, ten thousand? something like that, correct? And we *know* a whole lot more, don't we? Or at least maybe *you* do, and at least maybe *Jack O'Connell* does. But as for myself, I think I'm more or less the same girl I was when I was Kathleen Strawn and I saw that quiet sobersided Oscar Sellers and it didn't matter how old he was on account of I wanted to marry him anyway. Which I did. And since that time so many changes have come, but not inside *me*, do you understand?"

"Yes."

"I hope this time it's right for you."

"Thank you. Jack is a good man."

"I hope so."

"He believes in heart and imagination. They're probably his two favorite words."

"That's fine," said Mama. She finished the last of her hot chocolate. Then: "A person who has a good marriage . . . will we get to a point where that person stands out in a crowd?"

I said nothing.

"Is maybe all our new knowledge about the wrong things?"

". . . maybe," I said.

"That's too bad," said Mama.

I gathered up the boys a few minutes later. Mama kissed them all, and she helped me buckle their galoshes and wrap them in their coats and scarves. The boys and I walked home, and there was snow, and the boys laughed and sprawled. They did not *walk* with me as much as they *ran* and *lurched.* Don had bought a used car, and it was parked at the front curb. The family car had been awarded to me in the settlement. A small trailer was attached to Don's car. He was loading the trailer with boxes of his clothing and his papers and his books and I don't know what all else. The boys clustered around him, and he laughed with them, but he said nothing to me. I shooed the boys inside the house. Don went in and out several more times, fetching the last of the boxes. He stowed them securely in the trailer, then covered them with a small tarpaulin. He came into the house and told me he would be stopping at my mother's place to say goodbye, and then he would be on his way back to La-Belle. He spoke flatly. I said nothing. He telephoned me about ten minutes later. Mama had collapsed and died while watering her green things. A stroke, the doctor said. I wept at her funeral, but I was not sure why, or for whom.

BLAH & BLAH & BLAH

The Soeder name is not an insignificant one in Paradise County, and so there was a sight of comment after the elderly Mrs Louise Soeder, widow of Hans Soeder, a grain merchant, died in the Paradise Valley Memorial Hospital early in the morning of October 6, 1977, a cold and damp Thursday. Mrs Soeder had been born Louise Henrietta McClatchy on April 23, 1894, which made her eightythree at the time of her death. She had suffered for years from a nervous disorder that somehow had loosened her bones, causing her to wobble and shake, but the primary cause of her death was listed as heart failure. Later that day, while sitting in cushioned rockers in the Paradise View Nursing Home, Mrs Soeder's three closest friends discussed her death. They all were elderly widows, and their names were Henshaw, Martin and Hamner. And Mrs Martin said: "*Heart failure?* What sort of a cause is *that?* Why, *everybody* dies of *heart failure,* for heaven's sake . . ."

And Mrs Henshaw said: "At her age, does it really make all that much difference? She just *stopped,* and I expect that's all really needs to be said about the thing."

And Mrs Hamner said: "And at least *her* children let her stay in her own house until just about the end. We ought to envy her, you know that?"

And Mrs Martin said: "No."

And Mrs Hamner said: "What?"

And Mrs Martin said: "I treasure every day. Even now. Even though the girls have to help me on and off the potty. I mean, look out the window there. Look at the golds. And think back on the mists from this morning. Oh, the golds and the browns and the reds. I don't mind this. I mean, better this than nothing."

And Mrs Hamner said: "Oh."

And Mrs Martin said: "The girls are very good at helping me on and off the potty. Oh, I *know* it's their *job* and all, but *still* . . ."

And Mrs Hamner said: "But that doesn't mean I have to like the *name* of this place, does it? At our age, to be sitting in a place called *Paradise View*. I mean, *really*."

And Mrs Henshaw said: "Well, at least it's optimistic. It could just as well be called Devil's View, you know."

And Mrs Martin said: "Today is Thursday, isn't it?"

And Mrs Henshaw said: "All day."

And Mrs Martin said: "That means baked apple for dessert tonight, doesn't it?"

And Mrs Henshaw said: "Yes. And in two more days our children will come out to see us. It'll be Saturday, and this morning on the *Today* show that fellow Lew Wood gave a longrange forecast that seemed to indicate our part of the world just might be clear."

And Mrs Hamner said: "Lew who?"

And Mrs Henshaw said: "Stop that, Bernice. You sound like an owl. Or somebody trying to cry."

And Mrs Martin said: "I remember a song; it had something to do with boo hoo, how much I love you. Something like that."

And Mrs Hamner said: "Well, all I was trying to *say* was that I wouldn't know Eleanor's precious Lew Whatshisname if he kissed me with rosy lips. I never watch the *Today* show. I need my beauty sleep."

And Mrs Martin said: "Which is why you miss so many breakfasts?"

And Mrs Hamner said: "Yes. I'm not all that fond of Special K. If I want to eat wet wallpaper, I'll buy it myself so at least I'll get the *color* I want."

And Mrs Henshaw said: "Bernice, I swear, you always have been a scandal, and you always will be."

And Mrs Hamner said: "I'm taking that as a compliment."

And Mrs Henshaw said: "It was meant as one."

And Mrs Martin said: "Poor Louise. Ah, but, well, at least now she knows the answer. To whatever lies Beyond, I mean."

And Mrs Hamner said: "Let's not talk about Beyond. Not *today*. Most days, fine, whenever you bring up Beyond, I don't mind a bit. We have nice discussions, and I enjoy them. But we were too close to Louise, and I . . . and I . . ."

And Mrs Martin said: "I'm sorry, Bernice. I didn't mean to make you cry."

And Mrs Henshaw said: "Bernice . . . Bernice . . . *there* . . ."

And Mrs Hamner said: "Yes. All. All right. I'm. Ah. I'm sorry."

And Mrs Martin said: "We have to be brave. How much else is left to us? Baked apples? Our *children?* Tell me, how can we call them children anymore? My Charlotte is *sixty*, and her husband, that Wes Izor, he's sixty*two* if he's a *day*. And he *looks* older than the hills out beyond your grandma's outhouse . . ."

And Mrs Henshaw said: "But what else do we have if we don't have our children? I mean, so all right, maybe we've stuck them in time, and we don't see them as old as they really are, but is that such a terrible sin? What else *is* there for us?"

And Mrs Hamner said: "I don't like it when the conversation gets like this. Please stop."

And Mrs Henshaw said: "All right. I'm sorry."

And Mrs Martin said: "We ought to be talking about *Louise* anyway. I expect she was a little too bossy, and I never did care much for the way she brewed a pot of tea . . . too strong and *then* some. And I expect she boasted too much on her *precious* and *perfect* sons, what with the one being in the Legislature and the other being a Lutheran minister, whoop de do and tra la, and she was no better than the rest of us when it came to gossiping, and she wore the most *awful* and *jimmied* Eastern Star formal gowns, and myself I never much liked her heliotrope or whatever it was she always absolutely *splashed* on her neck and her bosom. But what the heck, are any of those things all that terrible?"

And Mrs Hamner said: "But what about that Phil Cooper?"

And Mrs Martin said: "*Phil Cooper?* Why, that was a good forty years ago, and Hans already was dead, and so what if Phil Cooper did call on her. She was a healthy woman. And Phil never was all as wicked as most people made him out to be."

And Mrs Hamner said: "*Phil?* Did you call him *Phil?* Sounds mighty familiar to me."

And Mrs Martin said: "Well . . ."

And Mrs Hamner said: "*What?*"

And Mrs Martin said: "Louise wasn't the only widow in town in those days."

And Mrs Henshaw said: "And you always were prettier than she was."

And Mrs Martin said: "Thank you."

And Mrs Hamner said: "Why, Providence Martin, *I'm* not the scandal at all. *You* are. You and *Phil Cooper* . . . well, I never would have *imagined* . . ."

251

And Mrs Martin said: "Louise was sort of young and sort of pretty, but I was sort of younger and sort of prettier . . . and so . . . well, he was polite and considerate, and we danced in the front room after the kids had been put to bed . . . the radio . . . Russ Columbo . . . Ben Bernie . . . I don't know who all . . . and he never hurt me, and nothing was promised . . . and . . . oh, dear . . ."

And Mrs Henshaw said: "Good for you, Providence."

And Mrs Hamner said: "I give you credit."

And Mrs Martin said: "You *do?*"

And Mrs Hamner said: "Absolutely. At the time, maybe I wouldn't have. But *now* I do. And that is the God's truth."

And Mrs Martin said: "He never really had much use for Louise. He claimed she talked too much."

And Mrs Hamner said: "Well, I can believe *that.*"

And Mrs Henshaw said: "Tell me something, Providence. Do you know why he, um, left town?"

And Mrs Martin said: "No. He didn't say a word to me. He just *vanished*, that's all. It was a typical Phil Cooper thing to do. Went with the sort of person he was. I suppose he couldn't face up to hurting me, and so he left like a thief in the night. Ah, but those things happen. And anyway, what little time I had with him was better than no time at all. I'm not complaining."

And Mrs Hamner said: "Remarkable."

And Mrs Martin said: "If you see one of the girls, flag her down."

And Mrs Hamner said: "Do you have to use the potty?"

And Mrs Martin said: "I *will* have to . . . by the time one of them comes sashaying along . . ."

And Mrs Henshaw said: "I wonder when the calling hours will be for Louise. I expect George will take us in the minibus if we ask him, don't you? Huh. I wonder how she looks."

And Mrs Martin said: "Dead."